GALAXY'S EDGE
EDITED BY MIKE RESNICK

ISSUE 14: MAY 2015

D1476360

Mike Resnick, Editor
Jean Rabe, Assistant Editor
Shahid Mahmud, Publisher

Published by Arc Manor/Phoenix Pick
P.O. Box 10339
Rockville, MD 20849-0339

Galaxy's Edge is published in January, March, May, July, September, and November.

www.GalaxysEdge.com

Available by subscription (www.GalaxysEdge.com) or through your favorite online store (Amazon.com, BN.com, etc.).

ISBN: 978-1-61242-268-8

Advertising in the magazine is available. Quarter page (half column), $95 per issue. Half page (full column, vertical or two half columns, horizontal) $165 per issue. Full page (two full columns) $295 per issue. Back Cover (full color) $495 per issue. All interior advertising is in black and white.

Please write to advert@GalaxysEdge.com.

FOREIGN LANGUAGE RIGHTS: Please refer all inquiries pertaining to foreign language rights to Spectrum Literary Agency, 320 Central Park West, Suite 1-D, New York, NY 10025. Phone: 1-212-362-4323. Fax 1-212-362-4562

Contents

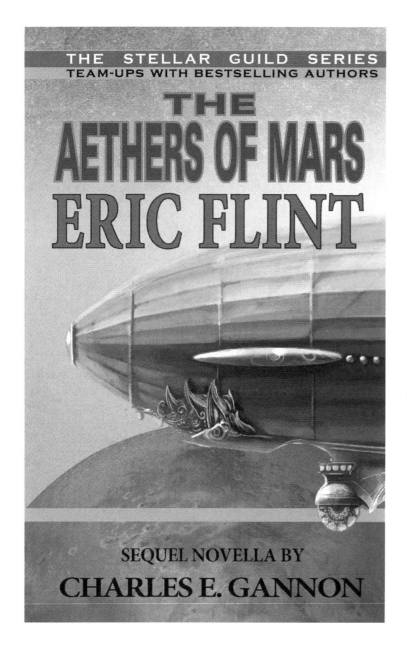

THE STELLAR GUILD SERIES
TEAM-UPS WITH BESTSELLING AUTHORS

THE
AETHERS OF MARS
ERIC FLINT

SEQUEL NOVELLA BY
CHARLES E. GANNON

THE EDITOR'S WORD

by Mike Resnick

Welcome to the fourteenth issue of *Galaxy's Edge*. We've got a new *Draco Tavern* story by Larry Niven in this issue, plus new stories by Tom Gerencer, Jennifer Campbell-Hicks, Anna Wu (translated by Ken Liu and Carmen Yiling Yan), C. Stuart Hardwick, and Sean Williams, plus reprints by such stellar writers as Harry Turtledove, Nancy Kress, Alan Dean Foster, and Michael Bishop. We also have the conclusion of our serialization of Michael Flynn's *Melodies of the Heart*. And we introduce the team of Jody Lynn Nye and Bill Fawcett as our book reviewers. To round it out, we feature Gregory Benford's science column and Barry N. Malzberg's anything-he-feels-like-writing-about column. Joy Ward's interview is with David Brin. To top it off, we feature a Robert A. Heinlein story that has, to date, been seen by only a small handful of people, its sole previous appearance being in a *very* limited edition.

I was recently re-reading a wonderful book that came out half a dozen years ago called *Seriously Funny*. It's by Gerald Nachman, a man who, like myself, never thought much of the stand-up comedians of his/my youth, such as Milton Berle, Henny Youngman, etc., who just stood there and told jokes that other people wrote for them—and who also finds almost all the comedians of the past twenty years totally unfunny. (I'll include 95% of Saturday Night Live and 100% of SCTV in the unfunny group. The only two bright spots in the past quarter century have been Rita Rudner and, very occasionally, Dennis Miller.)

The book concentrates on the "new wave" of cerebral comedians that never played the big rooms, rarely made films, and have been pretty much forgotten these days. But they were the cream of the crop, and there are long, thorough chapters on them:

> Mort Sahl (still the most brilliant of this bunch)
> Mike Nichols and Elaine May
> Tom Lehrer
> Lenny Bruce

> Ernie Kovacs
> Jean Shepherd
> Sid Caesar
> Bob Elliott and Ray Goulding
> Shelly Berman
> Jonathan Winters
> Woody Allen (before his movies)
> maybe a dozen more

Then there's *The Compass*, a book by Janet Coleman, on the Compass Players, the most remarkable comedy group ever assembled. They started at Jimmy's, also called the Compass Bar, about two blocks from the slum apartment where I lived when I was attending the University of Chicago. Most (not quite all) of them were undergrad students at the university, and in the three years they existed prior to moving to an abandoned Chinese laundry on Chicago's Near North Side and reopening in 1959 as The Second City, they numbered the following in their troop:

> Mike Nichols and Elaine May
> Jerry Stiller and Anne Meara
> Alan Arkin
> Severn Darden (far and away the most brilliant of them all)
> Shelly Berman
> Barbara Harris
> Andrew Duncan
> Ed Asner
> Eugene Troobnick
> Mina Kolb
> Paul Sand
> Del Close

That's a hell of a comic line-up. I actually belonged to a Second City workshop when I was in college back in 1960 (before the original troop, which has never been equaled, moved to New York and got bought off, one by one, by theatrical and film producers). I got to do scenes with Barbara Harris, Andy Duncan, and Gene Troobnick. The original Second City Players made three LP records—brilliant, cerebral, and long out of print—and I also have some audio tapes of them as they workshopped some of their improvisations. Never been anything like them for sheer talent. (The comics who replaced them as each went on to bigger things never came close.)

Somehow the subject got around to this on New Year's Eve, at one of the Cincinnati Fantasy Group's rotating parties. Two ex-Chicagoans, who also attended the University of Chicago before moving here and are just a couple of years younger than Carol and me, remembered almost all the above. But the other two dozen or so people, none of them culturally backward, knew only Nichols and May (most hadn't actually seen or heard them, but knew they were a team), Woody Allen, Shelly Berman, and Jonathan Winters—a tiny handful, and far from the best of the comics.

Are these talented people all due to become nothing but historical footnotes, their brilliance piled onto history's junk heap? And what does that say for the most innovative writers in *our* field?

What about some of the cutting-edge British comics? The hottest ticket in London in 1961 and New York in 1962 was *Beyond the Fringe*, an evening of brilliant humor by four young people, two of whom were Peter Cook and Dudley Moore. I have a video of the performance…but except for those same two ex-Chicagoans, no one at the party had even heard of it, and half of them hadn't even heard of Cook and Moore.

I remember going to Manhattan in the late 1960s, looking for writing assignments by day, and hitting the small clubs at night after catching a play on Broadway. We discovered the Ace Trucking Company (remember them?) with Fred Willard, Stiller and Meara, a couple of others. We saw Gerry Matthews and Madeleine Kahn break into the biz with tiny, hilarious reviews at Upstairs at the Downstairs, where a lot of the songs were written by newcomers (and eventual superstars) Cy Coleman, and the team of Tom Jones and Harvey Schmidt. Again, does anyone remember them, or are we doomed to watch HBO and Showtime comics who think endlessly repeating the word "fuck" is both hilarious and cutting-edge?

I hope not. I mean, I know each generation is growing up dumber than the last, but please tell me that Andrew Dice Clay is not the spiritual godfather of the next generation of successful comedians. And that (fill your choice among pretentious hack writers here) will not be remembered as the no-

holds-barred author who changed the face of science fiction.

The publisher would like to congratulate Mike Resnick and Kary English for their Hugo nominations. Mike Resnick has been nominated as Best Editor (Short Form) and Kary English's story "Totaled" (Galaxy's Edge No. 9) has been nominated for Best Short Story of the year.

Kary has also been nominated for the John W. Campbell Award for Best New Writer.

Robert A. Heinlein was the tallest of our field's giants. This story has previously appeared only in a 2,000-copy set that sells for $1,500.

FIELD DEFECTS: MEMO FROM A CYBORG

by Robert A. Heinlein

From: X-Model 69-606-ZSCCC-75-RAH (formerly "Robert A. Heinlein")

To: Complex Cyborg Corporation, an Unequal Opportunity Employer

Attn: Messrs. G. Zebrowski & T. N. Scortia

Subject: Above Model—Field Defects In

1. Help!

2 a. Neuroelectronic engineers indeed! That you should have such chutzpah! Before you took me out of the Box I told you that all my homeostasis was fubar, shaking like jelly. One of you—the uglier one if that be possible—patted me on my dexter gluteus maximus and plonked that it would all steady down once I was on my feet. Drek! I'm no longer shaking like jelly; I'm flapping in a gale. About Richter scale 6.7 at a guess. Worse yet, parts of it in positive feedback. I'm heading for a door, see? A big wide door and I change course a trifle to avoid the right side of the door frame—and walk right into it. Landlord wants *me* to pay for the damage. I told the puking obso to have his lawyer send the bill to ComCyCorp and to demand triple damages.

b. That's not half of what my shyster is going to do to you. Your big selling point, your convincer, was your NeverFail Neoflesh Everready Priapus Eternal. Correct, it never fails. I see a babe with jugs like Venus, a prominent pudendum, and a How-about-it? eye and at once my mouth waters. No, not that way, you throwbacks, I long for giant malted milks and juicy cheeseburgers. Worse yet, I get up in the morning, go to the jakes and am standing at the pot when I whiff frying bacon. *Spung!* Up like a fencepost and I micturate on the ceiling. Followed by a gob of wasted synthosemen. Who crossed those nerves?

Can't either of you count up to XII with your shoes on?

c. Worse still, when I try to be philosophical about it, roll with the punch, and be My Own Best Friend, here's what happens: I strip down, stretch out on the bed, and think about apple pie à la mode. Old NeverFail engorges at once, maybe 20 cm high, and thick to match; I can barely get my fist around it. Complaints? Oh, nothing much, a mere detail. No sensation. None. I told you not to use teflon. Or Elmer's Glue. What happened? Don't ask *me*; you're the "experts." But obviously the thick network of dermal pseudonerves no longer comes to the surface. Permanently detached or broken. Perhaps if you used tiny helices with some give to them— But not you two. I'll take my guarantee to General Motors' Johns Hopkins Division and have it done right. They'll send the tab to you and maybe you can get Medicare and Triple-A to split it. Maybe.

3. Don't go away; I'm not through. That "technologist" you sent out to "service" me. The bedpan hustler with one walleye and Parkinson's Disease. I was stretched out on the rack and clamped and he started to remove my skull piece without shutting me off. I reminded him, gently—after all, everyone makes an error now and then. "Thorry, Thir," he answered, very politely, and did shut me down before any real damage was done. Then he flushed out my hippocampus … with *Drano!* I saw the can. Then he "cleaned" my amygdala cerebelli with his thumbnail, explaining happily that it was so much gentler than a curet. If I could have moved, I would have bitten his thumb off. But I don't hate him; he's just an unfortunate minus. But as for you two—As soon as I'm over the side effects of the shotgun antibiotics I've been taking to offset my "servicing," I'm going to call at CrummyCyCorp, loaded past the red line with ATP, switch to SuperSpeed, breeze past your guards like the Invisible Man, go straight to your offices, jerk down your pants, and set fire to the hirsute thickets around your testes. If you have any. What day? Don't worry, you'll notice it when it happens. But I won't take it out on your geek. I did tell him what I thought of him. Didn't faze him. He just shrugged and said, "Thorry, thir, tha'th not my department. If you'll examine your guarantee, you'll thee that for one full year you can

alwayth go back into the Box at no charge to you. And a ten-year Box privilege with only a nominal charge for labor and parth."

4. *Insult to Injury.* Gentlemen, if you'll pardon the word, you are *not* going to get me back into that Box! If GMC-JH can't repair me, I'll go to Volkswagen-Übermensch, make a deal with a waiver that permits them to photograph and *publish* pix of your work (in the *International Journal of Cyborg Surgery and Prosthetics*, no doubt, with my signed and sworn statement), as they uncover it in rebuilding me. But you'll see me before then. In this morning's mail arrived this week's *Science* magazine…and I saw your full page ad on the inside front cover: There was that picture of me (taken without my knowledge or consent), bare as a *Penthouse* centerfold, with old NeverFail rampant. I could have shrugged that off. After all, I'm fairly handsome; my mother always said so…and old NeverFail *is* impressive—by appearance, not function. But underneath it said: Our Improved and Perfected *Production* model 69-606-ZSCCC (my emphasis added). Call our toll-free number, and some more garbage. That tore it! Oh, I'll sue, of course. But you'll see me much sooner. Watch Channel Four Wednesday evening for their 11 p.m. adults-only-anything-goes show with Johnny ("Jack the Ripper") as host and X-Model 69-606 et cetera as guest star. With *Science* magazine. With the studio warm enough for skin. With a pot installed to let me demonstrate how I must stand on my hands to pee.

Hope you are the same,

X

X-Model 69-606-ZSCCC-75 (formerly Robert A. Heinlein)

Copyright © 1975 Robert A. Heinlein. Copyright © 2003 The Robert A. & Virginia Heinlein Prize Trust

NOTES

In 1975, Heinlein received a book edited jointly by his friend Thomas N. Scortia and George Zebrowski, titled *Human-Machines* (Random House/Vintage, 1975). It was a theme-anthology of stories about cyborgs—computer-human hybrids, part organic and part machine. The book was affectionately dedicated "For Robert Heinlein, who taught us both." On November 30 that year, he wrote them both a letter thanking them for the dedication, wondering precisely *what* it was he had taught them both:

> Thanks for that most pleasing dedication. Not to believe editors' promises? Or always make certain that copyright is in *your* name, not the publisher's? Or don't grant *anything* but the specific right they are paying cash at the bedside for? If you learned any one of those points from me, I'm pleased, as I learned the hard way and hate to see any writer get taken by the gonifs.

> *Bob*

But this was a P.S. The letter itself was a fictional consumer complaint from Robot Heinlein to his creators—the first short fiction he had written in thirteen years, whimsical and entertaining, a side of Heinlein we have seen only too rarely in his fiction, though there always for friends and colleagues. The text of the letter was graciously provided for the Virginia Edition by George Zebrowski. It is reprinted here with permission from George Zebrowksi and The Robert A. & Virginia Heinlein Prize Trust.

Thomas N. Scortia was a physico-chemist who worked in the aerospace industry until the early 1970s and was also a well-regarded author of science fiction stories and novels. With Frank M. Robinson he wrote The Glass Inferno, a bestseller and major motion picture. His short fiction is collected in Caution, Inflammable! and The Best of Thomas N. Scortia.

George Zebrowski is best known for his John W. Campbell Award-winning novel Brute Orbits, the classic Macrolife, and Cave of Stars, recently chosen as one of the best SF novels since 1985. A collection of stories with Jack Dann, Decimated, is from Borgo/Wildside Press. All his fiction is available from Gollancz's SF Gateway (http://www.sfgateway.com/) and Open Road Media ((http://www.openroadmedia.com/).

Jennifer Campbell-Hicks is a Writers of the Future Finalist. Her recent sales have been to Orson Scott Card's Intergalactic Medicine Show, Flash Fiction Online, *and* Nature Futures. *In her day job she's a newspaper editor. This is her first appearance in* Galaxy's Edge.

SHORE LEAVE

by Jennifer Campbell-Hicks

A knocking rattled the old wooden door with such force that Elise imagined the whole world on the doorstep, trying to get in. She stopped playing with her seashells and colored rocks on the rug on the living room floor and listened. All she heard now was howling wind and rain pelting at the windows.

"What was that, Mama?" she asked.

Mother set aside her needlepoint, smoothed her skirt, and stood from her rocking chair. She took down the rifle from the mantle. The fireplace crackled and popped with a warming blaze, the only light besides an oil lamp on a corner table. Mother's long brown hair shimmered in the firelight.

"Stay behind me, Elise," she said.

Mother went to the front door, in a tiny space that cut through the center of the house between the living room and the kitchen. Across from the door, a narrow spiral staircase led up to two bedrooms on the second floor and then higher still to the lighthouse tower, where Father was tending to the flame, as he did every night.

Elise sat on the bottom step. She twirled her hair, the same deep brown as Mother's, around her small fingers. She twirled only the hair on the right side. On the left were just a few wispy strands. That was her bad side.

"Is it a stranger?" she asked.

"Course it is. Who else?"

"Was there a shipwreck? Is he a sailor?"

"Hush, and stay back. If anything happens, you run up to the tower to get your father, understand?"

A thrill shivered up Elise's spine and tingled through the scars that covered half her face. In all her seven years, she couldn't remember seeing another person besides her parents.

Mother unlocked the door and cracked it open. An icy wind gusted in, along with raindrops that splattered Elise's dress. Elise craned to see past her mother.

The man was tall, fit, and clean-shaven. He wiped rainwater from his eyes with a damp sleeve. Lightning cracked behind him in the night sky, illuminating for a moment the narrow point on which the lighthouse was built, sloping down to the rocky shore and the storm-tossed waves that crashed against it.

"Good evening, ma'am," the man said.

"What do you want?" Mother asked sharply. She held the rifle between them.

"My name is Benjamin March. I'm a first lieutenant on the *Cabrillo* in the Intergalactic Fleet. I'm afraid I have to impose on your hospitality. I've been out hiking the coastline, but I got turned around when it got dark and started to rain, and the storm was bad enough to disrupt my link to my ship."

"You're lost?" Mother asked.

He nodded and wiped his face again. "I couldn't see a thing but the lighthouse beacon, so I followed it. May I come in?"

Elise held her breath. The man spoke strangely, with vowels too sharp and a cadence almost like he was singing. She didn't know what a fleet was, or a lieutenant, but they sounded wonderful and she wanted to hear more. She sat quieter than a mouse on the step because if she made even the slightest noise, Mother would remember she was there and turn the man away.

Instead, after a long moment, Mother opened the door wider. "You better not try anything. I have a gun, and my husband is upstairs."

"Understood, ma'am." The man stepped over the threshold, dripping. "I'm obliged to you."

Mother shut and locked the door. "We can't feed you. We grow everything ourselves, and there's just enough for the three of us. But you look about my husband's size. I'll get you some clothes to change into while yours dry. You can spend the night down here on the floor, but I want you gone first thing in the morning."

"I have rations, and money to pay for your trouble." He patted the bulging pack on his back, which Elise hadn't noticed before. "Thank you for your kindness, and the Fleet thanks you."

Mother snorted. "I don't want your money, and I don't want anything from the Fleet. I'm only helping a fellow human being in need. I'll get you those clothes."

She swept past Elise, up the spiral stairs.

Outside, thunder crashed.

The man wore brown pants and a black shirt with a picture on his chest in white of a crossed branch and sword. His wet hair stuck to his forehead. He took off his pack and laid it on the floor, then saw Elise.

"Hello," he said.

Elise pressed herself against the staircase rail, turning her bad side away, into the shadows. But she had been raised to be polite. In a small voice, she said, "Hello. Who are you?"

"Benjamin. My friends call me Benji."

"Can I call you Benji?"

"I'd like that."

"Are you a sailor?"

"Of a sort. What's your name?"

Just then Mother called from upstairs. "Elise, come here!"

Elise turned to scramble up the stairs. She knew better than to stall when Mother used that tone. After a few steps she stopped and whispered down at the dripping man.

"My name is Elise. It's nice to meet you."

The clock in the living room struck one, its gong echoing through the house. The storm had stopped an hour ago, but Elise couldn't sleep. Her jaw and cheek throbbed. Mother always said the throbbing was ghost pain, but it felt real enough to Elise.

She slipped out of bed in her nightie. The house was pitch black, but she left her lantern on her bedside table. She didn't want to draw attention with the light. She tiptoed past her parents' room, where Mother was sleeping, and downstairs.

Benji sat on the rug beside the fireplace, the blaze faded to a flicker. In his hand was a strange small lantern—thin, flat and rectangular. The lantern had no flame, but its light glowed across Benji's face. He was looking at it and frowning.

From the bottom of the stairs, Elise watched him. His face was angular, his chin cleffed, and his blond hair spiked. He wore overalls belonging to Elise's father, and Elise giggled at how baggy they were on his thin frame.

Benji glanced up. "Shouldn't you be asleep?"

"Shouldn't you?"

"When I'm on my ship, this is when I'd be on my shift."

"Like how Papa works at night?"

"Exactly like that."

Elise edged into the living room but, still wary, she kept out of arm's reach. "Papa never leaves the lighthouse. Why did you leave your ship?"

"Because I'm on shore leave."

Confused, she said, "But you didn't leave the shore. You came to it."

Benji chuckled. "Shore leave means my ship is in orbit and I have a few days on the surface before we leave again. Most crew members stay close to the shuttle port, but I like to explore. This time I got lost. Thank goodness your lighthouse guided me."

She shrugged. He was using words she didn't know again, like orbit and shuttle port.

He said, "I bet you get a lot of lost folks here."

"You're the first one I can remember."

"Really?"

She nodded and looked at her feet.

"Can I ask you something, Elise?" Benji said.

"Sure. I guess."

"What happened to your face?"

Her embarrassment grew. She covered her bad cheek with her hand, the skin bumpy and rough under her palm, and backed toward the stairs. She shouldn't have come down.

"Wait, I'm sorry. I didn't mean to upset you." He beckoned to her. "Please, come sit with me. I want to show you something." When she hesitated, he added, "Don't be scared. I won't bite."

"I'm not scared," she said. To prove it she marched over to sit beside him, but she didn't take her hand from her face. "I see rock cats and rattlesnakes all the time when I walk to the shore. I'm not scared of them, and they *do* bite."

"I like you, Elise. You'd make a good officer someday."

She perked up. "On your ship? On the ocean?"

OATHS AND MIRACLES

NANCY KRESS

A GENETIC THRILLER — STARRING ROBERT CAVANAUGH

STINGER
NANCY KRESS

A GENETIC THRILLER STARRING ROBERT CAVANAUGH

He blinked. "The ocean? No, not that. The Fleet. Here, look at this."

He held out his rectangular lantern.

Elise gasped. It wasn't a lantern at all. There were moving pictures on it. Forgetting to hide her face, she touched the metal, cool and sleek.

"What is it?" she asked.

He gave her an odd look. "Haven't you seen a communicator before?"

"No."

"Strange. Actually, you don't have much tech around here." He glanced around the living room, at the rocking chair and the stone fireplace and the small corner table decorated with shells. "No tech at all, in fact. Do you have electricity? Wireless? Mod generator? How about a transport?"

Elise shook her head to every one. She had never heard of those things.

"Wow." Benji rubbed his chin. "I was going to show you my ship on this." He waved the communicator. "But I can see that'll only confuse you. I know another way." He unfolded his long legs and stood. "Would you go outside with me?"

The night wind chilled Elise through her thin nightie as they stood beside the vegetable garden, and she hugged herself to keep warm. Above them, the lighthouse beacon shined, illuminating waves breaking against the rocks. The clouds had cleared, and the sky sparkled with thousands of stars.

Benji knelt beside her and pointed at the sky. "Do you see those stars in a cluster? Good. Now look to the left. There's one light by itself. That's the space port. My ship is there."

Elise stared at the tiny light in wonder. She felt as if a hand had grasped her heart and squeezed. "A ship that sails the stars?"

"There are thousands of those ships, exploring other planets, other stars, meeting other species, some nice, some not so nice." His eyes grew far away. "I've seen the great ice caves of Thor and the sentient forests of New Wales. Sometimes it can be dangerous, but it's always exciting. There's nothing else like it in the universe."

"Oh," Elise breathed. "Can I go?"

"When you grow up."

She fought down her disappointment. She didn't want to wait. "Will you come get me when I'm grown, so I can go with you?"

"Maybe I will, kid."

He ruffled her hair. Elise couldn't help but notice he only touched her good side.

She chewed her lip and skimmed her fingertips over her scars, drawing a line from her jaw, up the slope of her nose, through her forehead and over her scalp back down to her ear.

"It was a fire," she said.

"What?"

"My face. There was a fire when I was a baby, and I got burned. Mother says I'm lucky to be alive."

"I'm sorry," he said.

He looked at her with so much pity that she had to turn away. "I have to go," she said and ran inside, then turned in the doorway to wave. He waved in return.

✿

The next morning, Elise wanted to hear more about sailing among the stars. All she found in the living room were Papa's overalls, folded on the rocking chair. Benji had returned to his ship in the sky.

"It's for the best," Mother said at the kitchen table over a breakfast of porridge topped with a dollop of strawberry jam. "We don't need his kind here."

"I liked him," Elise said.

"It's best you forget about him. Finish your breakfast and get on with your chores."

Her chores took all morning. After a lunch of thick bread and tomato slices, she rested in her room before her afternoon lessons in letters and numbers. There, she noticed something next to the lantern on her bedside table, something she had missed when she had woken up that morning.

She picked it up, a sleek, thin rectangle of silvery metal. On the back was an etching of a crossed branch and sword. Her excitement built. Benji had not left her empty-handed, after all.

He had left her his communicator.

✿

Years passed. Life at the lighthouse stayed the same, only Elise changed.

On the day before her 18th birthday, she walked to the tidal pools to harvest clams. She wore her father's old pants and suspenders and carried a grass basket she had woven herself last summer. The sun shone warmly, and Elise took her time strolling through the sage scrub that grew everywhere around the lighthouse.

On a sandy bank above the tidal pools, she pulled off her boots and rolled her pants cuffs to her knees. A dolphin leaped in the waves nearby, while a fishing boat passed in the far distance. Gulls cawed and dived for fish.

Elise took her communicator from her pocket and slid it inside one of her boots. She had never dared to show the communicator to her parents, and most of the time she kept it hidden beneath a loose floorboard in her bedroom. But she brought it with her when she went walking, which was the only time she could use it unobserved. With it, she had learned about the universe.

She massaged her fingertips over her scars from jaw to forehead, to keep them from stiffening up, then braided the hair on her right side into a long brown plait. As her fingers worked, her mind wandered to earlier that morning.

"You have your mother's hair," Papa had said at the kitchen table, after she had woken up and before he had gone to sleep. "You have my eyes and my stubbornness, but you have her hair."

Elise hadn't known what to say to that. Mother's hair was gray like an overcast sky, and so were her cheeks that once had been rosy pink from the sun. It was as if something had leeched out her color and left her a ghost of herself.

"She's sick," Elise had said.

The words had come out before she could stop them. She hadn't meant to bring up the subject, but she had been thinking about it for a while.

Papa sliced an apple with his pocket knife. His bushy beard was streaked with gray, and his eyes tired and dark-rimmed.

"Your mother is fine," he said.

"She needs a doctor." Doctors were a piece of modern life that she had learned about from her parents, not the communicator. "Let me go to the city and bring back help."

"You've never been to the city."

"I can do it."

"No."

"I can go and be back in a few days."

Not only would such a trip help Mother, but it also would be Elise's chance to finally see civilization and a shuttle port and maybe even a spaceship.

"I said no." Father's eyes bored into her across the table. "Your mother and I love you as you are, but other people would see your face and…" He trailed off.

Elise didn't want him to stop there. "And what?"

He shook his head.

She said, "I'm not afraid of what anyone might think."

"That's because you've never experienced how cruel people are. Besides, if you went for a doctor, they would put your mother in a hospital. They would hook her up to machines and pump drugs into her body. No. She'll get better on her own."

Elise couldn't mask her fear. "What if she doesn't?"

Papa bit an apple slice in half and chewed. "The people out there have lost touch with what it means to be human. I was one of them once, I'm ashamed to say. Very ashamed. So was your mother. We came here when you were a baby to reclaim what's simple and right, and we vowed we would never go back, not for any reason."

"Not even to make Mother well?"

"Not for any reason. Don't ask again."

After that, Elise had to let it go. She lacked the life experience to agree or disagree with him, and she respected the choices he and Mother had made. Still, she sorely wished that she could make up her own mind on what kind of life she wanted for herself.

With gulls circling overhead, she scrambled down some boulders, left her basket on the bedrock beside the tidal pool, and waded into the cold, calf-deep water, careful to avoid shell fragments that could cut her bare feet.

Low tide was the best time to dig for clams, when the water was still and clear. She spotted one on the bottom and plunged her hand into the shallow water to scoop out sand. Her fingers closed around a shell, and she plucked it free.

A voice said, "Well done."

She whirled around.

A man sat on the bedrock, watching her.

Elise wondered whether she was dreaming.

"Benji?" she said.

"You remember me?"

"How could I forget?"

He had grown a straw-colored beard that was closely trimmed, but otherwise he hadn't changed. Elise guessed that was because of the space travel. She had read on the communicator that time slowed as a person approached the speed of light.

"What are you doing here?" she asked.

"I was invited." He took a communicator from his pocket, a new one. "You sent me twenty-one messages in a month. I was starting to feel harassed."

She blushed. "Sorry about that."

She had sent the first message a few weeks after Benji had left her the communicator. She had asked him to come back and take her with him on his ship. When he didn't write back, she had tried again and again. Eventually she had given up.

She waded to shore. The bedrock was dry now and crawling with thumbnail-sized crabs. At high tide, all this would be underwater.

She tossed her clam into her basket, then sat beside him and cleaned out wet sand from between her toes. "It's been ten years."

"I know."

"How long for you?"

He picked up a smooth rock and tossed it into the tidal pool. *Plop* went the rock and spread ripples over the surface. "Nine months."

"I turn eighteen tomorrow."

"Happy birthday."

"Thank you," she said, but he had misunderstood why she told him. She didn't want birthday wishes. Eighteen meant adulthood. It meant she could do what she wanted. Eighteen meant she could enlist.

She picked up a rock of her own and threw it into the water. "I've been planning to go to the city. My parents don't know about it."

"Alone?"

"Yes."

He whistled through his teeth. "The city is a tough place. Dangerous. Especially for a girl who's never been more than a mile from her home. There's a lot worse than rattlesnakes and rock cats in the back alleys."

"You think I shouldn't go?"

"I wouldn't advise it."

"Well, then. Who do I know who knows the city? Who could be my guide and help me avoid the dangerous parts?"

She felt clever for how she had twisted that back on him, but Benji didn't look impressed.

"I'm not a guide," he said.

"Please? I wouldn't be any trouble. Just take me to the Fleet recruiting station. You'll never hear from me again."

He studied her, as if she were a particularly strange bug he had found on a leaf. "You want to enlist?"

"More than anything."

"What about your life here?"

"This isn't a life," she said. Here, she felt like the clam she had caught, trapped in a tiny pool with a whole ocean *right there*, tantalizing her, just out of reach. "If you're not here to help me, why did you come back?"

"I don't know," he admitted. "I guess I wanted to see how you were getting on. You stuck with me. A little girl living on the edge of the world."

"I'm not a little girl anymore."

"No you're not," he agreed.

"I can make my own decisions." On a hunch, she asked, "How old were you when you enlisted?"

"Eighteen."

"Then help me," Elise implored.

His lips tightened into a thin line. He stared at the ocean, but not at her. "I don't know…"

"Is it my face?" She remembered what Papa had said that morning. "I don't care if people stare. So what if they say cruel things? I'm stronger than that. I know who I am." Then she added so quietly she could hardly hear herself, "You made me want to go to the stars. Help me get there."

Benji said nothing.

Up the slope behind them, over the sand and sage scrub, the lighthouse stood against the clear blue sky. Her whole life had revolved around that tower. It seemed big, but it wasn't. It was actually very small and insignificant.

Then there was Benji, who seemed to her the embodiment of the entire universe. He was the ice caves of Thor and the forests of New Wales. He was the space port and the Fleet. He represented everything she wanted.

If he rejected her, it would be as if the universe had rejected her, too. She didn't know what she would do then.

Finally, he said, "My transporter is over that ridge." He pointed. "I'm leaving in two hours. If you're not here by then, I'm going without you."

Elise couldn't contain herself. She threw her arms around him. When she let go, she said, "There are things I need from the house."

"Two hours," he said, but he was grinning at her excitement.

She tossed the clam from her basket into the pool, then climbed over boulders to the sandy bank with her basket in hand. Her communicator went into her pants pocket, her boots onto her feet. She picked up the basket and set off running.

The way was all uphill.

At the lighthouse, Elise opened the front door and stood there until she had caught her breath. Her chest burned, and sweat dripped down her face—smoothly on one side and through the paths of her scars on the other.

She tiptoed up the spiral staircase, careful to skip the step with the creaky board, into her bedroom.

On the other side of the stairs, in her parents' bedroom, Papa was sleeping and likely Mother, too. She slept a lot nowadays.

Elise didn't have a pack, or a bag of any sort, to put her things in. She had never needed one. So everything went into her grass basket. Clothes, hair brush, toothbrush, cake of soap, lotion for her face. When the basket was full, she took a last look at her room before sneaking downstairs.

A dry coughing came from the living room.

Elise froze.

"Darling, is that you?" Mother said. Darling was what she called Father.

Elise couldn't slip away unnoticed now. Resigned, she said, "No, it's me."

"Elise. Would you come here?"

Helpless to do anything else, she set her basket by the stairs and went to find out what her mother wanted.

The curtains were drawn shut, and the living room was dark except for flickering light from the fireplace. The air was hot and stale.

Mother sat in her rocking chair, a wool blanket draped across her lap and another wrapped around her thin shoulders. Her face was drawn and pale, and her hair hung in dull, limp strands the color of ash.

"Stoke the fire," Mother said quietly. "And put on another log. I get so cold."

Elise did. "It's warm outside. I could take you out to the garden."

"The sunlight hurts my eyes. Sit with me."

Elise had hoped the fire was all Mother wanted. She didn't know how long it had been since she had left Benji or how much longer he would wait, but she couldn't leave without raising her mother's suspicion.

She knelt by the chair. "Do you need another blanket?"

Mother patted her shoulder. "I'm fine. Your father told me that the two of you had an argument this morning."

"It was about you."

"So I heard. But you must not argue with him." She took a breath, and soft rattling noises fluttered in her chest, like a nest of moths. "I'm dying."

"Don't say that."

"There's no use denying it. Doctors can't save me. At most, they might extend my life by a few weeks or months, but I would spend them like this"—she gestured to her chair—"or worse. I don't want that. If it's time for me to go, then I will go, and that's my choice. I am only glad that you're here, Elise."

"Why?"

"Your father will need you when I'm gone."

That made her feel guilty. "Surely we wouldn't stay here. Not without you."

Mother coughed, a dry hacking that made her double over. Elise could only watch. When the spell had passed, Mother said weakly, "There's something you need to know about your father. A long time ago, he was in the Intergalactic Fleet."

Elise was shocked. "No. He was a captain. He had his own ship." That was what she had always been told.

"Yes, he had a ship, but a starship not a sailing ship. He was ordered to secure a treaty with a human colony on the planet Ryman. The colonists had refused intergalactic control, and there had been bloodshed on both sides. The negotiations took a long time. I went with your father. You were born on that planet, and you were almost old enough to walk when the treaty was signed."

Elise heard the words, but they made no sense. Perhaps Mother was delirious. Still, Elise didn't interrupt. She feared that if she did, Mother would not finish, and Elise needed her to finish.

"We were preparing to leave," Mother said, "when your father learned that the treaty was a ruse and the Fleet planned to attack now that the colony wasn't expecting it. He warned them, but it was too late. The colony was wiped out as an example to others who would defy the Fleet. We barely escaped." She touched Elise's scars with her fingertips. "That attack was the fire that did this to you, and your father was charged with treason. He said he would expose the Fleet's actions as a violation of intergalactic law, and for that reason the trial was never held. He was exiled instead. *We* were exiled. Here." She looked into the fire, her eyes far away.

Elise tried to wrap her head around that. "He said we came here to get back to what was simple and right."

"That's true in a way. We could have chosen another place. A city, perhaps. But we chose here, as far from the Fleet as possible. Did you think we lived here because of the lighthouse? Who needs a lighthouse when there's global positioning? No. We wanted isolation. We chose this. The main thing to remember is that your father can't leave."

"Why not? How would anyone know?"

"They watch us."

Elise felt punched in the gut. "Benji?"

"That kid who got lost all those years ago?" Mother smiled sadly. "No, not him. They have satellites. They don't need spies." She patted Elise's hand. "So you see, your father is lucky to have you." She leaned back in the rocking chair, exhausted. "I need to sleep. Thank you for listening to the ramblings of a sick woman."

But Elise didn't go. She sat, stunned.

Everything she had believed about the Fleet, the romance of space that she had built up in her imagination until it had become as real to her as the rocks and the ocean, had been a lie. The Fleet killed innocent people, tricked and betrayed its own officers, sent good men into exile for doing what was right.

Her heart broke.

Then she remembered. Benji was waiting.

She could still go to him, and he would take her to the recruiting station. Ten minutes ago that thought had excited her. What did she feel now? Dread? Uncertainty? Disgust?

In any case, she couldn't go. Not now that she knew the truth.

She settled in next to her mother's chair.

"Actually," she said, "if it's all right with you, I think I might stay here for a while."

Mother died that winter. Elise and her father buried her beside the garden. Six years later, Papa stepped in a rattlesnake nest and died after two days of fever. Elise buried him alone.

For days she debated what to do next. She had stayed because of Papa. Now that he had gone, she should, too. But where?

If Benji were here, he could help her. Elise had not seen him since that day by the tidal pool. When she hadn't returned after two hours, he had gone, as he had promised he would, and had not come back.

In the end, though, she decided she didn't need him. She had her father's stubbornness and her mother's courage. Benji had shown her a larger world, for which she would always be grateful, but she was the one who had to go get it.

At sunrise, she stood in front of her parents' graves. The breeze smelled saltier than usual.

Beside her feet lay a backpack that she had cut and sewn from the living room curtains and filled with her clothes and other possessions, along with some food and water. Behind her stood the lighthouse, its windows boarded up with driftwood.

Elise didn't know why she had bothered with the driftwood, except that she couldn't stand the thought of the windows broken, and snakes and birds finding their way in to make homes in the fireplace, under the stairs and in her parents' bed.

"I know how you feel about the Fleet," she said to the graves, one blanketed in wildflowers and the other a fresh mound of dark dirt. "But the Fleet is only as good or bad as the people in it. You were good. You tried to do the right thing, and so will I."

She knelt and put a hand on each grave.

"I'll work to make the Fleet better so that what happened to you and to the colonists of Ryman never happens again. I promise."

She stood, slung her pack over her shoulders and took her communicator from her pocket. She pulled up a map to the city. On foot, it would take days to get there.

"Better get going," she said.

A gull cried in answer.

Elise turned her back on the shore and started walking.

Months passed, or years, depending on how she measured time. Elise was an ensign on a freighter that delivered supplies to space ports across the galaxy—not the most exciting of starts, but a start, nonetheless.

She parked her transport a mile from the lighthouse, amid the sage scrub. She wore long pants and boots. Her T-shirt and backpack were printed with the Fleet logo of a crossed branch and sword.

Elise breathed deep. On her ship, the temperature was controlled and the air recycled. She had missed the salt tang in her nose and the ocean spray on her skin.

She had missed home.

In the distance, dark thunderheads built over the ocean. A storm was coming in.

Elise hiked toward the lighthouse. She spotted its tower as the first drops fell. Soon she was close enough to make out details. The driftwood had been taken down from the windows and the chipped, faded exterior was repainted. A generator rumbled, powering electric lights that shone through the windows.

The house had occupants, Elise realized, though she shouldn't be surprised. Someone would always want the isolation of the lighthouse.

The storm worsened. Lightning flashed. Elise huffed up the hillside, her boots crunching on wet sand, and reached the top as the gloom darkened a little, signaling dusk.

Her hair, which she had cut short like a man's since joining the Fleet, stuck to her forehead. Her bad side throbbed from the exertion of the hike, and she massaged her temple.

The new people had built a low, white picket fence around the house, and Elise unlatched the gate and walked through. She was pleased to see her parents' graves lay undisturbed beside the garden.

She knocked.

A woman opened the door a crack and glared. "What do you want?" she said sharply.

A girl of five or six with huge blue eyes and curly yellow hair peeked around her mother's legs.

Remembering another girl from long ago, Elise smiled at them both. "Good evening," she said. "I'm sorry to impose on you, but I've been out hiking and I seem to have gotten caught in the storm. May I come in?"

Harry Turtledove is a Hugo winner, a frequent bestseller, and has been called "The Master of Alternate History" by no less an authority than Publishers Weekly. He and daughter Rachel recently wrote On the Train, *a Stellar Guild book published by Arc Manor/Phoenix Pick. "Hi, Colonic" was first published in* I, Alien, *a DAW Books anthology released in 2005.*

HI, COLONIC

by Harry Turtledove

Some people say probing other planets for intelligent life is an exciting, romantic job. As far as I'm concerned, that only goes to show they've never done it. Me, I do it for a living, and I'm here to tell you it's nothing but a pain in the orifice. The air smells funny even when you can breathe it, the animals smell even worse (and taste worse than that, half the time), and even when we do find people they're usually backward as all get-out. If they weren't, they would have found us, right? Right.

Another planet from space. If I've sensed one, I've sensed a thousand. Third planet from a medium-heat sun. Water oceans. Oxygen atmosphere. Life. Oh, joy. We weren't even the first ones here. This place had been checked a bunch of times over the past fifty local years. Always nothing. So why did we go back again? Orders. If I don't do the work, they don't pay me. Even when I do do the work, they don't pay me enough, but that's a different story.

Down we went, into the atmosphere. Iffspay—he's my partner—and I rolled dice to find out who got stuck wearing the calm suit. I give you three guesses. The calm suit we needed for this planet is the most uncomfortable one in the whole masquerade cabinet. It's bifurcated at the bottom, it's got tendrils near the top, and then an awkward lump at the very top. Guess who got to put it on. I'll give you a hint: it wasn't Iffspay. I think he uses loaded dice.

"This is all a waste of time," I grumbled.

"We're here. We might as well do it," Iffspay said. He would. Of course he would. He got to lie back in the ship and soak up nutrient while I was out there doing the heavy lifting.

The atmosphere on this one was really noxious, too. Way too much carbon dioxide for a stable climate, plus oxides of nitrogen and assorted vile hydrocarbons. I made damn sure the purifier in the calm suit was working the way it was supposed to. You could fry yourself on air like that.

To add insult to injury, the weather was fermented. Antigravity or not, round flat aerodynamic shape or not, we bounced around enough to turn your insides inside out. Iffspay was doing the flying, which didn't help. As a pilot, he doesn't know his appendages from a hole in the ground. I thought he was going to fly us into a hole in the ground, but he didn't. Don't ask me why. Somebody out beyond the cosmos must like him. Don't ask me why about that, either.

Rain pounded us. "I'm supposed to go out in this?" I said.

"I would have done it if I'd lost the roll," Iffspay said virtuously. He would have bitched all the way, too. Am I lying? If you've ever met Iffspay, you'll know I'm not. You can't tell me that's not him, segment by segment.

"Just find some of them so we can run the tests," I said. "We'll get another negative and we'll go on to another world. And when it comes to finding out who wears the calm suit next time, I'm going to roll your dice."

"What's that supposed to mean?" he asked, as if he didn't know. Ha!

Before we could really start quarreling, the heat-seeker indicated a target. Three targets, in fact, grouped close together. That actually cheered me up. If we caught all three of them, we could finish this planet in one fell swoop. I wouldn't miss putting it behind me, not even a little bit I wouldn't.

Trouble was, they were at the edge of a swamp. I worried that they might escape into the water or into the undergrowth, calm suit or no calm suit, before I could slap the paralyzer ray on them and we could antigravity them up into the ship. And if they did—if even one of them did—we'd have to go through this whole capture-and-release business somewhere else on the planet, too. Once was plenty. Once was more than plenty, as a matter of fact.

"As we lower, put on the full display," I told Iffspay.

"We're liable to scare them off," he warned.

"Yeah, yeah," I said. "If we do, we'll try somewhere else, that's all. But the data feeds say they usually gawk. They're photosensitive, you know."

"All right, already." Iffspay complained, but he did it the way I wanted. He had to, pretty much. If he'd been going out, I would've done it his way. I wondered how much the rain would hurt the locals' photosensitivity. Light is so unreliable. Since most planets rotate, half the time there isn't any. Evolution does some crazy things sometimes.

I have to give Iffspay credit. He didn't fool around when it came to the display. He had it radiating every frequency the locals could perceive, going from the high end to the low in rhythmic waves. He cranked the air vibrations way up, too. I could sense some of those myself. They seemed to go right through me.

I checked the heat-seeker. By the taste, the locals hadn't moved. That meant—I hoped that meant—they were fixated on the show the ship was putting on. I struggled into the calm suit and went down to the exit orifice. "I'm ready," I told Iffspay, exaggerating only a little. "Go on and shit me out."

The mild obscenity made him mumble to himself, but out I went, floating in midair. Rain thudded against the calm suit. Considering all the crap in the atmosphere, the rainwater probably wouldn't have done me much good, either. Maybe I was lucky being in the suit, even if it was uncomfortable.

And the locals still didn't try to escape. I can't tell you exactly how much I resembled them—how do you evaluate a sense you haven't got yourself?—but it must have been close enough for government work. I was glad the suit had its own powered heat-seeker; the rain would have played hob with the one I was hatched with, which naturally isn't anywhere near so strong.

I wanted to get really close before I paralyzed them, for fear all that water coming down out of the sky would attenuate the beam, too. And I did. I got so close, my instruments could tell they were emitting air vibrations themselves. The ones from the ship had much more pleasing patterns, but I wasn't there to play art critic.

Ready...Aim...The calm suit's appendages aren't as sensitive as real ones, so I squeezed the control inside just as hard as I could. "Got 'em!" I told Iffspay. "Bring me back, and bring them in, too."

"Keep your integument on," Iffspay said. There are times when I'm tempted to turn the paralyzer on him. Leaving him unable to communicate would be all to the good. That's what I think, and nobody's likely to make me change my mind.

Up went the locals, one by one. Iffspay saved me for last, just to annoy me. He did, too, but I wasn't about to let him smell it when I got back to the ship. He was bustling around when the antigravity beam finally pulled me back aboard. The locals were all lined up neatly, ready for us to start doing our latest check. Two of them emitted significantly more heat than the third, which meant they had more body mass.

All three of them also went on emitting high-amplitude air vibrations. "Why are they doing that?" Iffspay asked irritably. "Aren't they supposed to be paralyzed?"

I had to check the manual before I could answer him. "It says paralysis only inhibits gross motor functions. If it inhibited all movements, they'd die."

I got out of the calm suit. I didn't need it any more, and we'd made the capture. The paralyzed locals weren't going to interfere. As I put it back in the closet, the amplitude of their air vibrations increased even more. "They're still sensing us somehow," I said. "Those waves have to be voluntary."

Now it was Iffspay's turn to check the manual. Yeah, yeah, I know—when all else fails, read the instructions. At last, he said, "I think they're photosensitive to some of the wavelengths we use for heat-seeking."

"Oh. All right." That even made sense. "I wonder if those were alarm calls, then. They might have been surprised when they perceived me changing from something like their own shape to my own proper one."

"Who cares?" Iffspay said. "Let's get them analyzed, and then we can analyze the data—not that there'll be any data to analyze. We'll do it by the book, though."

"By the book," I agreed. And, by the book, we did the two bigger specimens first. We had to check the manual again to make sure just where to analyze them. Iffspay thought the orifice emitting the air vibrations was the one that would take the probe, but he turned out not to be right. Evolution was even crazier than usual on that planet, you betcha.

And the manual didn't exactly match the specimens we had. By what it said, the orifice should have been accessible once we figured out where the space fiend it was. But the locals had integuments more complicated than what the manual showed. Good old Iffspay was all for cutting right on through them. Iffspay never was long on patience, I'm afraid.

"Let's try peeling them instead," I said. "That way, we're less liable to injure them."

"Oh, all right," he said sulkily. "It'll take longer, though."

I was the one who got to peel them. Since it was my idea, Iffspay didn't want thing one to do with it. I wasn't too thrilled about it, either, not getting started. I kept thinking about gross and fine motor functions. If the locals weren't perfectly paralyzed...well, they'd splatter me all over the walls of the ship.

But I managed to peel the first one without doing it any harm I could detect—its heat signature and the kind of air vibrations it emitted didn't change at all—and without getting hurt myself. Once I'd taken care of the hard part, Iffspay grabbed the glory. He bent the local into the position the manual suggested and threaded in the probe.

"Well?" I asked.

"Well, nothing," Iffspay answered. "The computer can check me later, but there's nothing. A big, fat, juicy nothing. So much for that."

"Don't prejudge. We've still got two more to go," I said, though I wasn't what you'd call optimistic about them, either.

"Go on and peel the next one, then," Iffspay said.

"Why me again?" I asked him. "How come I get stuck with all the hard stuff?"

"Because you did such a good job the last time," he answered. Iffspay tastes smooth, no two ways about it.

After letting out a few last bitternesses of annoyance, I got to work on the second large local. Fortunately, everything went well. In fact, it went better than it had the first time, because I'd had the practice of doing it once. I reached for the probe once I'd got the local into the position—I did it myself that time—but Iffspay already had it in his appendage.

"This is the last lump," I said angrily. "You're going to peel the third one, and I'm going to do the analyzing. And if you don't like it, I'll talk to a lawyer when we get home. There *are* limits to how much you can impose on people." I had really had it.

Iffspay could tell, too. "Fine. Fine!" he said. "Don't get all disconnected from your nutrient provider. You want to analize the third one, be my guest. Meanwhile, though..." He inserted the probe. He tried to go on as if everything were normal, but my talk about lawyers had put a bad smell in his chemoreceptors, let me tell you. After he withdrew the probe, he added, "Nothing again. Not even a hint. If you want to waste your time with the last one, be my guest."

"I want to perceive you peel it," I said. "That should be funny enough to go on the planetwide sensorium special."

"You'll find out." Now I'd got Iffspay mad. I could taste it. And, of course, when he got mad, he got clumsy. I wish they *would* put the recording of the botch he made of that peeling job on the sensorium special. He'd have an offer to do sitcoms so fast, you wouldn't believe it. The local's air vibrations increased in amplitude, too. I don't think it much cared for what was going on.

After what seemed like forever, Iffspay turned to me and said, "There. All yours."

I took the probe. But it didn't want to do what it was supposed to. I had to feel around near the target area. "You bumbling idiot," I said. "There's still a layer of integument here. The other two had this layer—weren't you paying attention when I dealt with them? Once you get this down, *then* it's pay dirt."

"Well, take care of it, then, if you're so smart," he said.

"Oh, no. The deal was you'd peel this one and I'd probe it. You finish your job, and then I'll do mine."

He made a stink about it, but he did it. I suspected there'd be some long, nasty silences on the way to the next star. Well, too bad. I know what my rights are, by the Great Eggcase, and I know when to curl up for them.

"I hope you're satisfied now," he grumped when he'd finally got the peeling right.

"Couldn't be happier," I told him, just to smell him fume.

And I meant it literally. This time, the analizer went in just as smooth as you please. I extended an appendage through it—and made contact!

Photosensitive creatures use energy waves to talk. I suppose you could talk with air vibrations, too, though I've never heard of any intelligent races that do. Too much ambiguity either way, as far as I'm concerned. Taste and scent, now, those are universal languages. No doubt about 'em.

"Hello, there," I said. "How are you doing?"

"We're fine," came the answer. "Hooked on to the intestinal wall here, kicking back and living the life of Reilly."

Even universal languages have dialects. I'm still not sure what a Reilly is. But I got the point. They were happy where they were. "Do you need anything?" I asked.

"No way, José," they replied without the least hesitation. My name isn't José, but I didn't bother calling them on it. "We're happy right here, you better believe it."

"Okay," I said. "Now that we've finally found you, we'll probably send you an ambassador or something before too long."

"Whatever. No hurry. No worries," they said. "You guys are free-living, aren't you?"

"Oh, sure," I said. "We have been for a long time. We think hooking up with nutrient when we want to is easier than staying tied to a host."

"We like it better this way," they told me. "We can ease back and relax and go along for the ride. Beats working—who needs technology if you've got a tasty host? From what we've smelled, free-living makes people pushy."

"I didn't know you'd met Iffspay," I said.

"Hey, don't drag me into this, you flavorless, unsegmented thing," Iffspay said, neatly proving my point.

"What's an Iffspay?" the planet's intelligent lifeforms wanted to know.

"Nothing much—he's my partner here," I replied, just to smell Iffspay fume. He didn't disappoint me, either. Iffspay is a reliable guy.

The locals said, "Nice to meet you and everything, but we'd really like to get back to what we were doing. Some of our segments are going to break off and go out into the world to find new hosts."

Ah, the simple pleasures of parasites! It almost makes me long for the eons before we were free-living. Things were simpler then. They...Well, enough. When a worm starts getting nostalgic, he's the most boring creature in the bowels of the Galaxy. And so I won't. I just won't.

I unthreaded the analizer and said, "Well, we'll have to be careful placing the locals back on the ground now that we know some of them are inhabited."

"Tastes like you're right," Iffspay agreed. "Who would've thunk it? All these negative reports, and now this!" Then he let out a bad smell. "Think of all the forms we'll have to fill out on the way back to Prime."

I did a little farting of my own, too. I hadn't thought of that. I hadn't wanted to think about it. "Can't be helped," I said, and he knew damn well I was right again. He set the local hosts back where we'd found them. Old Iffspay does have a nice appendage on the antigravity when he wants to, I will say that for him.

And then we flew away. As we headed for the next star on the list, I started in on some of that miserable, vermicidal paperwork.

Some things are too big to be fully comprehended. Willie and Al and Little Joe had only the vaguest idea how they'd all ended up back in their duck blind in an Arkansas swamp with their pants around their ankles. What had happened to them beforehand was, mercifully, even vaguer.

Pants still below half-mast, Willie stared up at the sky—and got rain in his face. "We are not alone," he said...vaguely.

"Yeah," Al murmured, slowly and wonderingly pulling up his jeans.

"Reckon the two o' you are," Little Joe said. "Not me." Solemnly, Willie and Al nodded, though they didn't quite know what he meant. Which was okay, too, because neither did he.

Copyright © 2005 by Harry Turtledove

Their MAJESTIES' BucKETEERS

L. NEIL SMITH

An Agot Edmoot Mav
Murder Mystery

C. Stuart Hardwick is a Writers of the Future winner, a Baen Memorial Finalist, and a James White Award semi-finalist. His work has appeared in Writers of the Future #30, In Flight Magazine #30, and Tides of Possibility. This is his first appearance in Galaxy's Edge.

LUCK OF THE CHIEFTAIN'S ARROW

by C. Stuart Hardwick

I once was a ship's bell, high and proud, and all the glories of creation rolled past my horizon in cloaks of mist and birdsong. Now I'm a coin, spare change, and Sturgle's gone and lost me. He's seventy-three, shrewd, with round wet eyes and an easy smile, and I see his mind as plain as any, the old faker. He was stalling, turning the chess board inside out in search of escape. Murray, his customary opponent, had started drumming his fingers while the benches collected suited young office workers with lunch bags and novels and predatory eyes for the tables. Sturgle feigned having forgotten his pills and dug in his satchel pocket as if the bottle were somehow hidden in the once-gold lining. When it finally popped out, his change came with it and spilled across the table, and the penny I now inhabit fell into the weeds.

I know he saw me. His yellow eyes tracked me as I rolled through the numismatic fray, but then he thought of the bishop and snapped his fingers and turned back to Murray and the game. He bought himself another five moves and lost his lucky penny—and isn't that the way of life?

Now I'm stuck in a fold of green, the soil near enough to scent the air, and Sturgle's shuffling off, arguing with Murray over which shop once sold a *real* cup of coffee and greeting the joggers and stroller-bearers crowded under the April sun. Later, he'll remember. He'll make a little fuss and start to retrace his steps. Then he'll notice a hangnail or a young girl's smile and he'll forget again. And that's the trouble. I was never meant to be forgotten, to know mankind, to dread unknown tomorrows.

At first, I'd hoped Sturgle might be the one finally to release me, but he was a little too proud and bitter, made so by his time in the war, so I gather. Which war that was, exactly, was never quite clear, but it was one of machinery and commerce, not of blood and muscle as in earlier times. I came from that older kind of war, from a short, desperate struggle fought and forgotten long before the first of mankind's histories were written.

I started in the dreams of a Siberian shaman called Chotasuan and in the cunning of his chieftain's schemes. In the frozen forests above what is now China, the living was hard and the people hardy. For generations, the fish-eaters had spread into Shiwei territory, up along the rivers, ever northward and inland. They claimed the most sheltered campsites for their settlements, and the Shiwei gave way till they backed into the hills beyond the wind-blown forests where the moose and roe deer wintered. Rather than risk starvation or war, the chieftain sought a new land on which his people could still live in peace. North across the few remaining valleys to the southern steppe, he knew there would be bison and wood and sheltered draws in which to camp until spring, but he also knew the old tales of jealous neighbors.

The way proved long, the ridgetops high, and the skies were the colors of blizzard. A party went ahead to scout and hunt, but returned no news until an elder found them scattered across a bloodstained glacier within sight of the open plain. Boot tracks led west through patchy snow, toward a smoke-stained horizon and the pointed huts familiar from ancient stories of the bloody Joura clan. It was too late in the season to turn back, and with the strongest of the fathers dead, the tribe could go no farther. It would be war after all, or extinction.

The apprentices raised the broad roundhouse of birch poles and hides and built a fire safe from the wind. The council assembled around it. Chotasuan sang prayers, threw citrus-smelling herbs, and jingled his rattles and charms. The elders passed around an old copper blade, a knife bartered from the fish-eaters and once prized for peeling vegetables. They peered through the flames, chanting and spitting beseechments. They fired and pounded in the fish-eater way, using stones and flints to pound and carve the metal into a broad arrowhead edged with serrated wind-charm.

Chotasuan, his people's tears reflected in his own, sprinkled the coals with lichen crumbs and settled, cross-legged, into the spirit walk. The now-gleaming point was pressed to his palm. He drew in the prayer smoke and called on my brethren to enter and guide it and deliver the tribe from disaster and death. And so we did. And so I became.

I was hafted by sinew to a cedar shaft and fletched with snow crane feathers. A war party crept from the pines and west through boggy fields of paper-tipped cotton grass. The arctic sky was gray and growing darker. The horizon blurred with windblown frost haze. Joura huts rose like flints above the brittle grass, and the wind was touched by woodsmoke.

The huts circled a bonfire and a yard crisscrossed by Joura hurrying with hand-sleds and hide-bound parcels. In the center stood the khanling in his pointed fur hat, casting shadows through the fire-lit snowfall and directing preparations for the coming storm. When the chieftain saw him, he raised his simple bow and drew my fletching to his shoulder. With a yell meant to beg the spirits passage for the life he was about to claim, he broke silence and cover and let me fly.

I was happy enough to oblige. The winds by now were biting, but I steered the point through gusts and driving snow, across the grass and rocks and forming drifts, and into the khanling's heart. It was a powerful heart, and I felt the surprise of its owner as he fell, its warmth as he lay dying, his pride ebbing to fear for his death, for his tribe's huddled children, for children yet to come.

A small cut, and one man's loved ones would starve while another's lived. How had I been the one to swing that balance? For ages beyond imagining, I had been nothing so impressive as an atom. I had witnessed whole stars birthed and aged, their substance scattered to forge new worlds. Death was hardly new, yet here was loss measured not by entropy or erosion, but by depth of despair. Finally I had substance and some measure of will. Only now did I feel small and cornered. I recoiled from the bloodied trap.

It was not quite the slaughter it seemed, however. Joura fingers pulled me back into the firelight and the battle. Still out in the grass, indistinct through the whipping flurries, stood thirty Shiwei warriors, each hooded and furred and pitched to one side in the unmistakable stance of archers waiting to strike. I knew these were mostly elders whose backs had not been so straight in many seasons. I knew that only a few actually held bows, only some with arrows capable of taking more than a songbird at such range. But the Joura didn't know. They only knew their leader had been felled by an arrow shot straight and true through a wall of blinding snow, and they imagined its waiting brothers. They broke and ran, grabbing only what was packed for the storm or could easily be slung on their backs. They left me to the snow and the Shiwei to their abandoned supper. The chieftain had gambled. He'd saved his people at the cost of one life, and left the others time to flee and regroup further west before the blizzard overtook them.

The storm passed and I was left to ponder this world of men. The dead were carried up into the trees and tied. Chotasuan presided over their wind burials. There followed three days of mourning and three days of fasting and rest. When the tribe ventured across the steppe again, the grass was buried, the sunlit snow blinding, and the bison distracted, their heads deep in the drifts after forage.

A hunting party set out against the breeze, but the Shiwei had no experience with animals of such fearsome size and disposition. They approached with wooden spears, hoping to isolate a calf. Then the wind shifted. The calves retreated, and the cows closed ranks. The bulls turned and snorted white mist. A few of the largest charged, brown-gray hulks loping through belly-deep snow and hoof-kicked ice. They leaped on the hunters and knocked them down, snapping spears and bones alike. One made straight for the chieftain, who with only his bow for protection, had me already nocked and ready.

Muttering prayer, the chieftain leaped down to try a desperate belly shot. The horns sliced the snow and spun him. They shifted and stabbed and gored. The beast reared. The chieftain swung me up, and in an instant, I was buried in bone and the dark and heat of a thrashing, dying monster.

That was the last I saw of the Shiwei tribe. The chieftain died with the same thoughts as the khan-ling. The bull was abandoned to the wolves, and I to the ice and soil.

And I was glad to be forgotten. I wanted nothing but to take my leave and rejoin my brethren who know neither death nor eternity. For them, the end of the universe and its beginning are the same instant. They see all but perceive little, whereas I, now compressed to the vantage point of human thought, understand everything but see only through the nearest of my kind, not much beyond the bounds of the earth, which is to say virtually nothing. Yet that meager glimpse held all the horror I had known, and I welcomed escape, back to the impassive void.

Instead, I lay trapped in the soil, witness through the scattered prism of my brethren as civilization struck its sparks across the globe. At last I knew the ebbing tide of time. I knew the hopes of mothers everywhere, the despair of fathers forced to watch them shattered, the countless miracles forged by mankind's genius, and as often cast onto pyres.

Foraging gave way to farming, apprenticeship to university, squabbling for sustenance to industrialized warfare. On I waited, till the serrations flaked from my verdigris edges, till I wondered if one day I'd flake off with them and remain there forever, privy to mankind's every triumph and tragedy, yet marooned in isolation.

I couldn't blame Chotasuan. He hadn't understood the power he was wielding any more than Nero's engineers would later understand the cement that sealed their aqueducts, or the crew of the *Enola Gay* their bomb. These shamans of science knew little enough, having coaxed enough secrets from their world to remake it, improve it, and have a go at its destruction. Chotasuan knew nothing. He lived by hope and hunger, moored by tradition and guesswork, buffeted by forces he could no more understand than an ember caught in a whirlwind.

He interpreted these forces as spirits and hoped that if he turned to them in earnest they might offer guidance. He could not conceive to ask for more. And so his spirits answered in the only way they could, with an emissary of their own construction—with me. Thus acquainted, he might have learned everything. He might have ruled the earth, fed it, and

set its people free among the stars. Instead, he asked only for what he could understand, and the tiniest sliver of what I am was expended to steer a shaft through a snowstorm.

And so I came to be a knot of awareness twisted into the substance of the world. And if that substance had been bone or wood or stone—anything that any shaman had ever so invested before—it would have worn and decayed and been taken up again by life, and I'd have been released. But somehow the copper held me.

When I finally emerged, the bison and glaciers were gone, the landscape was verdant, and the snow had withdrawn up the mountains. I was warmed again by daylight, free to act and to guide—and finally to seek my escape.

A gaunt boy with pinched black eyes and broad shoulders pried me from his muddy plow. He wiped and looked me over well and showed a sun-darkened smile.

"Mother!" he called, hurrying me over to a stooped-backed woman, a kindly looking thing with thirty finger rings and one good eye. He held me out like a prize and asked, "What will the old man say to this?"

"Show respect," she said, gently cuffing his cheek. Then she gripped his hand to steady me under her gaze. "What is this, a talisman?"

He nodded. "I will ride to Fevralskoye in the morning and offer it in payment."

"No." She took me up for a closer look and wiped me with her thumb. "I'll go myself."

The mother tucked me in her basket with the garlic and kale and carried me into her house, a simple, tin-roofed shack of whitewashed wooden planks. She bound me to a leather cord and hung me from a peg where I waited, buried in folds and furs while she tended a daughter delirious with fever.

At first light she appeared in a deerskin caftan richly appointed with beads and embossing and colored with bright ochre dye. She gave the boy his instructions, slipped me around her neck, and set off on the back of a stocky black Panje horse that never broke a walking pace and seemed to be constantly chewing.

We rode through ragged fields of oats and rye and along a rushing, cobbled stream. When we passed clumps of purple meadowsweet, good for fever tea, I tried to guide her to them. I swung to one side and tugged at the cord, but she only swatted as if to shoo an insect. Further along, she stopped and dismounted to slip past a log in the path, a fallen birch with rings of medicinal bracket fungus. Again, I pulled and twisted and tried to make her see. She held up the cord and stared. She even wet a finger to test the wind. But then she clucked and climbed back on the Panje's back and continued on her way. Reduced from spirit guide to ornament, I was obliged to await our appointment.

We continued east through wooded hills to a settlement where rows of wooden houses faced deep-rutted lanes and dray horses hauling people and tools by the wagon load. The people moved with industry, and the air filled with oil smoke and engine noise and Russian conversation. We passed all this by, and in the wooded hills, found a clutch of metal-roofed log houses with shutters and carved pediments over the windows.

We stopped near a circle of Tungus farmers who had gathered around a great open fire. They all watched a dancing man whose brightly painted buckskins, high ruddy cheeks, and mask of carved, inverted antlers gave him the look of a jovial demon. The mother dismounted and spoke to a distracted young man who called himself "second-spirit" to this shaman. When he laid eyes on me, his face grew bright and he asked three times after the ailing child's name. Then he broke through the crowd and laid me around his master's neck. The shaman's eyes sparkled and he nodded at the woman. Then he resumed his prancing with blue and yellow ribbons coiling behind like the tail of a strutting game cock.

I could have done much for this shaman. Manifest as I was, I could have answered the prayers of all his petitioners, guided them to medicinal herbs and seams of gold, and found their stolen goods and missing loved ones. Instead, they paid the shaman to prance and spin and left no less abject than they had arrived. The shaman grew little richer and no wiser, and I remained as marooned as ever. Chotasuan's people had barely understood our kind or how to receive our guidance. These later folk had forgotten

even how to seek it. To the shaman, I was payment, a valuable bauble and token of ancient authority. He went on as before, asking the spirits to work magic beyond their powers in words none could hear, save for me. With his cavorting dance and drunken nights, I could no more reach him than wash away the stench of his hides and sweat.

By the time the great trans-Siberian railroad opened, the shaman's wanderings had taken him south and west and into contact with the smallpox. He died without the counsel of the spirit walk, and his country seemed ready to follow. Protests over peasant indenture ignited strikes and mutiny and armed confrontation. From a sack in a crumbling hovel, powerless and ignored, I witnessed pretty frontier streets fill with wasted blood as young men and women with common dreams fought to the death to achieve them. Was this to be my lot then? Mute witness to tragedy?

While I lay buried, humanity had levered the natural proclivities of my brethren into powerful technologies—and confused success for understanding. Like children playing at silhouettes, they had peered ever deeper into shadows and ever farther from the lights that made them. I could not see their future, but I knew secrets yet undiscovered, and that strong lenses can set fire even in the hands of the blind. Mankind's imperfect vision had grown powerful indeed—well beyond that of the brutes who called me fourth. The wants that haunted their simple lives were now met a dozen times over for a dozen times as many, yet mankind's jealousy was greater than ever. Every invention was turned to warfare. Every act of genius left unintended ripples. And there *was* genius, more than on a million other worlds scattered through the trackless void. Mankind was a marvel, but his cherry tree dreams were never far from nightmare. I had witnessed destruction on a cosmic scale. Now I knew the meaning of loss. I understood now the agonies of those ancient chiefs and I did not wish to see them replayed by the billions.

I was stuck. If I could have chanted and breathed the lichen smoke, if I could have entered the spirit walk myself, then I would have sought my escape. But then I'd have already been free, wouldn't I? No, I could only be released as I was called, by someone with the guileless innocence of old Chotasuan.

Someone who, given a glimpse of real knowledge, would use it to free me and not to set this world ablaze. In finding this savior, I would have to be cautious. Better to endure another billion tortuous nights than see as many children consigned to hellfire. And time, if recent events were a guide, was running out.

✿

After the revolt, the shaman's second bartered me to an innkeeper who traded me for boots. I made my way south in a trader's pocket, down the Amur to Khabarovsk, and through several more hands to a scrap merchant's forge. I emerged from the furnace unfazed and no less hobbled, but now in the form of a fine bronze bell. I was crated and shipped down to Vladivostok and there, mounted on the forecastle of the merchant steamer, *Stepenny Posadnik*.

Little in nature can match the organic unity of a sea captain at his watch, breaking his fast with steaming black coffee, his bridge alight with salmon glimmers mirrored from the Okhotsk Sea. Captain Gorbatov was a hard man bent to hard labor and accustomed to the ocean's tyranny of boredom and sudden terror. Despite this—or because of it—he found solace in the rhythms and simple beauties of his world: the life-carpeted rookeries in Schastya Bay, the winter ice north of Sakhalin Island, the plumes of purple mist blown by white belugas at twilight. I soaked it all up, fascinated by the living networks that found their roots in the sea and by this creature, man, who made so much of so little. I wondered, given the right man, what might be done to point his way, not through battle, but toward the enlightened future available to, and imperiled by, no other being.

When the Bolsheviks seized power, the Japanese came to defend their frontier—or perhaps to push it northward. *Posadnik*, was a name they might know from the earlier confrontation at Tsushima island, so the captain had it painted out with *Kazantsev*, the name of a childhood friend. He learned to say *Konnichiwa* and *Sayonara* and to drink the odd glass of saki, though he found it weak as rain water. He survived the revolution and the border tensions and went on plying cereals and coal up and down the coast for many years, but the Japanese were no longer

the aloof neighbors they had been. Their incursion into Manchuria finally convinced him the waters between the two nations had grown too dangerous. To the north, Stalin was rebuilding Nikolayevsk at the mouth of the Amur. Captain Gorbatov applied to take his pension there.

As a bell, I suffered from a slow, wasting corrosion caused by impurities in the scrap from which I'd been cast. So when the good captain retired, I was retired with him and installed in a fancy metal frame on a post beside his porch step.

Captain Gorbatov had grown old and his children had grown old. His granddaughter, Katya, had a child of her own when she was widowed by Stalin's madness and received word that her grandfather was drinking. By the summer of 1938, she was living with him and clerking for a fish packer. On a moonless August night there came a knock at the gate in the high, paneled fence that screened the captain's garden. Katya carried a lantern out through the yard, pulled back the bolt, and spoke at length and with some energy to the shadows. Finally, she stepped aside to admit a tall, blond woman in a long pleated skirt and woolen vest. The woman scowled, swept dubious eyes over the too-late vegetables that overfilled the yard, and threaded her way up the path.

She introduced herself as Tamara Ulyanov, an ethnographer from the Russian science academy, and produced a typewritten letter. Gorbatov unfolded the paper as Katya held the light for him. The letterhead bore a sword and sash and the words, "*Blut Und Boden.*" The woman spoke as if she'd grown up in Leningrad, but the letter was written in German.

"What's this to me?" the captain said.

"That is from General Secretary Sievers of the German Ahnenerbe. He has requested our assistance in gathering certain ethnographic data, and for diplomatic reasons we have been instructed to—"

"Spy on the Jews—our neighbors."

"Hardly spy, Captain. We have been asked to assist with a survey of certain anthropological and anatomical—"

"I ask you again, grazhdanka..."

"Ulyanov."

"I am not a Jew, Tamara Ulyanov. My granddaughter here, is not a Jew. There are no Jews among all the many graves of Nikolayevsk-on-Amur so far as I know."

"We are looking also for certain artifacts." The woman ran her eyes over me, then looked back at the captain.

He regarded her, his big toes poking through tattered slippers and digging the nails into the soft rotted ends of the porch boards. He rested a hand on my steel frame. "What would you want with the memento of an old sea captain?"

"Rather more than a memento, I think."

Katya was reaching to hang the lantern back by the doorway. Now she spun back around with the light. "Deda, what is it? What does she mean?"

The woman answered. "I am told your grandfather tells certain stories when his tongue is sufficiently moistened."

The captain studied a sprig of knapweed growing amidst the dried blooms of his chrysanthemums. "Stories, yes..."

"Deda, shush!" The hinges squeaked behind Katya the way they always did when too much weight was on the iron knob. To the woman, she said, "My grandfather is prone to drink. Never you mind his stories."

The woman stood in the captain's shadow. She studied his face. She studied me. Her nose was straight, her complexion unlined by disappointment. Finally she said, "There is no point in denying what your protestations have already confirmed. Show me the bell. Show me how to use it. My associates will make you a wealthy man."

At this, the captain stood tall. "What use have *your associates* for a half-rotten bell?"

The woman's eyes were fixed, her smile, sullen. "Do not insult me, Captain. What use had your freighter for a bell that sounds its own collision? That gives three day's warning before a typhoon? What use, now, has a warship?"

Of course she was right. War was coming. The captain could well imagine my utility to the fuhrer's navy. Even he, however, could not fathom the danger I posed in the hands of the Reich. I had learned sympathy for earthly affairs through the eyes of the people around me, but Chotasuan had asked for a guide, not a conscience. Once the Ahnenerbe worked out how to pose their questions, I'd have no choice

but to answer. They would waste time on nonsense, of course—pointless queries about their mythical master race and other myths that would prove useless to their cause. Then they'd turn me over to their war ministers. If they asked, I could tell them where Zhukov had deployed his troops and what Churchill fed to his code breakers. Without meaning to, I'd help them starve twenty million Russians and exterminate whole races. I'd teach them how to build the neutron bomb and teleport it into Roosevelt's bedroom.

The captain could not foresee these things, but neither was he a fool. "Communists are the sworn enemies of anti-semitism, isn't that what Stalin says?"

The straight nose dropped a bit. "Of course. Racial chauvinism deflects the working people from striving against capitalism." Her eyes sparked like embers in the lamplight. "But what is good for the people is not always what is good for the state."

The captain nodded. "I think you can let yourself out, Tamara Ulyanov."

The woman blanched. "Let us sit and talk," she said. "Your bell can help the fight against Jewish cultural domination. Hitler may not be a true friend, but he *is* a true nationalist." She stepped closer and spoke more softly. "You want to be on the right side of history, don't you, Captain?"

The captain moved to block the steps. "And if I don't see history as you would like? What then? I suppose your *associates* will send their bar brawlers around to steal from an old man?"

She stiffened. "There are greater dangers in this world than petty thugs."

The captain stood his ground. "Of that, I have no doubt. Good night, grazhdanka."

The woman demurred and stepped back. "Very well then, but I urge you to consider my words. Good night, Captain."

She withdrew, and before she'd even reached the gate, Katya filled the captain's ears with frozen whispers. "Deda, what are you doing? She's the same kind who turned my Stefan over to the Gulag. Do you think she will leave us in peace?"

As the gate spring whined through the garden, she allowed a stronger voice. "Call her back! Give her what she wants."

"Go check on the baby," he said.

"Deda... Dedushka, please..."

"Go! Take her in the back room."

Katya stared for a moment, then withdrew, leaving the lamp swinging from its hanger. The captain turned and ran his finger around my rim. "What of it, bell? Will Tamara Ulyanov leave us be?"

The Ulyanov woman had been right. While at sea with the captain, a few close calls had necessitated my sounding the alarm on my own initiative. My mass was now such that I could only shift it with difficulty, but one good clank against the striker was sufficient to rouse a drunken watch—and to ignite the captain's interest. Once he learned I could answer him, he swore off drink for half a voyage and became convinced the others would rise against him for sorcery. In time, we came to an understanding. I'd give one good tip for yes or a more subtle double waggle for no. The slow, rocking nod I gave now needed no prior definition; it had just the character of a head shaking in despair.

The captain nodded, glanced at the still-creaking gate, and tramped into the house. In a moment he returned and hollered after the woman. He gave my frame a sudden jerk, and I flipped and rang like the call to mass. Seconds later, the woman reopened the gate.

"Yes?"

"I've changed my mind," said the captain. With one hand against my stanchion, he let the other wave dismissively at the gate. "Well, come in," he said. "Don't stand in the damp." He was wearing his white skipper's cap.

The gate swung shut and the woman picked her way back up through the darkness of the sheltered garden.

"You can have my old bell," the captain said. "You can wrap it up and take it to the fuhrer himself if that is your wish, but on this one condition."

The woman stepped around a tomato plant set in a large clay pot in the center of the path. "And what is that?"

His jaw set, the captain pulled from my shadow an old but formidable carbine. Before the woman could do more than gawk, he raised it level and fired. She fell, and he hurried down the steps and past her through the shadows. He peered through the gate, bolted it tight, and returned to poke the body with the carbine. He stooped to collect the woman's hand and rolled her off of his cauliflowers.

"First, you must say, please," he said.

The door crashed open and out flew Katya. "Deda, what is it?" She saw the body, then ran down the steps to his side. "What...what have you done? Do you think—"

"I think it is dark and the neighbors will understand there are snakes about."

"You fool! She'll have others who know she was coming here. You should have called the NKVD!"

"And if she is a traitor, they would have shot her for me. But if she was acting for the state as she claimed..."

Katya shivered. "You'll be shot. Or sent to the camps like Stefan."

"Yes," he said, "These things may happen. But you and the bell will be safe."

"What?"

"And my great granddaughter, of course."

"Deda! Why?"

The captain squeezed his granddaughter's shoulder and looked into her eyes. "Katya my child, it's true a man must pick his battles, but enemies are sometimes like in-laws. Some you choose, others you only learn to recognize at a safe distance." He wiped a tear from her cheek. "Now go inside and gather your things," he said, "I have some gardening to do."

The old man had set his course. Neither Stalin nor Hitler was to have me. He would sacrifice himself for what was more to him than life. And I would help him—for what was more than freedom.

✿

The body was interred beneath a plot of winter cabbage. By morning, the captain had cut down my stanchion, fixed me to a wooden base, and packed me in his steamer trunk with a few cherished belongings. Thus provisioned, he hitched up the wagon, a meager contrivance with two spoked wheels and a basket just large enough for Katya to lie in with the trunk and her daughter and a cover of carrots and greens. The captain was taking no chances.

As the Panje was no more than a pony, the captain walked alongside, guiding her through the early mists and around the worst of the mud toward the river. The wharf was a dizzy line of ship's masts and funnels and yellow brick warehouses with bright metal roofs, all new since the revolution. The captain checked and rechecked a telegram that he'd already consulted several times. Finally, he found the berth where *Stepenny Kazantsev*, newly refitted, sat building up steam for departure. He deflected an inquisitive dockhand and soon was embracing the vessel's new skipper and speaking quickly and earnestly in his ear.

The conversation, through hushed, went on for several minutes. Then the skipper directed his deck hands up toward the bow while Captain Gorbatov walked the wagon across the ramp and into the hold and tied the Panje to a railing. By the time the sea doors were shut and the crew had gone to stations, the baby had grown restless. The captain hurried to free her and his granddaughter from the vegetables.

"Vasili Gregorovich is not happy," he said, popping the latches on the steamer trunk, "but he cannot refuse his old master. We are expected in the wardroom. In case of trouble, this will explain for us, eh?" He pulled out a bottle of vodka and gave his granddaughter a wink. "Even those children in the NKVD have grandfathers who sometimes pine for the old days, yes?"

✿

When next the captain appeared, the hold was dark and the ship had sailed and come again to rest. He transferred me to a carpetbag, then climbed through a hatch and down the side of the vessel, down a set of steel rungs to a motor launch loaded with flour and sugar and four other men bound for shore. We'd steamed north and moored at a lightering buoy off Ayan, a once-important port on the sea of Okhotsk, all but abandoned since the civil war and the closing of the rail line decades earlier. The port had fallen to ruins, and the town was so derelict, there weren't even any police to meet the launch. Snow-specked mountains, pink in the setting sun, slept around the city. The supplies were offloaded onto push carts, and the men set off past darkened warehouses to a nondescript brick depot, conspicuous for its unbroken windows. As arrangements were made for the flour, the captain stopped in the lee of the broken-down security shack. He made

surreptitious glances at the others as he unbuttoned his greatcoat, then he crouched and opened my bag.

"I don't know what you are, bell, nor whence you came, but you've always been true enough, though I've asked you for naught. Now I must plead for my Katya. Steer her as you have me—and give me this one night of folly—and you'll more than make up for an old fool's tongue."

He had come here to gamble. The five men from *Kazantsev* were joined by five more from the town. All knew each other well except for the captain, who was vouched for by two who'd sailed under him. He carried me into the depot, past rows of oak barrels set standing on end and past wooden crates stacked like tenements. In an office in the back, the shades and bolts were pulled and the working papers cleared from the tables.

The captain wisely avoided games that would have required me to see into the future or affect events beyond my control. Godori was played for kopecks using tiny floral cards of a Chinese design. Players only had to call "go" or "stop" to see their bets doubled or held. I knew the minds and cards of the participants, and the gentle tap of my rim against his boot was sufficient to indicate the wisest move. He kept my bag by his side and worked patiently, losing just often enough to keep his body parts intact. After Godori came higher stakes and poker, and in the final hours, a move to a disused cold store reclaimed as an office, and the company of a tattooed man named Mirzoyan to whom all the others deferred.

By dawn, the captain had slipped off into the mountains, and I was back on *Kazantsev*, steaming for the Aleutians with Katya. The captain had returned only long enough to kiss his sleeping granddaughter and return me to the trunk. "Vasili Gregorovich is a good communist," he had said, "but his father was with the White Guard. He will risk everything to save my Katya now, just as I risked everything to save his family from Triapitsyn during the war."

He pulled out the bottle, worked loose the cork, and tipped the mouth to his lips.

"If the Jews frighten the Germans," he said, "perhaps it is only that they know one thing: there are some things greater than nations."

For a moment, I thought he might empty the bottle and manage yet to spoil all his plans, but he only patted me and pushed in the cork, then closed me into the bag.

✿

West of Japan, *Kazantsev* met the steamer, *Puget Clipper* and exchanged illegal American machine parts for illegal white caviar. A hefty bribe and a few choice threats bought Katya passage to the United States. In these years between the wars, security was not very tight on the west coast and a pretty girl with a hungry child wasn't given a second look. The wad of greenbacks folded around my striker opened doors and bought groceries until she was more than settled. By the time the Japanese attacked Pearl Harbor, she was seeing a boy who sold Fordson tractors in Seattle and who would later win a medal building airstrips in the Solomons.

Never once did Katya ask anything of me. Time was running short and she was my best hope for release, but the captain had entrusted me with her welfare, and I never invited communication that might have somehow exposed her, or that might have invited questions to which she could not bear the answers. She never learned of the captain's cancer. She never knew that death by gunfire had been his choice, that it had been precipitated by the vodka bottle, stuffed with a rag, set alight, and thrown through the window of a government office to help cover and purchase her escape. I had known from the captain's thoughts, of course, and when the wartime scrap drives were announced, I knew it was time to finish what he'd started.

It was a sunny spring morning when the loudspeakers paused outside the rented houses of Crawford Loop. Katya was nailing in a picture hook and I sat on the mantle. When the truck stopped outside, I swung with all the force I could muster, enough to clank, to overturn my base, and to crash to the concrete hearth. Softened by corrosion, I broke like a clay flower pot. Katya shrieked and flew down beside me, her eyes filling with tears. I saw in her memories the captain and her Stefan and the others she had left or lost. She thought her nailing had made me fall, that she had spoiled her only keepsake of their lives. She touched the red tassel by which the captain had often rung me and hugged the striker to her chest.

The loudspeaker echoed again: "Make sure they're sunk, bring out your junk." I—now just a fragment bearing a word of Cyrillic script, waggled and jumped as if to say, "Go on Katya, go and tip me into the bin." It was her patriotic duty to her adopted homeland, after all.

"All right, bell."

✿

A scrap barge carried me to California, where I was smelted and rolled and trucked to the mint. I became the last copper penny struck before wartime production shifted to steel. Then it was cash drawers and pockets up and down the coast, till an Army airman named Sal Litvack decided I was lucky and slipped me in his wallet. Rather than luck, I nearly earned him a section-eight. So I held my peace while he hunted submarines off Catalina and then built houses in Philadelphia. After the war, he left me in a shoebox of mementos and medals meant to have been sealed in his casket. But his grandson rescued me and put me under glass, and *his* grandson sneaked me to school to buy chocolate. Another year and several hands carried me to Smith's Drug in Fairhill, and the baseboard where Sturgle found me, a very rare coin indeed.

And so here I lay. Mankind has tamed the Earth, sprinkled its deserts with ersatz suns, and ventured beyond its skies. He's grown invincible, indomitable, like some hardy, sprawling vine that paints the hillsides with waving color till it chokes out the trees and the roots are gone and the earth all slides away. Technology tends and protects him, but it was adversity that made him wise, the hunt and struggle that honed his creative spark. And what nature makes, she as quickly begins to erode. The hammer lost man his jaw muscles, the stone knife his canines, the lever the bulk of his strength. What will ease and plenty cost him? How long will the machines support him once the minds that made them have atrophied?

The greatest danger to humanity was never war, famine, or plague. It was success. Very soon, mankind must push beyond the grist of nature's mill or slip and fall beneath it. I'd hoped perhaps a small spark in the right place might yet break the wildfires to come. I'd hoped there was time yet to strike such a spark. But here I am. The soil looms close, a dark and quiet crypt in which to remember the chieftain's children and a million million others, and millions yet to come.

Sun-dappled green flicks past and tumbles—spins faster and faster until I'm sickened by the simple frenetic intensity of motion. Then I'm lying flat and still. The sun warms my metal. A stroller wheels past and a child bends to examine me. Her sandy curls hang loose against the cloudless sky. Her hazel eyes squint against the sunlight. She picks me up with bitten nails and cracks a gap-toothed smile.

"Look, Momma. Poppa says if it's heads-up it means good luck."

The mother, pushing the stroller, smiles back. "Come along my duckling."

The girl balances me on the crook of her finger, flicks me into the air, then catches me with a clap. Each time she peeks between her palms, she smiles and tries again. All the way home, I always land heads-up.

Jessica turns out to be eight and a precocious reader. Her headboard is stacked with books from H.G. Wells to Douglas Adams. A T-shirt draped over a straight-backed chair bears the famous image of Albert Einstein sticking his tongue out for the camera, which gesture she gleefully returns as she empties out her pockets. No Ouija board under this bed, but she has something even better. Someone has made her a table, butcher-block style, tiled with glued-up alphabet blocks. As I bounce onto the lacquered surface, I try to roll as I did on Sturgle's chess table, but only manage an unnatural flip onto a half-open gum wrapper.

"Lucky penny," Jessica says. Then she sings, "Penny for a ba-all of thread. Anoth-er for a needle," and flips me a few more times, giggling each time I come up heads. "Silly penny," she says, scrunching up her eyebrows and parroting the stern tone she has doubtless heard from her mother, "what am I going to *do* with you?"

Quick now. I fling myself from her palm and bounce across the table. I careen around, only just veering in time to avoid flying down into the socks and dust bunnies hiding under her box spring.

Round and round the table I roll, feeling my mass and getting the lay of the letters. If I watch my speed, I can spin across any letter, and so spell out a message as I roll. And so I begin.

"A-S-K...M-E...Q-U-E-S-T-I-O-N-S..."

Jessica's mouth falls open and her lollipop threatens to fall. She doesn't understand, not just yet, but there's time yet. At long, long last, there's time.

Copyright © 2015 by C. Stuart Hardwick

Michael Bishop is the author of more than thirty novels. He is a multiple Nebula and Locus Award winner, and a multiple Hugo nominee. This is his first appearance in Galaxy's Edge. *This story was previously published in* The Door Gunner *and* Other Perilous Flights of Fancy.

THE ANGST, I KID YOU NOT, OF GOD

by Michael Bishop

The ztun stunned us. They had observed that certain arrogant superpowers and certain stateless fanatics gripped Earth in a brutal vise, and they were appalled. Outraged on our behalf, the ztun intervened. After parking their light cruiser in disguised orbit around Earth, they dropped microscopic chemical "seeds" into our atmosphere. These reacted with our terrestrial gasses, rendering any human indigene—and *only* human indigenes—comatose for from twenty-four hours to an entire year, depending on the innate bellicosity of those incapacitated. You could say that the ztun *gassed* us, but really they reconfigured our air. The ztun stunned us, for our own good.

The ztun do not discriminate among "civilized" worlds in exercising either their judgment or their powers. They reconnoiter the dense core and the diffuse spiral arms of our galaxy making their lists and checking them twice. They determine which sentient species are naughty and which nice and chemically correct every instance of the former. The magic grains by which the ztun reconfigure a planetary atmosphere stymie the worst bullies for a full local year, but let the lowly and the peaceful resume their lives after only a single day of oblivion. By the time the ztun stunned us human beings, they had already "gassed" a dozen intelligent species in our galactic vicinity. Then they abducted the most warlike leaders, to psychoanalyze in the long transit to their home world.

As an analogy, let me cite the gassing of the Moscow Opera House, decades ago, when Islamic separatists seized that building and held its occupants hostage. The black-clad rebels threatened to blow everyone up if the Russian leader refused to stop the war in Chechnya and to grant it independence. Wisely or foolishly, the Russian authorities used a secret gas to knock out everyone in the Opera House, terrorists and hostages alike. Unfortunately, so crudely did this gas work that, although it ended the siege, it also killed many of those gassed, including one hundred and twenty hostages.

The ztun, however, are better chemists, physicists, astronomers, engineers, and general technophiles than those bumbling Russians. Indeed, they excel at such tasks, lacking peers in the known universe. And so, when altering the atmospheres of worlds with morally pesky and/or deficient intelligent species, they rarely take a life. Those autochthons that accidentally die the ztun regard as martyrs to their ethical cleansing of yet another reprehensible species.

"We've done you a favor," the ztun argued. "Uprooted your vilest weeds and taken them home to re-pot as hollyhocks."

"Roses," I said to my shipboard counselor. "The hollyhock's a gaudy plant with no poetic resonances."

"We know hollyhocks," Counselor Ztang said. "And, believe me, we find them lovelier than your run-of-the-trellis Bobby Burns roses."

I belonged to a small caste of bellicose entities whom the ztun had chosen to take home to their small planet orbiting the star Spica (274 light years from Earth). The inside of their light cruiser—what I'd seen of it—resembled a cross between a brand-new sewer system (lots of tubular passages, metal ladders, and oddly placed manhole covers) and a high-tech playground (redwood monkey bars, cedar-sided slides and swings, and crumbly peat-moss-carpeted floors). The decor stemmed in part from the fact that the ztun are lanky humanoid legumes with lianas for limbs and yellowish pods for bellies, butts, and heads. However, I spent most of my time in a metabolic-suspension berth—the ztun call them beds, of course—to avoid the effects of aging, which the ztun escaped by sprouting new appendages every few days.

Every other alien captive *also* went into a suspension berth. At length, I met five others. Counselor Ztang brought us together now and again for—well, *group-therapy sessions.* Previously, you see, I had served the Half Vast Rocky Mountain Hegemon as commander-in-chief of its Global Interdiction & Liberation Force. So I bridled when Ztang told me to sit, to speak, or to pay more attention. Who did Ztang think he was, anyway? And why should a man of my status kowtow to a yellowbelly bean like him, even under threat of instant molecular dispersal?

Well, circumstances change minds, and rapping with my alien therapy mates gave me to understand that rank is relative and life a fleeting dream—when it isn't an outright outré nightmare.

At my first session, Ztang introduced me to the chief decapitationist of an inner planet of 61 Cygni A (11.2 light years from Earth). We met in the main therapy cabin, where a mother-of-pearl mist imparted a gothic surreality to our talk. The air in this cabin was Omnirespirable O (the ztun designation for a universally life-supporting mix), and Ztang gave my partner and me DNA-coded translator scarabs. I put mine in my ear, but the reptilian Cygnusian stuck his to his cobalt-blue throat. The lizard called himself a "toidi," his name for the dominant intelligent species on his home planet, and, frankly, he stank, like a combo of sour apricots and snaky sex.

"Go ahead," Counselor Ztang urged the toidi. "Tell General Draper who you are and why you're here."

"Call me Al," the lizard said. And then he wept, exuding from his skin a ruby-red oil that lent his signature B. O. a sweet fecal undertone.

"Gaaah," I said.

Our scarabs translated, rendering my *"Gaaah"* into late-empiric English as *"Al's scent borders on the putrid."* Al noted that he could say the same of mine, so Ztang broke out a spray bulb to neutralize the odors gagging us both.

Al admitted authorizing all the political decapitations in the predominant nation on the only life-supporting planet circling 61 Cygni A. He admitted having the victims' severed heads placed atop the cactus-ringed rocks marking their family burrows. Al felt no remorse for this brutality, though, which he claimed had kept his nation from plunging into cold-blooded anarchy. Ztang's mouth fringes rippled, but he said nothing.

I spoke into his silence: "Counselor, how can a species that's poisoned the air of twelve planets presume to teach *anyone* nonviolent behavior?"

My mind turned inside out. An indivisible blackness came upon me.

But my *second* official gathering included the toidi again and an energy creature from Epsilon Eridani IV (10.7 light years from Earth). This creature, with a head like an otter's, flickered unpredictably in and out of view. She answered to the name Seyj and smelled of stale Worcestershire sauce and fried plastic—until Ztang neutralized her scent with his papaya-shaped spray bulb.

Seyj and her kind lived amid a system of charged fields that the chief political entity on her planet generated and withdrew at whim, often killing fellow "caparoina"—as all intelligent Eridanians were called—hostile to its policies. The ztun believed that Seyj herself had authorized the withdrawal of fields resulting in two million caparoina deaths. Like Al, however, Seyj insisted that her actions had saved her world from both barbarism and commercial stagnation.

Ztang eyed me meaningfully. "Please, General Draper, reintroduce yourself to Al and tell both him and Seyj what most troubles you this morning."

The bean terrified me. What if my words again rendered me *non grata*? Sensing my reluctance, Ztang lifted a finger pod and swore that nothing I uttered would expel me from his good graces.

"In that case," I said, "what most frets me today is the impunity with which you judgmental ztun have butted in all over our galaxy."

Al gasped and sweated his ruby sweat. Seyj's head pulsed out of view, leaving only the gray outline of her body behind.

And, yes, an indivisible blackness seized me.

But Counselor Ztang forgave me. A week later, in a new session, I met a seven-armed, chitin-plated sentient caterpillar from the Tau Ceti system (11.9 light years from Earth). This caterpillar, Kaa Lotcharre, had invented a liquid incendiary called "spark tar," which flowed across the countryside igniting the enemy upon contact and reducing him to ash. Lotcharre—scientist and tar master—boasted of his expertise as a materials engineer and a genocidal assassin. Al and Seyj, brutal decapitationist and ruthless force-field manipulator, sat unmoving, visibly cowed. I laughed—derisively, I admit—and was slammed *a third time* into indivisible blackness.

Eventually, I met two more war criminals, the last in my group of six: a jellyfish with front-facing eyes and a living slab of ochre granite that pulsed with ennui and a large inner constituency of agitated flecks of mica. The jellyfish hailed from Groombridge 34 (11.6 light years from Earth), smelled vaguely like cotton candy, and answered to a name something like Gilneta. The granite slab had originated on a planet orbiting Lacaille 9352 (11.7 light years from Earth). A hermaphrodite named Bacmudsorak, it locomoted on a rubbery foot and secreted a musky slime that it shoved backward to create a pressure gradient enabling it to move forward. Bacmudsorak kept many crystalline personalities within its body and felled its foes by sending subliminal bolts of igneous music at them via headache-inducing radio frequencies.

I said nothing when Counselor Ztang introduced me to Gilneta, the jellyfish, and so escaped early banishment to my suspension berth. But during my next session, with Bacmudsorak on hand in the guise of a glowing, lopsided coffee table, I tapped my feet to some sort of heavy, heartfelt, subliminal music.

Al's wattles undulated, Seyj's head pulsed in and out of view, Lotcharre's seven arms writhed, and Gilneta's iridescent violet bell swayed as if combers from a fearful oceanic storm were pounding her. As for Counselor Ztang, his runners grew and shrank in beat-driven cycles, and the beans in his pods rattled like a set of traps. Bacmudsorak thrummed, and everyone jived. Don't ask me what that rock confessed to, but, unlike the rest of us, it did communicate a candid remorse.

Over our next few meetings, against my expectations, Al, Seyj, Kaa Lotcharre, Gilneta, Bacmudsorak, and I *bonded*.

Al lamented the inevitable heartbreak of cold-bloodedness in most toidi family relationships. Seyj confessed the trauma of learning that a sister caparoina had a bipolar electrical orientation, and Kaa Lotcharre observed that few citizens of his war-torn land could manage the complex excruciations of metamorphosis without breaking; indeed, he had spun silk about himself at least three times to *escape*

adulthood rather than to *trigger* it. Gilneta opened up, lamenting the nettlesome nature of jellyfishhood, particularly one's dependence for transport on methane swells and cetacean nudges. Bacmudsorak, swearing us all to secrecy, noted that early in its igneous development, it had harbored a millennia-long case of pyroclastic envy against a pit mine of collateral laminates. Even Counselor Ztang, usually one shut-mouthed bean, let slip that a virulent fungal smut had almost derailed his aspirations to enter the ztun space force.

And I, Myron "Pit Bull" Draper?

Well, I acknowledged that I had secured my high position in the Rocky Mountain Hegemon by boinking President Bobeck's wife, Eustace, and diverting a thousand shares of my own dirty-bomb stock to the portfolio of the Secretary of War. I also admitted my teenage affair with a comely creature on an Alberta sheep ranch, tossing hand grenades at protected wolves, paying a heroin addict to put a nail bomb in the mailbox of a peacenik fag, and using tax monies to indulge my three-decade-old pink-shoe fetish. I reckon I got carried away.

My support group listened closely. Seyj fought hardest to withhold judgment, I believe, and the disappearance of her head for part of this session no doubt bespoke the intensity of her ambivalence. Ztang dehisced, scattering a rattle of seeds across the floor, but everyone else offered upbeat, if bemused, encouragement.

When next we met, Seyj declared that of all us captives in the ztun therapy cabin, only I interposed artificial accoutrements between my body and their optical equipment. In short, I wore *clothes*.

"So?" Bacmudsorak said.

My refusal to appear nude, Seyj noted, left me open to accusations of betraying, at best, my human vanity and, at worst, a therapy-thwarting lack of candor.

Actually, Kaa Lotcharre wore a cap, a kind of yarmulke, but he, Al, and Gilneta called for me to shed the uniform in which the ztun had tweezered me aboard their ship.

Eventually, I gave in. What else could I do?

Instantly, the jellyfish from Groombridge 34 orbited my bipedal self, swimming about me as if in water rather than air. Seyj sent her head over to gape at me, and Al palpated me from neck to knee as I indignantly squirmed. Kaa Lotcharre shrugged seven times, eyeing me from afar.

"I presume that's your reproductive unit," he said. "But on the basis of its shape, not its size."

Pate to pediment, I flushed a bioluminescent red.

Seyj's head rebounded back to her flickering otterine form. "Ornament yourself again, Draper," she said. "You're not really hiding much, and after our last few sessions, I no longer relish playing the bully."

I obeyed, not so much out of embarrassment as from a sudden-onset chill, and I never appeared before them again minus my military blues. Which made me wonder just how "civilized" they could be, if none of their species had hit upon the concept of clothes for fashion, warmth, and intimidation.

And so, meeting and sleeping, sleeping and meeting, we passed our time aboard the ztun ship, *Conquistador*. The ties among us hired warmongers and genocidal maniacs grew tighter, more profound. Before my abduction, I would *never* have believed that the tidal dependencies of a jellyfish could elicit my sympathy, that the spiritual longings of an off-red slab of granite could influence my own, or that a whiff of lizard could render me maudlin. Which proves that astonishing links exist among the sentient creatures in our galaxy, and that even mercenary paladins from different planets pine for interspecies amity.

Although we never shared a meal—the ztun had foreseen major problems in our doing so—we shared our hang-ups and hopes, and we strove to forge a humane unitary personality from our separate barbaric faults.

Over time, we even touched one another in our suspension berths, via disorienting dreams, a few of which suggested the work of Hollywood & Whine vid directors. I often got on Bacmudsorak's frequency, and occasionally on Kaa Lotcharre's. Owing to their dreams, I soon understood that the caterpillar regarded metamorphosis as a personality-annihilating form of death, and that the Big Slab had a petrifying existential horror of the end of the universe, which it saw as nigh and certain rather than far off and theoretical. I mean, some of this stuff we had never even

talked about. In dreams begin derangements, I guess, and although none of us greatly minded getting to know our therapy mates better through our nightmares, we soon began to resist Counselor Ztang's commands to wrap up our regular sessions and to return to our beds.

"You're acting like sprouts," Ztang scolded. "Putting off bedtime for as long as you childishly can."

So off we'd slink to our coffins, where Al dreamt of cannibalizing a head that he had severed, Seyj emitted bursts of psychic energy that crisped our nerve endings, and Gilneta broadcast visions of juvenile polyps attacking leviathans in underwater grottoes as roomy as outdoor rodeo arenas. And we all quivered in unison, full of fret and dread, not to mention longing for a *regular* group-therapy session.

Then, during one such meeting (until that point, trauma-free), poor Gilneta up and died. One moment the medusa drifted about in the mother-of-pearl mist; the next, her tentacles dropped, her bell collapsed, and she plummeted like a defective parachute. The spray that Ztang used to neutralize our competing stinks failed, and the cabin filled with a stench commingling the odors of rum, kelp, and necrotic coconut meat.

Everyone froze—even Bacmudsorak looked a bit more rigid than usual—until Lotcharre inched across the floor and disposed of Gilneta's corpse by eating it. This act struck none of us as disrespectful, owing to the reverence with which Lotcharre ate and our own lack of relish for seafood.

After this incident, Bacmudsorak's nightmares worsened. Most of these dreams put the slab at their center: It turned red as lava, for example, and flowed downhill into a quenching pit; or broke into crystals as tiny as frost filaments and melted; or eroded over centuries into squishy sea sand. Then, in a nightmare of my own, Bacmudsorak set itself up in my old hometown as a tombstone:

GENERAL MYRON "PIT BULL" DRAPER

R. I. P.

I could not wake up. In fact, I would have died in my sleep if Lotcharre had not projected at me a dream in which the caterpillar did a clumsy impersonation of the Hindu goddess Kali. Then he grabbed a hookah and blew smoke rings. These rings had started to turn red, blue, and yellow, and to fuse into butterfly wings, when I finally slid out of nightmare and back into picture-free sleep.

At our next session, Ztang delivered a lecture. He informed us, brusquely, that our death fears were foolish and that Gilneta's demise should comfort rather than bum us out. Ztun science had discovered that our expanding universe was closed rather than open, and this fact meant that the universe would not diffuse into "a tenuous blanket of matter and antimatter debris," via the deterministic engines of the heat-death hypothesis, but would "cease its outward motion and contract." This action, in turn, would one day lead to a new Big Bang and the prospect of a fresh cycle of star making and civilization building.

I said, "Then we ought to call it the Big Boomerang!"

Nobody congratulated me on my coinage. (Maybe our scarabs had failed to find good equivalencies for *boomerang*.) Indeed, Bacmudsorak protested that, by *its* species' calculations, the universe lacked sufficient matter to generate the gravity necessary to prevent it from expanding forever. Lacking such a brake, the universe would never end, but persist unto eternity, in ever-widening, frigid darkness. Gilneta's death had made Bacmudsorak profoundly aware of this fact, and Ztang's recitation of a more optimistic formula for the fate of the universe could not persuade the Big Slab to renounce the real truth as it perceived it.

Ztang argued that although most other species' astronomers had failed to account for as much as ninety percent of the universe's mass, the ztun knew with certainty that dark matter and dark energy sufficient to halt and reverse universal expansion actually existed. This dark matter, he told us, consisted of particles that do not influence nuclear reactions, i.e., neutrinos, WIMPs (weakly interactive massive particles), and hypothetical quantum-level *ztun ztones.* The dark energy, on the other hand, arose not only from a tangle of fields dispersed throughout the vacuum at the subatomic stratum, but also from the hidden gravity-imparting properties of the angst of God.

"The angst of God?" we captives chorused.

"I kid you not." Counselor Ztang explained that although the religions of many sentient creatures either denied the need for a creation-triggering deity or held that God would "never suffer angst," the ztun had authenticated God's existence and conducted experiments confirming the prominence of divine dread among those dark energies still undetected by *our* species. And it was divine dread—the angst of God—that would keep the cosmos from slipping into ceaseless entropic decrepitude.

Silence—a localized entropic decrepitude—greeted Ztang's speech. We captives glanced at one another and then at Ztang, hoping that he would document his claim or die as our poor jellyfish had done. Ultimately, Lotcharre asked Ztang what the alleged deity had to feel any angst *about.*

"The unrelieved, inventive brutality of intelligent creatures against their own kind." Ztang looked at me and added, "The inhumanity of humanity, if you will, to its very self."

Ouch, I thought. Lotcharre lifted his seventh arm, as if saluting God, and with his other six arms embraced himself. Seyj's head faded from view, and the scorch of fried plastic wafted from her body. Al hunkered down like a lizard on a rock, and the mica in Bacmudsorak's topside manically twinkled.

"Now, do you see why we intervened in your worlds' affairs?" Ztang asked self-righteously.

Oh, man. I hated Ztang in this mode. Although I nodded, I tuned him out to think of what I most missed about my previous life: brown-nosing aides-de-camp, taking my paychecks in foldable cash, and net-surfing for pink shoes.

Bacmudsorak began to thrum, broadcasting to each of us, Ztang included, a beat that made our internal fluids ebb and flow erratically. "You want to lessen God's angst," the rock said.

"Right," Ztang said. "Very good."

"And by lessening God's angst, you will diminish the supply of dark energy at large in the universe."

"Maybe," Ztang said warily.

"And by lessening this dark energy," Bacmudsorak pursued, "you will guarantee the open-endedness of the cosmos, its heat death, and the suffocation of every contingent intelligence but God's."

"No." Ztang's various yellow pods had already begun to mottle.

"Yes," Bacmudsorak said. "Logic leads to a single conclusion, namely, that the ztun have aligned themselves with entropy and against the—"

I blurted, "*The force that through the green fuse drives the flower.*" Where had this line come from? Oh, yeah: from a postcoital session with Eustace Bobeck in a cabin at Camp David. She had written her masters thesis on Dylan Thomas.

Ignorant of my sources, Bacmudsorak finished its own sentence: "And against the powers of life and regeneration."

✿

What can I say? That was the last time the slab of granite from Lacaille 9352 met with us as a responsive entity. At our next meeting, Ztang had Al, Seyj, Lotcharre, and me sit around Bacmudsorak in its common default mode, that of a tabletop. We did not session, though. We played five-card stud, praying that no one would piss Ztang off again. Once, Lotcharre laid down his best hand with a loud slap, but our rebuking looks dissuaded him from taking the pot.

When we finally arrived on the ztun home world, the ztun stunned us again by canceling their re-education programs. (In a superfluity of budget consciousness, the ztun masses protested that their leadership had prioritized long-term cosmic health over their desire for bread and circuses, and demagogues made great capital of the "waste" implicit in trying to teach funny-looking, uneducable aliens how to play nice.) As a result, I went to work as a consultant to the producers of a mass entertainment about armed conflict, whom I introduced to the transgressive pleasures of gunplay and sensational explosions. I had so many pods, flowers, and stems flying around the set that you would have thought we were using a Salad Shooter.

The next day the director fired me, and I went into full-time begging mode, asking the government for return passage to Earth. Eventually, the Powers That Be relented and by light cruiser sent me home.

✿

Here on Earth, everything had changed, and changed again. Even so, my fellow Western Hemispherites grasped me to their bosoms and appointed

me to direct their Self-Defense Legions. The Easties soon picked a fight, and tomorrow an all-out war will likely begin. Still, but for the unfortunate angst of God, I could aver, "Life is good, my compatriots"; after all, I have work to do, a pet man-o'-war in my heated swimming pool, and a garden full of outsized purple hollyhocks.

—for George Alec Effinger
Copyright © 2004 by Michael Bishop

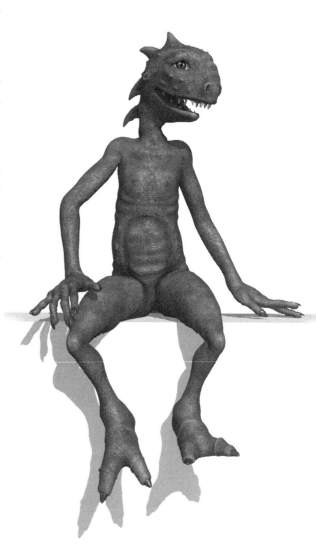

Australia's Sean Williams is the author of more than forty novels (including five New York Times bestsellers in the Star Wars *series), more than one hundred stories, and five collections. His latest novel is* Crashland, *second in the* Twinmaker *series. This is his first appearance in* Galaxy's Edge.

THE DARK MATTERS

by Sean Williams

The one thing she cannot think is that she's crazy.

Susan Barker is a small teenager with brown hair. Her weight is within the healthy band, and when she talks her eyes are still. When her therapist responds, however, her gaze moves constantly, roving around the office as though looking for something.

"They live in the shadows," she says. "They come out at night."

"Why?"

"Which part?"

"Let's start with the shadows."

"They can't stand the light because they're fragile. They're all that's left of us when the matter is gone."

Her eyes skitter about as her therapist takes this in.

"If I turned out the lights now, would they come?"

"No, because you're here. They like it when I'm alone."

"What do they do when you're alone?"

"Nothing but press in real close, all around me. I can feel them. It's like the darkness has weight, although I know that's impossible. They don't have any weight. They're just..."

"Ghosts?"

"No. That's not the right word. They're...echoes... of all the versions of me who went into a d-mat booth and didn't come out the other end."

The therapist taps the tips of his fingers together. The reference to d-mat ghosts is unexpected. Ever since the invention of matter transmission there have been people afraid of being disintegrated. They talk of zombies, of souls ascending to heaven long before the physical body has grown old and died, of half-remembered screams as the lasers go to work...

"Not just me, other people, too," Susan goes on. "Sometimes I can feel my mother next to me, and my ex-boyfriend on top of me. They come because they know me."

"Why?"

"Just because, I guess. Look, I know what you're going to tell me. You're going to tell me I'm wrong. But I know I'm not wrong. Life is complexity—that's what I learned in biology—but what difference does it make if complexity is born or grown or made out of nothing? As soon as someone steps from a booth, they have a new soul to replace the one in their old body. And meanwhile the old soul is set free. The old soul can wander for years before it gets home, where of course there's no room for it anymore. So it just... sticks close...remembering who it was and not feeling bad about it, I guess. It rejoices in me. It loves me, and so do all the others."

"That's an interesting theory, Susan."

"If you don't believe me, that's okay. I know I'm right. And if you put me on drugs like my parents want, that's fine too. You can even lock me away. It won't make any difference. They'll find me again. We'll always be together. Just so long as you turn the lights out sometimes, they'll come."

The therapist nods, even though she is wrong.

That wasn't what he was going to say at all.

✧

The one thing I cannot admit that is that she's right.

Not about the source of the dark ones, although her theory haunts me through the following sessions, and haunts me still when I get home, where I close the windows carefully, ensuring that no glimmer can enter my chambers and halls. I turn out the lights. The darkness is perfect. Through long practice I have learned to navigate without use of my eyes. I feel my way through dinner and toilet, never fumbling, never stumbling, all my other senses heightened.

I sense them gathering like soft breaths of night. They know my routine. As I lay down to sleep they press in around me, touching me everywhere—my cheeks, my eyelids, my throat, my stomach, my scrotum, the soles of my feet. So often mistaken for puffs of air, they are present even here in the blackened stillness of my room, where there can be no breezes.

Susan was right. There are things that live in the night. And she is not the only one who feels them.

The first patient to come to me with this complaint was a physicist. He explained the sensation away by evoking neutrinos that sluice constantly through us, unseen and unfelt. Why shouldn't some of them stick and form negative images of us, particularly when we ourselves, as users of d-mat, spend so much of our lives as incorporeal energies?

Then there was the social scientist who evoked impressions cast in a collective consciousness, psychic eddies that survive much longer and travel much farther than they would have in times before d-mat.

A biologist thought it was the forgotten flora that inhabits our bodies—on our skin and in our guts—that lingers when we have moved on, like the skeleton of a leaf when the rest has crumbled away. So similar to Susan's metaphor.

I know that they are the memories of my past selves, the ghosts of lost emotions, saved by d-mat from forgetfulness in the memory of the universe. Therefore I do not fear sickening and wasting away as some of my more superstitious patients have. I wish only to keep my dark ones close and bask in their affinity.

Shadows press in around me. I open my arms in welcome.

✧

The one thing you can be sure of is that we've always been here.

Sometimes you have banished us unknowingly, with your electric light and your cities. Sometimes you welcome us back, as in this world of plenty, where technologies powerful enough to manipulate matter at its basest level allow everyone the luxury of a darkened bedroom.

We are here, waiting for the lights to go out. Desiring you. Loving you. Hungering for you.

We come from the shadows to whisper, sweet nothings.

We come to feed.

Copyright © 2015 by Sean Williams

Nancy Kress has won five Nebulas, two Hugos, a Campbell Memorial and a Sturgeon Memorial, and recently co-authored Arc Manor's Stellar Guild novel, New Under the Sun. *This is her fourth appearance in* Galaxy's Edge.

MARGIN OF ERROR

by Nancy Kress

Paula came back in a blaze of glory, her Institute uniform with its pseudo-military medals crisp and bright, her spine straight as an engineered diamond-fiber rod. I heard her heels clicking on the sidewalk and I looked up from the bottom porch step, a child on my lap. Paula's face was gen-emod now, the blemishes gone, the skin fine-pored, the cheekbones chiseled under green eyes. But I would have known that face anywhere. No matter what she did to it.

"Karen?" Her voice held disbelief.

"Paula," I said.

"*Karen?*" This time I didn't answer. The child, my oldest, twisted in my arms to eye the visitor. The slight movement made the porch step creak.

It was the kind of neighborhood where women sat all morning on porches or stoops, watching children play on the sidewalk. Steps sagged; paint peeled; small front lawns were scraped bare by feet and tricycles and plastic wading pools. Women lived a few doors down from their mothers, both of them growing heavier every year. There were few men. The ones there were, didn't seem to stay long.

I said, "How did you find me?"

"It wasn't hard," Paula said, and I knew she didn't understand my smile. Of course it wasn't hard. I had never intended it should be. This was undoubtedly the first time in nearly five years that Paula had looked.

She lowered her perfect body gingerly onto the porch steps. My little girl, Lollie, gazed at her from my lap. Then Lollie opened her cupped hands and smiled. "See my frog, lady?"

"Very nice," Paula said. She was trying hard to hide her contempt, but I could see it. For the sad imprisoned frog, for Lollie's dirty face, for the worn yard, for the way I looked.

"Karen," Paula said, "I'm here because there's a problem. With the project. More specifically, with the initial formulas, we think. With a portion of the nanoassembler code from five years ago, when you were…still with us."

"A problem," I repeated. Inside the house, a baby wailed. "Just a minute."

I set Lollie down and went inside. Lori cried in her crib. Her diaper reeked. I put a pacifier in her mouth and cradled her in my left arm. With the right arm I scooped Timmy from his crib. When he didn't wake, I jostled him a little. I carried both babies back to the porch, deposited Timmy in the portacrib, and sat down next to Paula.

"Lollie, go get me a diaper, honey. And wipes. You can carry your frog inside to get them."

Lollie went; she's a sweet-natured kid. Paula stared incredulously at the twins. I unwrapped Lori's diaper and Paula grimaced and slid farther away.

"Karen—are you listening to me? This is important!"

"I'm listening."

"The nanocomputer instructions are off, somehow. The major results check out, obviously—" *Obviously.* The media had spent five years exclaiming over the major results.

"—but there are some odd foldings in the proteins of the twelfth-generation nanoassemblers." Twelfth generation. The nanocomputer attached to each assembler replicates itself every six months. That was one of the project's checks and balances on the margin of error. It had been five and a half years. Twelfth generation was about right.

"Also," Paula continued, and I heard the strain in her voice, "there are some unforeseen macro-level developments. We're not sure yet that they're tied to the nanocomputer protein folds. There might not be any connection. What we're trying to do now is cover all the variables."

"You must be working on fairly remote variables if you're reduced to asking me."

"Well, yes, we are. Karen, do you have to do that *now*?"

"Yes." I scraped the shit off Lori with one edge of the soiled diaper. Lollie danced out of the house with a clean one. She sat beside me, whispering to her frog.

Paula said, "What I need…what the project needs—"

I said, "Do you remember the summer we collected frogs? We were maybe eight and ten. You'd become fascinated reading about that experiment where they threw a frog in boiling water but it jumped out, and then they put a frog in cool water and gradually increased the temperature to boiling until the stupid frog just sat there and died. Remember?"

"Karen—"

"I collected sixteen frogs for you, and when I found out what you were going to do with them, I cried and tried to let them go. But you boiled eight of them anyway. The other eight were controls. I'll give you that—proper scientific method. To reduce the margin of error, you said."

"Karen—we were just kids…"

I put the clean diaper on Lori. "Not all kids behave like that. Lollie doesn't. But you wouldn't know that, would you? Nobody in your set has children. You should have had a baby, Paula."

She barely hid her shudder. But, then, most of the people we knew felt the same way.

She said, "What the project needs is for you to come back and work on the same small area you did originally. Looking for something—anything—you might have missed in the protein-coded instructions to successive generations of nanoassemblers."

"No," I said.

"It's not really a matter of choice. The macrolevel problems—I'll be frank, Karen. It looks like a new form of cancer, one nobody's ever seen. Unregulated replication of some very weird cells."

"So take the cellular nanomachinery out." I crumpled the stinking diaper and set it out of the baby's reach. Closer to Paula.

"You know we can't do that! The project's irreversible!"

"Many things are irreversible," I said. Lori started to fuss. I picked her up, opened my blouse, and gave her the breast. She sucked greedily. Paula glanced away. She has had nanomachinery in her perfect body, making it perfect, for five years now. Her breasts will never look swollen, blue-veined, sagging.

"Karen, listen—"

"No—you listen," I said quietly. "Eight years ago you convinced Zweigler I was only a minor member of the research team, included only because I was your sister. I've always wondered, by the way, how

41

ROBERT A. HEINLEIN

EXPANDED UNIVERSE

VOLUME ONE

ROBERT A. HEINLEIN

EXPANDED UNIVERSE

VOLUME TWO

you did that—were you sleeping with him, too? Seven years ago you got me shunted off into the minor area of the project's effect on female gametes—which nobody cared about because it was already clear there was no way around sterility as a side effect. Nobody thought it was too high a price for a perfect, self-repairing body, did they? Except me."

Paula didn't answer. Lollie carried her frog to the wading pool and set it carefully in the water.

I said, "I didn't mind working on female gametes, even if it was a backwater, even if you got star billing. I was used to it, after all. As kids, you were always the cowboy; I got to be the horse. You were the astronaut, I was the alien you conquered. Remember? One Christmas you used up all the chemicals in your first chemistry set and then stole mine."

"I don't think trivial childhood incidents matter in—"

"Of course you don't. And I never minded. But I did mind when five years ago you made copies of all my notes and presented them as yours, while I was so sick during my pregnancy with Lollie. You claimed my work. Stole it. Just like the chemistry set. And then you eased me off the project."

"What you did was so minor—"

"If it was so minor, why are you here asking for my help now? And why would you imagine for half a second I'd give it to you?"

She stared at me, calculating. I stared back coolly. Paula wasn't used to me cool, I could see that. I'd always been the excitable one. Excitable, flighty, unstable—that's what she'd told Zweigler. A security risk.

Timmy fussed in his portacrib. I stood up, still nursing Lori, and scooped him up with my free arm. Back on the steps, I juggled Timmy to lie across Lori on my lap, pulled back my blouse, and gave him the other breast. This time Paula didn't permit herself a grimace.

She said, "Karen, what I did was wrong. I know that now. But for the sake of the project, not for me, you have to—"

"You *are* the project. You have been from the first moment you grabbed the headlines away from Zweigler and the others who gave their life to that work. 'Lovely Young Scientist Injects Self With Perfect-Cell Drug!' 'No Sacrifice Too Great To Circumvent FDA Shortsightedness, Heroic Researcher Declares.'"

Paula said flatly, "You're jealous. You're obscure and I'm famous. You're a mess and I'm beautiful. You're—"

"A milch cow? While you're a brilliant researcher? Then solve your own research problems."

"This was your area—"

"Oh, Paula, they were *all* my areas. I did more of the basic research than you did, and you know it. But you knew how to position yourself with Zweigler, to present key findings at key moments, to cultivate the right connections…all that stuff you do so well. And, of course, I was still under the delusion we were partners. I just didn't realize it was a barracuda partnering a goldfish."

From the wading pool Lollie watched us with big eyes. "Mommy…"

"It's okay, honey. Mommy's not mad at you. Look, better catch your frog—he's hopping away."

She shrieked happily and dove for the frog. Paula said softly, "I had no idea you were so angry after all this time. You've changed, Karen."

"But I'm not angry. Not anymore. And you never knew what I was like before. You never bothered to know."

"I knew you never wanted a scientific life. Not the way I did. You always wanted kids. Wanted… *this.*" She waved her arm around the shabby yard. David left eighteen months ago. He sends money. It's never enough.

"I wanted a scientific establishment that would let me have both. And I wanted credit for my work. I wanted what was mine. How did you do it, Paula—end up with what was yours and what was mine, too?'

"Because you were distracted by babyshit and frogs!" Paula yelled, and for the first time I saw how scared she really was. Paula didn't make admissions like that. A tactical error. I watched her stab desperately for a way to regain the advantage. A way to seize the offensive.

I seized it first. "You should have left David alone. You already had Zweigler; you should have left me David. Our marriage was never the same after that."

She said, "I'm dying, Karen."

I turned my head from the nursing babies to look at her.

"It's true. My cellular machinery is running wild. Just in the last few months. The nanoassemblers are creating weird structures, destructive enzymes. For five years they replicated perfectly and now… For five years it all performed *exactly* as it was programmed to—"

I said, "It still is."

Paula sat very still. Lori had fallen asleep. I juggled her into the portacrib and nestled Timmy more comfortably on my lap. Lollie chased her frog around the wading pool. I squinted to see if Lollie's lips were blue; the weather was really too cool for her to be in the water very long.

Paula choked out, "You programmed the assembler machinery in the ovaries to—"

"Nobody much cares about women's ovaries. Only fourteen percent of college-educated women want to muck up their lives with kids. Recent survey result. Less than one percent margin of error."

"—you actually sabotaged…hundreds of women have been injected by now, maybe *thousands*—"

"Oh, there's a reverser enzyme," I said. "Completely effective if you take it before the twelfth-generation replication. You're the only person that's been injected that long. I just discovered the reverser a few months ago, tinkering with my old notes for something to do in what your friends probably call my idle domestic prison. That's provable, incidentally. All my notes are computer-dated."

Paula whispered, "Scientists don't *do* this—"

"Too bad you wouldn't let me be one."

"Karen—"

"Don't you want to know what the reverser is, Paula? It's engineered from human chorionic gonadotropin. The pregnancy hormone. Too bad you never wanted a baby."

She went on staring at me. Lollie shrieked and splashed with her frog. Her lips *were* turning blue. I stood up, laid Timmy next to Lori in the portacrib, and buttoned my blouse.

"You made an experimental error twenty-five years ago," I said to Paula. "Too small a sample population. Sometimes a frog jumps out."

I went to lift my daughter from the wading pool.

Anna Wu is a rising new voice in the Chinese SFF scene. She was nominated for the Chinese Nebula Award for Best New Writer in 2014, her fiction has been published in various Chinese venues, and she currently works as a screenwriter in Suzhou. This is her first appearance in Galaxy's Edge.

THE RESTAURANT AT THE END OF THE UNIVERSE

by Anna Wu

Translated by Carmen Yiling Yan and Ken Liu

At the end of the universe far away, there was a restaurant, and its name was The Restaurant at the End of the Universe. From a distance, it looked like a conch shell spinning silently in the void of space.

The restaurant was sometimes big, and sometimes small. The furnishings inside its walls changed often, as did the view outside its windows. It had a refrigerator that was always full of fresh ingredients; a cooking box that fried, baked, seared, steamed, and everything else; a clock that could regulate the flow of time within a modest area; and a melancholic android waiter named Marvin. A red lantern shone perpetually at the center of the restaurant.

Two people, father and daughter, ran it. They came from a place called China on a planet called Earth. Going by the *Traveler's Guide to the Milky Way*, the father was an exemplary specimen of the middle-aged Earthling male—perhaps even a few deciles handsomer than the median. He was black-haired and thin, and there was a scar on his left wrist. He didn't talk much, but was well-versed in Earth cuisine. If a customer could name it, he could make it. The daughter, Mo, looked to be eleven or twelve years old. She had black hair too, and big, round eyes.

The nearest space-time hub was a small cargo station, a singularity primarily used for Earth shipping. Of course, as a singularity, only organisms with a civilization rating above 3A—capable of uploading their physical bodies into the network—could use it.

Few guests came. Most hailed from Earth, but there were the matchbox-sized three-body people of Alpha Centauri, too; Titanians with their vast balloon forms, adapted to the atmosphere of Saturn; even dazzling silver Suoyas from the center of the Milky Way, fifty thousand light years from Earth. Intelligent beings of every shape and size might be seen in this restaurant's blurred concept of time and space: waving their antennae, dribbling their mucus, crackling and sparking their energy fields.

Virtual reality may hold infinities, but wander long enough in it and your soul feels a little lost. Every once in a while, people still want to put on a real body, eat a real meal, and reminisce.

There was a rule for everyone who ate here. You could choose to tell the owner a story; as long as it was interesting enough, your meal was on the house, and the owner would personally cook you a special dish. And you could eat while you thought of the countless civilizations rising and falling, falling and rising, at every instant and in every corner of the universe outside this restaurant, like the births and deaths of the sextillion stars.

Laba Porridge

He's not a regular, Mo thought. *This is probably his first time here.*

Today, the restaurant was furnished for a Chinese winter's night. There were five little tables made of rough-hewn wood and three guests sitting at them. The kitchen station was tucked into a corner. A man and a woman sat at the table under the red lantern. The woman looked to be from Earth, maybe a second-generation clone—her legs were unusually long and slim. The man was probably from Venus, with his bulky cranium and deep purple irises.

And there was an Earth man sitting by himself in a corner, mechanically turning the wine cup in his hand. His pale face was devoid of expression, and his temples were gray. The smell of alcohol poured off of him. Today was the Chinese Laba Festival, and the restaurant had accordingly prepared sweet Laba porridge, whose fragrance filled the room. Yet the man hadn't ordered it.

Mo had never seen eyes like his before: empty and dark as a dry well, they reminded her of the eyes of a dead insect.

While the business was still slow, Mo stuffed the menu into Marvin's hand. She waited.

Marvin took the menu and gazed at the falling snow outside the window, sighing. His eyes glimmered blue to indicate melancholy. "They've been dead for centuries. Why do they bother eating anyway?" he muttered, even as he ambled over to the Venusian's table on his short legs.

"Dad, that Earth man should have a good story." Mo slipped into the kitchen station, grinning. It might count as a gift of sorts—give her a group of people, and she could always pick out the one with the best stories at a glance.

Her father paused in his tasks. He stared at a pile of dishes, silent.

His expression was odd: interest, worry, disgust, perhaps even a little fear?

Time went by. The din of the restaurant floated around them as lightly as the snowflakes outside the window.

"Mo, I think you've heard of the Agency of Mysteries."

"All laws are one; all things are eternal," Mo said without thinking. The organization's motto—one Earth language version of it, at least. It was renowned in many eras and many planets. It ignored all interstellar laws and regulations and could provide any service imaginable—but only if your request was entertaining enough to catch its interest. And you couldn't buy its services with money; you had to... trade. What you needed to trade was a secret that no client had ever revealed. No one knew who the boss was, either—he was too clever to be caught by the space-time police.

"His name is Ah Chen. He was a client of the Agency of Mysteries."

Slowly, the father began to tell Ah Chen's story.

Ah Chen wrote novels, and he was twenty when his debut, a romance novel, shot him to overnight fame. At the celebratory banquet, his literary peers greeted him with ingratiating praise and admiration well-laced with envy. He was dazzled and drunk by it all the same.

But achieving fame at a young age is not always a good thing. That night, he met an admirer—his future wife, Ci.

Ci came from a renowned family of scholars. She was pretty and frail, but fiercely stubborn. Against her family's protests, she married the penniless Ah Chen. By day, she worked as a maid, washing and scrubbing until her hands were red from the dishwater. By night, she proof-read Ah Chen's drafts and helped him with research.

Three years later, the luster of the awards had long since faded, but the muses had not visited Ah Chen again in the duration. Writing was long, hard work, like a marathon run alone in the night, stumbling by touch and three inches of vision. Moods swooped and plunged, joy clawing into sorrow, as if to torment him with rain and snow.

As editors rejected his manuscripts again and again, Ah Chen came to discover his many weaknesses: he lacked the endurance to carry out plots fully, he wanted sufficient delicacy of touch, he was unable to draw from the strengths of other works and unite them in his own. Some of these weaknesses were real; others were only the specters of Ah Chen's insecurity.

He was young and idealistic. He couldn't endure the publishers' contempt; more than that, he couldn't face his own inadequacy. He began to drink, and every bottle of cheap alcohol was bought with Ci's long days and nights of labor.

One winter night, on Laba Festival, Ah Chen came home with the snow falling outside. He saw Ci smiling warmly at him. There was a pot of mixed grain porridge on the table, steaming.

"They say that Laba porridge originated when a rat stole many kinds of grain and hid them in its hole. Then poor people found the store and made it into porridge..."

Suddenly, Ah Chen's ears were ringing as if a clap of thunder had gone off in his head. Ci went on talking, but he was no longer listening. He heard nothing of her gentle sympathy, her willingness to live in poverty, her resolute lack of regret.

He rushed into the night, toward the Agency of Mysteries.

For a long time, Ci sat in the lamplight, alone. Her tears fell into that pot of Laba porridge, slowly cooling.

Ah Chen wanted five abilities from five Earth authors. The agency told him that as the universe conserved energy; abilities couldn't be "copied", only "transferred." Perhaps out of his last vestiges of conscience, or out of fear of disrupting his own universe's timeline, Ah Chen requested that his powers be taken from five other universes parallel to his own.

These five people were all the literary stars of their era.

A, a playwright. His output was great in both quality and quantity, and without equal for the next hundred years. Ah Chen wanted his mastery over plot structure.

B, a poet. The beauty and craftsmanship of his verses had won him acclaim as the greatest of poets. Ah Chen wanted his ear for language.

C, a suspense novelist and psychologist. At his peak, his works had triggered heart attacks in his readers. Ah Chen wanted his grasp of human psychology.

D, a science fiction author. His stories were strange, clever things, well-known throughout the galaxies. Ah Chen wanted his imagination.

E, a scholar of the classics and Buddhist. Weighty and thoughtful, his pen laid out the workings of history and the patterns of the world with the clarity of a black ink brush delineating white cloudscapes. Ah Chen wanted his powerful insight.

"Was Ah Chen a friend of yours?" Mo asked.

Her father smiled cryptically. "One of Ah Chen's targets was an alternate universe version of me. But that version of me found out and stopped him."

Mo wanted to ask further, but in the end, she didn't say anything.

Unlike most people, her memories began from only five years ago. She had opened her eyes to find herself lying in a spaceship with a middle-aged man and a big-headed android, fleeing for the ends of the universe. Before that... her memories cut off in an explosion of light.

Afterward, she considered the man her father. But he never told Mo what happened before the start of her memories. He never said anything he didn't want to say.

"Still, four abilities is a lot!"

"The universe obeys the laws of conservation. To get something, you have to give in return."

The Agency of Mysteries delivered A's ability first.

That night, Ah Chen felt as if his brain had been ripped out and forced through a red-hot wire mesh. His head seemed to split open. He howled and howled with pain.

Ci, whom he'd kept in the dark, quaked at his screams hard enough to nearly tumble off the bed. That entire night, wrapped in a thin sleeping robe, she kept Ah Chen's forehead and hands covered with hot towels. Watching him clench his hands into the bedsheets and refuse to go to the hospital, she could only stand helplessly *at his bedside. Every time Ah Chen screamed, Ci shivered too. She gripped his hands as hard as she could, terrified that he'd hurt himself as he thrashed and struggled.*

By the time the sky began to brighten, Ah Chen's face was as pale as paper, and Ci had wept herself empty of tears. Her mind held only one thought: If this man did not survive, she feared that she would not either.

When Ah Chen awoke in the morning, he found that the world in front of his eyes had taken on a sudden, perfect clarity.

Every piece of furniture, every drawer, every item of clothing, every pair of socks in the bedroom—abruptly, he knew where they were, how big, what color, for what purpose. He looked out the window. A group of neighbors were taking a walk in the commons. Behind every face was an identity, an age, and a list of relationships. Yesterday, Ah Chen couldn't even remember their names.

Her husband had awoken, but Ci saw on his face an eerie expression. Half delighted and half worried, she hurriedly put a hand to his forehead to check his temperature. Ah Chen impatiently brushed her hand away and herded her out of the room without a word.

He snatched up a book at random and started reading at the table of contents. His reading speed had increased five or six times. When he was done, he only needed to glance at the table of contents again, and the events of the book seemed to arrange themselves neatly into twigs and branches growing out of a few main trunks. Every knot, every joint was so clear. When Ah Chen closed his eyes, a few inharmonious branches stood out in sharp relief on the tree, and it seemed to only take him a second to realize how to fix these branches, how to fix this book—this book, which had been so praised and so successful in its sales.

Every edit Ah Chen noticed left him a little more breathless, a little more dizzy. Suspicion, amazement, and overpowering joy drove into him like waves in a tempest. He couldn't even wait long enough to boot up his computer. He grabbed a sheaf of paper and started to write.

With his front door locked tightly, he wrote more than a hundred beautiful plot outlines within the week. The beginnings were stunning, the middles fluid, the climaxes brilliantly fitting, the plot arcs graceful. Every one of them could be called a classic. He shook as he stroked his drafts. Now and then he broke into hysterical laughter.

However, in the course of this week, Ah Chen seemed to have caught some sort of obsessive-compulsive disorder. He rearranged all the furniture in his room, measuring each item's location to the millimeter; he sorted his clothes by color and thickness; he stuck a label onto every drawer. Everything had to be perfectly ordered. A single stain or misplaced scrap of paper was enough to scrape his nerves raw.

That week, Ci was forced to sleep in the living room. She would make three meals a day and bring them to the bedroom. One day, as she tiptoed in, she decided she would clean the room. The moment she opened the wardrobe, Ah Chen flew into a rage and slapped her.

A month later, the Agency of Mysteries brought B's ability. Ah Chen's ears became peculiarly sensitive to sounds; they left indelible marks in his mind. When he heard wind, music, thunder, or even the barking of dogs, every syllable seemed imbued with new significance. Poems, essays, haikus, and colorful slang rose from the pages as if given life, linking their hands and dancing, endlessly dancing, passing before his eyes one after the other like little fairies.

He wrote one beautiful poem after the next, but the sublime melody of his verses gave him no peace, not when A's powers of organization and structure howled at him from the darkness, "Order! Order!" while B's power insisted that the beauty of language came from ineffable spontaneity and inspiration. The two masters' mental states fought like storm and tempest, neither willing to bow to the other. Ah Chen felt as if his body had become a gladiatorial arena for his mind. He couldn't sleep; he shivered despite himself.

C's ability followed. What an abyss that was: a million faces, a million personalities, a million stories, a million different kinds of despair. Ah Chen finally understood the price C had paid to be able to write about those twisted souls and those unimaginable plots, the hell he had made of his own spirit. Ah Chen trembled, navigating through the blood, the tears, the white bones and black graves, as if he walked on thin ice; he very nearly fell. Without C's psychological tenacity, Ah Chen approached the precipice of suicide multiple times. Only through hard liquor, which temporarily numbed his brain, could he seek the smallest scrap of solace.

Day after day, tears washed Ci's face, and she soon fell ill. She couldn't understand how the handsome, scholarly, gentle man she loved could turn into a different person in the space of a night. Truth be told, Ci understood from history that the majority of authors' spouses led unhappy lives, enduring both material poverty and their partners' sensitivity, moodiness, and even unfaithfulness. She had understood it even before she married him.

Unfortunately, for many like her, knowledge and reason had never stood a chance before love.

This was all irrelevant. Ci lay in bed, weakly gasping for air. Remembering the slap, she closed her eyes. A tear slowly wended its way into her hair.

One day at dusk, Ah Chen was awoken by a strange voice.

"You thief."

Ah Chen's eyes snapped open. A man's face appeared in his mind, thin and long, its expression not quite a smile.

The face hadn't materialized in front of his eyes, and it wasn't projected onto anything. It had simply floated to the surface of his mind, clear and blurry at the same time. That's hard to explain. It was as if he had one good eye and one injured eye, and was trying to look at the world with both at the same time.

"Steal my imagination? Who do they think they are?" The man laughed.

Ah Chen grabbed wildly in front of his eyes, but caught only air.

"All laws are one; all things are eternal." The man looked at Ah Chen pityingly, slowly blurring into nothingness.

Ah Chen at last woke from his drunken stupor, and found that his vomit had already been cleared away by Ci, and that his blankets were aired and sweet-smelling. The setting sun shone into the room, and clarity seemed to flow into Ah Chen's heart. That was E's ability.

Humanity always reenacts the same bildungsroman. All the principles you learn through your struggles today had been written down by the ancients thousands of years ago.

There is nothing new under the sun.

"You went to such lengths to steal these things, and all for what?"

What have I done? *Ah Chen watched countless motes of dust dance in the setting sun's light.*

He seemed to see the history of literature slowly distorting in those four parallel universes as the butterfly effect rippled through space-time. Countless chains of causality broke apart, then joined again; countless people's fates altered with them.

He felt as if he was looking into each world: publishers' contempt as A seemed to run out of talent; readers mocking B for his clumsy language; E's wife yelling at him for his uselessness. C flogged himself in the dark of night, sobbing in agony.

He'd stolen each of their most precious possessions, and, drowned in alcohol, he'd trampled them into the dirt.

At this point, Ah Chen noticed something strange. E's wise, reasonable voice asked him, "Why do you feel no guilt? Why does your heart hold only regret, and not the pain brought on by your sense of responsibility? Why have you lost the ability to love another?"

Love? *Ah Chen thought dazedly.* What's love?

Oh. He'd traded love away at the Agency of Mysteries.

"Love was the most important thing of them all," E said tranquilly. "Technique and intelligence will let you see through the world, explain it, look down upon it, but they'll never make you a true master of literature. You have to let go of yourself, join yourself to the world without resistance or hate; use love, admiration, and respect to observe all living things, including humanity. This is the true secret of literature."

Ah Chen stood and opened the door to the dining room. Ci sat at the table, watching over a pot of steaming Laba porridge.

Ah Chen sat down stiffly across from her, like a puppet.

"You should eat a little." For the first time in many days, her eyes held the light and peace of knowledge.

Ah Chen took a mouthful. It was salty, not sweet. He raised his head, looking at Ci's pale face.

"Ah Chen, I don't know where you went the evening of Laba Festival. I don't know why you changed so much. But you must have a good reason for what you did.

"I waited for you the entire night. The porridge from that day, like today's, was salty." Ci forced a smile.

I should say something, *Ah Chen thought. In the end, he didn't say anything.*

"Ah Chen, I read your manuscripts yesterday, when you weren't looking. They're wonderful. I'm so happy."

Ci finally looked as if she were about to cry. Slowly, she took Ah Chen's hand in hers.

"Promise me, you'll keep writing."

Ah Chen was silent for a long time. "For you, I'll keep writing."

Ci slowly smiled. Her eyes shone with the same sweetness as they'd held just after the wedding, but it couldn't hide the grief at the corners of her eyes. The setting sun shone on her pale face, coloring it with a flush for the last time.

Her hand is so cold, *Ah Chen thought.*

"Ci...did she..." Mo's heart sank.

Her father continued to operate the cooking box slowly.

"Yes, Ci died the next day. Perhaps she saw that the last spark of light in her life—Ah Chen's love for her—was gone.

"Ah Chen lived alone after that, in the constant clash and torment of the powers in his head. You can't go back on a bargain, no matter how much you regret it. He sporadically wrote many bestsellers, won many awards, but he never remarried, never moved out of the house, and never read his own works. The books piled up in the corner of his study and gathered dust."

So her father was a science fiction author. Mo looked at him, her brow furrowed. *How do you know all this? How do you know a version of yourself from another universe? How many things are you hiding from me?*

The cooking box dinged. It was a bowl of Laba porridge.

Maybe it was just the chill from a snowy night, but when her father carried the porridge past her, it seemed to tinge the air with the cool, faint smell of salt.

At the other end of the restaurant, Ah Chen lifted his head. He saw the owner's long, thin face, and his eyes widened.

They conversed.

Mo hurried over to eavesdrop, but heard only their last words: "All laws are one; all things are eternal." She couldn't help but feel disappointed.

Her father turned and made his way back to the kitchen, leaving Ah Chen sitting stunned at the table. His gaze followed her father's retreating back for a while, and then slowly shifted back.

Gradually, a small smile surfaced on his face. There was a hint of desolation in it, as if he were reliving some memory.

In front of him was the bowl of deep reddish-violet Laba porridge, in which black glutinous rice, kidney beans, adzuki beans, peanuts, longan, jujubes, lotus seeds, and walnuts had been cooked until they'd turned slippery and soft, squeezed together like a family. The cool, faint smell of salt wafted from the bowl.

Ah Chen sat like that until the other guests had left one by one. The porridge had finally cooled.

He got up slowly. Mo hurried to open the door for him.

The smile was like the transient flash of a sparkler in the night sky. His eyes were empty again.

Without a glance for Mo, Ah Chen disappeared into the wind and snow.

The clock struck midnight; a gust of cold wind blew in, carrying powdery snow with it.

"Don't you want to know what we talked about?" her father asked slowly, as he wiped a plate dry.

"Yeah!" Mo thought of the look in Ah Chen's eyes and shivered despite herself.

"I told him that, a few days later, a certain book will win an award on Earth. It tells the story of a woman's undying love for a man, and the author's name is Zhang Ci. Ah Chen had written the book based on Ci's diary. I fear it's the last and only work he can write in this lifetime that will give him satisfaction."

Tom Gerencer, a graduate of the Clarion writing seminar, is a master humorist who has been turning out hilarious science fiction stories for sixteen years. He has just completed his first novel.

AND ALL OUR DONKEYS WERE VAIN

by Tom Gerencer

I found out one day that aliens had become intensely interested in my sandwich.

I couldn't blame them, exactly. It was a really good sandwich, as I am a really good side-cook, or I was before I lost my job down at Stu's House of Lunch Type Foods.

Good riddance, I say to that job. I mean, it wasn't glamorous, but the pay was lousy. Still, my reputation evidently preceded me in extraterrestrial circles, by which I mean to say the little bastards heard, somehow, about my proficiency with layered foods and certain condiments.

Now you put yourself in my position: I had just got up, turned on the television to one of those 24-hour Abe Vigoda marathons, and got myself a beer. Being unemployed in the great state of America in modern times may be a problem for some people, but to me, it was just a little slice of heaven. I'd got some crusty bread out of the fridge, which I had introduced, by way of a knife so sharp you could hide it in a notebook, to a few slices of Genoa Ham and some heart-breakingly fresh mozzarella that was still dripping from the brine they pack it in. A few roasted red peppers and some artichoke leaves, and the world is pretty much your oyster, unless you don't happen to like oysters, for some reason, in which case you are some kind of a freakshow and you ought to be examined.

So I'm in my underwear, I'm sitting in the lazy boy, I got my feet up on the coffee table because I broke that little lifter on the chair-arm when the cat got jammed down inside of there and died last August and I had to clean the thing out with a set of pliers and a shop vac. Terrible tragedy in the family, and the wife was not amused, let me tell you, since she got that cat, which I never liked anyway, as a

present from her uncle Steve, but there was nothing we could do about it.

They'll tell you curiosity killed the cat, but it's a lie. In my house, the cat was killed by excess leverage.

So anyway, I'm sitting there, and I'm watching Abe complain on the TV because his coffee tastes like motor oil, and this thing slithers out from under the credenza that I swear is right out of one of those dreams you get from too much MSG.

This thing—how do I describe this thing? You've never met my mother's Pomeranian, I'm guessing, so I can't refer you to its blocked salivary duct that hangs down as though it is choking on a light bulb. Anyway, the thing there in my living room looked kind of like it had been put together out of different-sized blocked salivary ducts from assorted Pomeranians and maybe schnauzers or possibly even Pekingese, all kind of interlinked. Furthermore, the thing moved like a snake, or like one of those old skinny guys who run the pawn shops—you know the ones—they have the thick white hair and the black eyebrows, big forearms, bulging eyes, usually they have people buried in the basement—and when it had slithered out into the center of my living room, it got up on its haunches and said, "Hi."

Again, put yourself in my position. You're sitting there in your underwear, you're just about to take a big bite out of a nice salami and mozzarella sandwich, you got some chips, a couple of pepperoncini for variety and a freshly opened coldie to add moral support, and here this thing from planet x or y or wherever the hell it was from comes out from under the credenza and it acts like you're old drinking buddies from the neighborhood.

I had the sandwich in my mouth at the time, which meant I almost choked, and that I spit out mozzarella with such force that at least three pieces of it became embedded in the paneling.

"I know you're busy," said the thing, in spite of the obvious problem that it didn't seem to have a mouth, "So I'll cut right to the chase. We'd like to buy your sandwich."

Now what the hell. I mean, I have never been one to say that life should be predictable or even that it should make sense, but there is only just so much insanity a guy can take. I am telling you, at any other time, I could have cared less, but first of all, my brother has been going around with a hooker since he was old enough to vote, and for another, my wife's mother just confessed to me the day before that she always thought I looked exactly like that guy on the mayonnaise commercial with the hooked nose and the receding hairline. So I spit out more of my sandwich and I said, "You want to buy a sandwich?" just to make sure I heard it right.

"Not just any sandwich," said the thing. "That sandwich."

I looked down at it. Notwithstanding that I had already taken a bite out of it, not to mention that I hadn't exactly what you call washed my hands before I made the thing, this creature in front of me was freakish, unholy, strange, et cetera. I dropped my sandwich on my chest and said, "What the hell are you?"

"Oh, now you dropped it," said the thing. "And I'm an alien, for your information. I'm from a planet in the cluster you refer to as M-31. You've heard of it?"

I hadn't. I guessed their PR was lacking, but anyway, I told it, "No."

It made a little sighing sound. "Well, it's pretty famous in some circles," it said. "It has some of the best Zreebock in the Universe."

"Some of the best what?"

"Zreebok," said the thing. "It's like your New York Pizza, only without the cheese, and the crust, and also it's alive when you ingest it."

Well, whatever, those were fighting words. There is nothing like our New York Pizza, barring New York Pizza. In fact, I had a theory that the deliciousness of the pizza varied with the inverse square of the distance from New York, having bought a slice one time in West Virginia and having regretted that particular culinary excursion for the remainder of my life to date. I explained this theory, as briefly as was possible, to the thing that perched there in the center of my wife's throw-rug, and it said, "You're right, actually. In fact, we've got pizza in M-31, which we copied after centuries spent spying on your kind, abducting you, and implanting little probes in you, and it's so bad that it can kill a donkey."

I didn't ask it what a donkey would be doing in M-31, or why it would be eating pizza, because, in my admittedly limited experience, you don't go into morbid culinary details where alien creatures are concerned. But I'm going to be a man here and admit that curiosity, evidently on a break from killing cats, had got the best of me, to the extent that I said, "Have we got Zreebok in New York?"

"You have," the thing said, "but your inverse-square law applies here as well. In fact, you know our Zreebok as a particularly nasty variety of Swanson Frozen TV Dinner—I believe it is referred to as a Salisbury Steak."

I almost came right out of my chair and re-educated the ugly little thing with the back side of the subwoofer from underneath my entertainment system. That was the first time the words "frozen" and "dinner" had been uttered within twenty feet of my living room by anyone who wasn't talking about dining in Antarctica.

"Look, alien or no," I said, "You don't bring up that Zreebok stuff again. I got kids," I said. Granted, they were at school, but bad food has a way of hanging on like fallout or unwanted relatives.

"Oh, but in our galaxy," the thing said, "Zreebok is delicious. It transports us to new heights of culture, art, and science. A nice dish of Zreebok, on my planet, is nothing short of a religious experience."

"You don't say," I said.

"No, I just did," the thing said. "And another thing, our Zreebok chefs are revered. We worship them. Anyone who can make a good dish of Zreebok commands the most supreme respect."

I was getting to like the sound of M-31. I mean, however much they might lack in the publicity department, anyplace where they look up to chefs has got to be okay.

"So you guys are interested in sandwiches?"

"Not sandwiches," he said. "That sandwich. The one there in your lap."

I looked down at it. It was a good sandwich, I had to admit, but it must have been even better than I'd thought to bring this thing across the universe. I mean, there's a little Greek place over on the East side that I happen to know serves up a dish of Souvlaki that's saved marriages, but the parking situation is so dismal that I haven't eaten there for years.

"The thing is," said the alien, jiggling his nodules, "your inverse-square law has been known to my kind for centuries."

"And?" I prompted.

"And it was foretold you would create that sandwich by one of our greatest prophets. He said you would sit right there, in that chair, and that you would be watching Abe Vigoda on the television."

"Yeah?" I said. "Did he mention anything about me being in my underwear?"

"That particular detail did not enter into the prophecy," said the alien. "However, he did say that sandwich would be one of the most delicious ever made."

I didn't doubt it. Not that I am cocky, but I have a talent. Some are born with musical ability, some are brilliant mathematicians. Me, I can put two slices of bread around some salted meat like you would not believe. It's an intuitive thing with me. You know, any other guy might slap some ham and cheese and condiments together and call it good. Me, I have a sixth sense about proportions, placement, textures, complimentary flavors. I once made a chicken sub that I am pretty sure expressed all the mysteries of Christianity in culinary form. That's how I met Alice. I was working at Stu's at the time and she was there for lunch. She took one bite and asked if she could have my children.

She has probably regretted it at times, in the same way some mid-century Germans regretted holding fund raisers for the Nazi party, but she says she still gets the shivers from my sandwiches.

I looked down at the sandwich, wishing that the alien had let me taste the thing, at least. There it sat across my boxer shorts, half demolished, slanting cheese onto the floral print, leaking oil onto my legs. It was not a pretty sight.

"You want this sandwich?"

"I have traveled an eternity to get it."

"But it's kind of wrecked."

"That's neither here nor there."

"No?" I said. "Where is it, then?"

"What I mean," the creature told me, "Is that we can rebuild it."

He sounded like the preamble to The Six Million Dollar Man. "What are you, gonna give it a bionic napkin?"

"That is none of your concern," he said. "What is your concern is that we wish to pay you dearly for it."

"What are we talking, dearly?"

"Let's just say you'll never need to worry about money again."

Well, call me cynical, but my mother always said that you should never count your chickens before they hatch, which was good advice, considering I have never ended up with any chickens.

"Clarify that a little, will you?" I said.

"How does a hundred million dollars sound?"

"For the sandwich?"

"Look," it said, "We really want that sandwich."

Evidently they did. Then again, for all I knew, it might be easy for them to cough up a hundred million. God only knew what the exchange rate was. "And what do you need it for?" I said.

"Do you want the money or don't you?"

Maybe I am nuts. Looking back on it, I think I must have been. But at the time, you've got to understand, I already knew that sandwich was a good one. And now this alien shows up and lets me know it's even better than I thought. And with all his talk about New York Pizza killing donkeys, I felt a great weight of responsibility settle on me. Like I was at a crossroads, or like Donna Richey had just asked me to sleep with her without a condom back in high school all over again. Seemingly innocuous decisions can be pretty jam-packed full of consequence. You learn that if you live long enough.

"If it means so much to you," I said, feeling my words hit the air like little tactical nuclear explosions, "then you can tell me why you need it."

The creature sighed. Some of his little bulbs deflated. "Very well," he said. "Your sandwich, there, is roughly fifty-three times better than a slice of New York Pizza, according to our prophet. He prophesied that if we were to take it back to M-31 and duplicate it using our own established culinary techniques, the effect would be, well, devastating."

"Worse than killing donkeys?"

"Much worse," the thing said, all the joy gone out of its voice. "Warring factions have been after that sandwich of yours for centuries, ever since the prophecy was made. You have no idea what I have gone through to get it, and I'm going to take it if I have to rip it from your disembodied fingers."

My mother's Pomeranian was never able to extrude huge, curving, knifelike things out of his salivary blockage. This thing didn't seem to have that handicap. I mean, it slid six of these long talons out of itself and started dripping something that did not look like it would prove beneficial to the complexion. Where it hit the rug, it smoked.

Still, I had a bad feeling about this. I wasn't at all sure I wanted the sandwich to fall into the wrong hands, so to speak. Who knew what untold destruction I might wreak. But I make it my personal policy never to argue with a horribly misshapen creature that can melt holes in the floorboards.

"Would you like a couple beers to take along?" I said. After all, it was probably going to be a long trip back, and space travel, I imagined, must be thirsty work.

A few hours later, I was scrubbing at the grease spots on the paneling when I turned my head a fraction and, as a result, I noticed that a Coke machine had somehow insinuated itself onto the center of my wife's throw rug. Before I could register my surprise at the intrusion, the Coke machine said, "Don't tell me it's gone already."

I wracked my brain for things whose absence might cause distress to talking Coke machines in general. Finding none, I remembered the sandwich.

"You from M-31?" I said.

"You're quick, you humans."

"You look like a Coke machine."

"I have chosen this shape out of your subconscious. Really, I could look like anything, including an ordered collection of blocked canine salivary ducts, if the need arose."

"I see," I said.

"I am a Scrobuloni," said the Coke machine.

"Sounds like a kind of pasta."

"It's a kind of alien, from your perspective," said the Scrobuloni. "Does the Xenne have the sandwich?"

"If you're referring to the thing that looked like all those salivary ducts, I'm gonna have to disappoint you."

The thing had slithered back under the credenza after handing me a fat cashier's check for a hundred-million dollars. At the time, I was obviously more than a little concerned about the authenticity of the currency, but those six-inch talons and the acid it

was dripping from them lightened up my scrutiny a bit.

"Oh, this is awful," said the Scrobuloni. "Do you realize what you've done?"

"Yeah. I sold a sandwich," I said, but it winked its lights on and off in a way it later explained to me was supposed to convey a sense of negativity.

"You've destroyed my world," it said.

It explained to me then that the Xennes lived on a planet not too far away, relatively speaking, from its own, and that their race was one of cruel, imperialist attitudes and appetites, kind of like the ancient Romans, only without the fig leaves or the pedophilia.

"For a while we'd held them back," the Scrobuloni said, "by abducting donkeys from your world."

"Donkeys?"

"Donkeys are brilliant three-dimensional military tacticians," said the Scrobuloni. "Granted, you have to modify them. Add extra brains. Increase their metabolic rate. And then there is the house training. Have you ever cleaned up after a genetically modified donkey? Just don't even try."

It shuddered, and it had a little moment, then, during which I was sure it relived unpleasant eschatological memories, and then it said, "Of course the pizza changed all that. A few slices of Xenne pizza, and all our donkeys were in vain."

The old inverse square law again. It didn't surprise me that New York Pizza could be used for evil as well as for good. I had become convinced, over the years, that the stuff was pretty much God's apology to the human race for all the crap he hands us. His little way of saying, "Look, death and taxes and your aunt's consumptive liver problems are a pain, I realize, but here's a little something for the effort." Of course a thing as divine as that is going to be a two-edged sword of sorts, by definition.

"So that's what they wanted the pizza for," I said. "It's a wonder Zreebok is only as bad as one of those frozen dinner things."

"Frozen nothing" the Scrobuloni said. "The Xenne lied to you. Zreebok is your atom bomb. You think the White Sands range was originally a military site? You naïve creature. It was a Xenne's failed attempt at opening a little lunch counter in the desert. That was the day they first learned how powerful the inverse-square law of culinary properties could be. Of course, our warring races had known about the law for centuries, like when one of our advance scouts accidentally dropped a light snack in Ancient China and caused the second invasion by the Mongol hordes. Or when a Xenne left behind the remains of a beverage and subsequently started World War II."

"Good God," I said.

"Yes, luckily in both cases the foodstuffs weren't very tasty, or the results could well have proven even worse."

It was a little more than I could take at that point without some means of refreshment. Speculatively, I popped a couple coins into the Scrobuloni's coin slot and bought a Mountain Dew.

"Don't do that again," it said. "It is extremely unpleasant."

"Sorry." I took a sip.

"You should be sorry. You've signed the death warrant for my world with that sandwich thing of yours."

Well. I'm not gonna sit here and say I didn't feel remorse. How can you not feel bad about causing the destruction of what was probably billions upon billions of sentient beings? But in the first place, at the time I'd made the sandwich, the inverse-square law had only been a sort of theory to me, and in the second, that Xenne thing had threatened to kill me if I didn't turn the sandwich over. What was I supposed to do? Risk my life for what was at best an admittedly wondrous comestible? Not this fat guy. Like my mother always says, on my death bed, my biggest regret will probably be that I'm about to die.

Still, you can't just go around destroying other worlds with your careless distribution of layered cheese and cold cuts, which is why I said, "What can I do about it now?"

"You can make me another sandwich," it said. "And make this one better than the first, if possible."

Now I ask you. Being that I have lived through the constant nervous aggravation of the cold war, does engendering an arms race make any sense to me? Not in the least. But when I told that to the Coke machine, it said it beat certain death and destruction and genocide, which again, I can't exactly argue with. But again, how did I know this guy was on the up and up, and that he wasn't the extra-galactic equivalent of another Mussolini, except with a lighted front panel and a wide selection of refrigerated beverages instead of shoulder pads and an anachronistic skinhead look? I mean I hate to let people down, but power is a dangerous thing, and I have never cottoned well to customers who make unreasonable demands.

"No," I said, therefore.

"What do you mean, no?"

"Clean the lubricant out of your coin slot," I said. "No. No means no, or haven't you been paying attention to the anti-rape publicity over the past couple of decades?"

"But our world," he said.

"Your world is going to be fine," I said. "You get the Xenne back here. You tell him I've got something for the both of you. A weapon that'll knock your socks off."

He tried to tell me I was being crazy, but I went after him with the fish tank, and he did this kind of rapid dematerialization thing that left me standing there in the aftermath, waving off the resultant puff of smoke and watching clownfish die all over the floorboards.

I spent the next four hours in the kitchen. I had never actually tried to make a dish that would outdo all the other dishes in existence, but then, I've never had the fate of civilizations on my shoulders, either, and I work relatively well under pressure, having done the lunch rush down at Stu's for years. I did things in my kitchen that day with fresh basil and garlic that would make a brave man weep. I pushed myself to the point of exhaustion and beyond, into the realm of madness itself, in my divinely inspired utilization of pine nuts and olive oil. When I was finished, I sensed that I would never cook again—could never cook again—that somehow the exertion of the feat had wounded me at a deeper level than I'd known existed under all that pasta-fed cellulite, that I'd broken myself, like the mold of a flawless sculpture must be broken to ensure that sculpture's singularity. I didn't know if God Himself had taken a hand in my pre-prandial preparations, but on the other hand I knew of no bookies in the immediate vicinity who were laying odds against it.

When I returned to the living room, the Coke machine was back, along with the collection of salivary ducts. They stood at opposite corners of the living room, like they were afraid they'd catch a fungus off each other.

"So you told him. Good for you," I said.

"I didn't tell him," said the Coke machine. "His prophet, evidently, had foretold this as well."

"He was a heck of a prophet," said the Xenne. "It's pesto, isn't it?"

I nodded. It was pesto. My mouth was watering just thinking about it. I tried to ignore it, but how can you ignore a work of art like that when you're holding it in both hands in a little dish, with a sprig of parsley stabbed into its lovely thickness? Get a job. It can't be done.

"This is really good pesto," I said, demonstrating my considerable talent for understatement. "I don't know what it will do in M-31, but it won't be pretty, let me tell you. You think the pizza was bad? Forget about it."

The two of them were trembling. The Xenne had extruded his curving knives again and was once again exuding acid, and the Coke machine was making a kind of threatening ascending-pitched warm-up noise like you get before an ungodly powerful laser beam cuts loose and fries somebody into the middle of next Tuesday afternoon.

"Now, look," I said, "I'm not giving this pesto just to one of you. I'm giving it to both of you. That way you can wipe each other out."

"You wouldn't do that," said the Coke machine.

In fact I would, as I had seen the solution on an old episode of *Star Trek* and it had worked like a charm for Captain Kirk and company.

"Either that," I said, "or you can talk to each other. Stop the fighting. Open up diplomacy. It's your choice, guys."

There was a tense moment, during which the only sound was a guy on TV, being beaten half to death by a marlin he'd caught that was twice as big as him. You could have used the tension to fill holes in sheet metal.

"Either that, or you can give me back the sandwich," I said to the Xenne.

"Never."

I shrugged. It was no skin off my nose either way, which, really, is the best position to be in when you're negotiating. "In that case, there's a third alternative"

I said, and I made a move as if to hand over the little dish of pesto to the Scrobuloni.

"Wait," the Xenne said. "Okay, okay. Take your sandwich back."

He produced it from somewhere out of sight and dropped it on the rug. I bent down, real slow like, in a way I'd learned from watching Al Pacino single-handedly arresting several high ranked mafia officials, and I picked the sandwich up. It was a little worse for wear, but it appeared to be the selfsame sandwich I had given him. I took a little bite, just to satisfy myself he hadn't pulled a swap on me, and nodded. I would know that sandwich anywhere. The Xenne might as well have tried to fool a jeweler with a set of plastic beads.

"Good for you," I said, and backed away from them.

Maybe I should have done something different, in retrospect. Maybe I should have gone ahead with my threat to give them both the pesto. Maybe I could have stopped their war for good. But it is my belief that in situations where you don't know the full scope of the story, the worst thing you can do is to play God, or some other sort of deity. I didn't like the idea of interfering where I didn't know the full score. I thought, in short, that the best thing I could do was not to have an effect at all. I say all of this as an explanation for why I dumped the pesto all over the sandwich and, in three heroic bites, I wolfed the whole thing down.

It made my eyes burn, I can tell you, all that garlic, all at once. And the taste of all those mingling, wondrous flavors gave me a momentary glimpse into the inner workings of reality. But that was nothing to what it did to the Xenne and the Scrobuloni. They shrieked and rushed me, but this time I was ready. I pulled out a Louisville Slugger that I normally keep in the closet in the event my bookie ever confuses real life with a movie.

You'd be surprised how easy it is to smash up a Coke machine, in spite of all of the protective engineering that goes into them, and I don't even need to tell you what a baseball bat can do, in the right hands, to what is basically a big pile of anatomical correctness.

So that's my story. Any relation to anyone, living or dead, is probably my fault. Especially the Xenne and the Scrobuloni. Last I heard, they had recovered from the beating and were suing me for publishing this. I found out about it when a guy showed up at the door, asked my name, and served me papers. Said he was an attorney. I said, "Like, at law?" and he said, "No, at plumbing." Ask a stupid question. But let them sue. After the lambasting I got from Alice when she got home from work that night and smelled the sheer amount of garlic on my breath, I figure I can handle anything. And anyway, she's let off me since I went back to work for Stu. I know I said I'd never cook again, but for one thing, the Xenne's check turned out to be as rubber as the tires on my Caddy, and for another, Stu doesn't seem to mind the absence of my former talents. In fact, he said the reason that he fired me in the first place was that I was such a prima donna in the kitchen.

"We don't want art, we want lunch," he explained to me, which was all well and good until last Thursday, when a donkey with an unnaturally bulging forehead walked in and asked me for a slice of pizza.

"I always wondered what the real stuff tasted like," it said.

Copyright © 2015 by Tom Gerencer

Multiple bestseller Alan Dean Foster is the author of the Humanx Commonwealth, *the Spellsinger series, and numerous early* Star Wars *books. This is his first appearance in* Galaxy's Edge. *This story first appeared in* Christmas Forever, *published by TOR Books.*

WE THREE KINGS

by Alan Dean Foster

It was overcast and blustery and the snow was coming down as hard as a year's accumulation of overdue bills. Within the laboratory, Stein made the final adjustments, checked the readouts, and inspected the critical circuit breakers one last, final time. There was no going back now. The success or failure of his life's work hinged on what happened in the next few moments.

He knew there were those who if given the chance would try to steal his success, but if everything worked he would take care of them first. Them with their primitive, futile notions and dead-end ideas! All subterfuge and smoke, behind which they doubtless intended to claim his triumph as their own. Let them scheme and plot while they could. Soon they would be out of the way, and he would be able to bask in his due glory without fear of theft or accusation.

He began throwing the switches, turning the dials. Fitful bursts of necrotic light threw the strange shapes that occupied the vast room in the old warehouse into stark relief. Outside, the snow filled up the streets, sifting into dirty gutters, softening the outlines of the city. Not many citizens out walking in his section of town, he reflected. It was as well. Though the laboratory was shuttered and soundproofed, there was no telling what unforeseen sights and sounds might result when he finally pushed his efforts of many years to a final conclusion.

The dials swung while the readings on the gauges mounted steadily higher. Nearing the threshold now. The two huge Van de Graff generators throbbed with power. Errant orbs of ball lightning burst free, to spend themselves against the insulated ceiling in showers of coruscating sparks. It was almost time.

He threw the final, critical switch.

Gradually the crackling faded and the light in the laboratory returned to normal. With the smell of ozone sharp in his nostrils, Stein approached the table. For an instant, there was nothing more than disappointment brokered by uncertainty. And then—a twitch. Slight, but unmistakable. Stein stepped back, eyes wide and alert. A second twitch, this time in the arms. Then the legs, and finally the torso itself.

With a profound grinding sound, the creature sat up, snapping the two-inch wide leather restraining straps as if they were so much cotton thread.

"It's alive!" Stein heard himself shouting. "It's alive, it's alive, it's alive!"

He advanced cautiously until he was standing next to the now seated Monster. The bolts in its neck had been singed black from the force of the charge which had raced through it, but there were no signs of serious damage. Tentatively, Stein reached out and put a hand on the creature's arm. The massive, blocky skull swiveled slowly to look down at him.

"Nnrrrrrrrrrgh!"

Stein was delighted. "You and I, we are destined to conquer the world. At last, the work of my great-grandfather is brought to completion." His voice dropped to a conspiratorial whisper. "But there are those who would thwart us, who would stand in our way. I know who they are, and they must be—dealt with. Listen closely, and obey...."

Outside, the snow continued to fall.

✿

In the dark cellar Rheinberg carefully enunciated the ancient words. Only a little light seeped through the street-level window, between the heavy bars. Seated in the center of the room, in middle of the pentagram, was the sculpture. Rheinberg was as talented as he was resourceful, and the details of his creation were remarkable for their depth and precision.

An eerie green glow began to suffuse the carefully crafted clay figure as the ancient words echoed through the studio. Rheinberg read carefully from the copy of the ancient manuscript in a steady, unvarying monotone. With each word, each sentence, the glow intensified, until softly pulsing green shadows filled every corner of the basement studio.

Almost, but not quite, he halted in the middle of the final sentence, at the point when the eyes of the figure began to open. That would have been dangerous, he knew. And so, fully committed now, he read on. Only when he'd finished did he dare allow himself to step forward for a closer look.

The eyes of the Golem were fully open now, unblinking, staring straight ahead. Then they shifted slowly to their left, taking notice of the slight, anxious man who was approaching.

"It works. It worked! The old legends were true." Unbeknownst to Rheinberg, the parchment sheet containing the words had crumpled beneath his clenching fingers. "The world is ours, my animate friend! Ours, as soon as certain others are stopped. You'll take care of that little matter for me, won't you? You'll do anything I ask. You must. That's what the legend says."

"Ooooyyyyyyyy!" Moaning darkly, the massive figure rose. Its gray head nearly scraped the ceiling.

✿

Within the charmed circle something was rising. A pillar of smoke, black shot through with flashes of bright yellow, coiling and twisting like some giant serpent awakened from an ancient sleep. Al-Nomani recited the litany and watched, determined to maintain the steady sing-song of the nefarious quatrain no matter what happened.

The fumes began to thicken, to coalesce. Limbs appeared, emerging from the roiling hell of the tornadic spiral. The whirlwind itself began to change shape and color, growing more man-like with each verse, until a horrid humanoid figure stood where smoke had once swirled. It had two rings in its oversized left ear, a huge nose, and well-developed fangs growing upward from its lower jaw. For all that, the fiery yellow eyes that glared out at the historian from beneath the massive, low-slung brow reeked of otherworldly intelligence.

"By the beard of the Prophet!" Al-Nomani breathed tensely, "it worked!" He put down the battered, weathered tome from which he had been reading. The giant regarded him silently, awaiting. As it was supposed to do.

Al-Nomani took a step forward. "You will do my bidding. There is much that needs be done. First and foremost there is the matter of those who would challenge my knowledge, and my supremacy. They must be shown the error of their ways. I commit you to deal with them."

"Eeeehhhhzzzzz!" Within the circle the Afreet bowed solemnly. Its arms were as big around as tree trunks.

✧

Stillman was cruising the run-down commercial area just outside the industrial park when he noticed movement up the side street. At this hour everything was closed up tight, and the weather had reduced traffic even further. He picked up the cruiser's mike, then set it back in its holder. Might be nothing more than some poor old rhummy looking for a warm place to sleep.

Still, the vagrants and the homeless tended to congregate downtown. It was rare to encounter one this far out. Which meant that the figure might be looking to help itself to something more readily convertible than an empty park bench. Stillman flicked on the heavy flashlight and slid out of the car, drawing his service revolver as he did so. The red and yellows atop the cruiser revolved steadily, lighting up the otherwise dark street.

Cautiously, he advanced on the narrow roadway. He had no intention of entering, of course. If the figure ran, that would be indication enough something was wrong, and that's when he'd call for backup.

"Hey! Hey, you in there! Kinda late for a stroll, especially in this weather, ain't it?" The only reply was a strange shuffling. The officer blinked away falling snow as something shifted in the shadows. He probed with his flashlight.

"Come on out, man. I know you're back there. I don't want any trouble from you and you really don't want any from me. Don't make me come in there after you." He took a challenging step forward.

Something vast and monstrous loomed up with shocking suddenness, so big his light could not illuminate it all. Officer Corey Stillman gaped at the apparition. His finger contracted reflexively on the trigger of his service revolver, and a sharp crack echoed down the alley. The creature flinched, then reached for him with astounding speed.

"Nnrrrrrrrrrr!"

✧

His head throbbed like his brother's Evenrude when he finally came around. Groaning, he reached for the back of his skull as he straightened up in the snow. Memories came flooding back and he looked around wildly, but the Monster was gone, having shambled off down the street. Eleven years on the force and that was without question the ugliest dude he'd ever encountered. Quick for his size, too. Too damn quick. He was sure his single shot had hit home, but it hadn't even slowed the big guy down. Wincing, he climbed to his feet and surveyed his surroundings. His cruiser sat where he'd left it in the street, lights still revolving patiently.

His gun lay in the snow nearby. Slowly he picked up the .38, marveling at the power which had crushed it to a metal pulp. What had he encountered, and how could he report it? Nobody'd believe him.

A figure stepped into view from behind the building. He tensed, but big as the pedestrian was, he was utterly different in outline from Stillman's departed assailant. Seeking help, the officer took a couple of steps toward it—and pulled up short.

The enormous stranger was the color of damp clay, save for vacant black eyes that stared straight through him.

"Good God!"

Startled by the exclamation, the creature whirled and struck.

"Ooyyyyyyyyyy!"

✧

This time when Stillman regained consciousness he didn't move, just lay in the snow and considered his situation. His second attacker had been nothing like the first, yet no less terrifying in appearance. He no longer cared if everyone back at the station thought him crazy; he needed back-up.

Too much overtime, he told himself. That had to be it. Too many hours rounding up too many hookers and junkies and sneak thieves. Mary was right. He needed to use some of that vacation time he'd been accumulating.

Body aching, head still throbbing, he struggled to his feet. The cruiser beckoned, its heater pounding away persistently despite the open door on the driver's side. Recovering his hat and clutching the flashlight, he staggered around the front, pausing at the door to lean on it for support. The heat from the interior refreshed him, made him feel better. He started to slide in behind the wheel.

The seat was already occupied by something with burning yellow eyes and a bloated, distorted face straight out of the worst nightmares of childhood. It was playing with the police radio scanner, mouthing it like a big rectangular cookie.

He'd surprised it, and of course it reacted accordingly.

"Oh <u>no</u>!" Stillman moaned as he staggered backward and an unnaturally long arm reached for him. "Not <u>again</u>!"

"Eehhhzzzzzzz!"

The wonderful profusion of brightly colored street and store lights slowed the Monster's progress, mysteriously diluted its intent. The lights were festive and cheerful. Even as it kept to the shadows, it could see the faces of smiling adults and laughing children. There were the decorations, too: in the stores, above the streets, on the houses. Laughter reached him through the falling snow; childish giggles, booming affirmations of good humor, deep chuckles of pleasure. Invariably, it all had a cumulative effect.

Memories stirred: memories buried deep within the brain he'd been given. The lights, the snow, the laughter and ebullient chatter of toys and candy: it all meant something. He just wasn't sure what. Confused, he turned and lurched off down the dark alley between two tall buildings, trying to reconcile his orders with these disturbing new thoughts.

He paused suddenly, senses alert. Someone else was coming up the alley. The figure was big, much bigger than any human he'd observed so far that night. Not that he was afraid of any human, or for that matter, any thing. Teeth and joints grinding, arms extended, he started deliberately forward.

There was just enough light for the two figures to make each other out. When they could do so with confidence, they hesitated in mutual confusion. Something strange was abroad this night, and both figures thought it most peculiar.

"Who—what—you?" the Monster declaimed in a voice like a rusty mine cart rolling down long-neglected track. Speech was still painful.

"I vaz going ask you the same qvestion." The other figure's black eyes scrutinized the slow-speaking shape standing opposite. "You one revolting looking schlemiel, I can tell you."

"You not—no raving beauty yourself."

"So tell me zumthing I don't know." The Golem's massive shoulders heaved, a muscular gesture of tectonic proportions.

"What be this, pbuh?" Both massive shapes turned sharply, to espy a third figure hovering close behind them. Despite its size it had made not a sound during its approach.

"Und I thought you vaz ugly," the Golem murmured to the Monster as it contemplated the newcomer.

"Speak not ill of others lest the wrath of Allah befall thee." The Afreet approached, its baleful yellow eyes flicking from one shape to the next. "What manner of mischief is afoot this night?"

"Ask you—the same," the Monster rumbled.

The Afreet bowed slightly. "I am but recently brought fresh into the world, and am abroad on a mission for my mortal master of the moment." It glanced back toward the main street, with its twinkling lights and window-shopping pedestrians blissfully unaware of the astonishing conclave that was taking place just down the alley. "Yet I fear the atmosphere not conducive to my command, for what I see and hear troubles my mind like a prattling harim."

"You too?" The Golem rubbed its chin. Clay flakes fell to the pavement. "I vaz thinking the same."

"I think I know—what is wrong." The other two eyed the Monster.

"Nu? So don't keep it to yourself," said the Golem.

"I have been pondering." Eyes squinted tight with the stress of the activity. "Pondering hard. What I think is that the season," the creature declared slowly, "is the reason."

"Pray tell, explain thyself." The Afreet was demanding, but polite.

The Monster's square forehead turned slowly. "The brain I was given—remembers. This time of year—the sights I see—make me remember. The time is wrong—for the command I was given. All—wrong. Wrong to kill—at the time of Christmas."

"Kill," echoed the Afreet. "Strange are the ways of the Prophet, for such was the order I was given. To kill this night two men; one of art and one of learning. Felix Stein and Joseph Rheinberg."

The Monster and the Golem started and exchanged a look. "I vaz to stamp out Stein alzo," muttered the Golem, "as vell as a historian name of Al-Nomani. Rheinberg is my master."

"And Stein—mine," added the Monster.

"Fascinating it be," confessed the Afreet. "For Al-Nomani is the one who called me forth."

"He is one whom I was to—slay," announced the Monster. "And this Rheinberg—too."

The formidable, and formidably bemused, trio pondered this arresting coincidence in silence, while cheerful music and the sound of caroling drifted back to them from the street beyond. Though least verbal of the three, it was again the Monster who articulated first.

"Something—wrong—here. Wrong notion. Wrong time of—the year. Everything—wrong."

"Go on, say it again," growled the Golem. "Not just Christmas it is, but Chanukah also. Not a time for inimical spirits to be stirring. Not even a mouse."

"The spirit of Ramadan moves within me," declared the Afreet. "I know not what manner of life or believers you be, but I sense that in this I am of similar mind with you."

"Then what—we—do?" the Monster wondered aloud.

They considered.

✿

Stillman blinked snow from his eyes. By now there wasn't much left of his cap, or his winter coat. He fumbled for the flashlight, somehow wasn't surprised to find that the supposedly impregnable cylinder of aircraft grade aluminum had been twisted into a neat pretzel shape.

He saw the cruiser and crawled slowly towards it. Nothing inside him seemed to be broken, but every muscle in his bruised body protested at the forced movement. The rotating lights atop the car were beginning to weaken as the battery ran down.

He was a foot from the door when he sensed a presence and looked to his right.

Three immense forms stood staring down at him, each all too familiar from a previous recent encounter. It was impossible to say which of the trio was the most terrifying. A clawed hand reached for him.

"Please," he whispered through snow-benumbed lips, "no more. Just kill me and get it over with."

The powerful fingers clutched his jacket front and lifted him as easily as if he were a blank arrest report, setting him gently on his feet. Another huge hand, dark and even-toned as the play clay his little girl made mudpies with, helped keep him upright. Trembling in spite of himself, he looked from one fearsome face to the next.

"I don't get it. What is this? What are you setting me up for?"

"We need—your help," the Monster mumbled, like a reluctant clog in a main city sewer line.

Stillman hesitated. "*You* need *my* help? That's a switch." He brushed dirty snow from his waist and thighs. "What kind of help? To be your punching bag?" He blinked at the Monster. "Uh, sorry about shooting you. You startled me. Heck, you still startle me."

"I—forgive," the Monster declaimed, sounding exactly like Arnold Schwarzenegger on a bad shooting day.

"Yeah—okay then. Well—what did you—boys—have in mind?"

The Afreet's eyes burned brightly. "In this Time, praise be, is it still among men a crime to set another to commit murder?"

Stillman stiffened slightly. "Damn straight it is. Why do you ask?"

The Afreet glanced at its companions. "We know of several who have done this thing. Should they not, by your mortal laws, be punished for this?"

"You bet they should. You know where these guys are?" All three creatures nodded. Stillman hesitated. "You have proof?"

The Golem dug a fist the size and consistency of a small boulder into its open palm. "You shouldn't vorry, policeman. I promise each one a full confession vill sign."

"If you're sure...." Stillman eyed the stony figure warily. "You're not talking about obtaining a confession under duress, are you?"

"Vhat, *me*?" The Golem spread tree-like arms wide. "My friends and I vill chust a little friendly visit pay them. Each of them."

☼

Stillman delivered the three badly shaken men to the station by himself. There was no need to call for backup. Not after his hefty acquaintances warned the three outraged but nonetheless compliant tamperers-with-the-laws-of-nature that if any of them so much as ventured an indecent suggestion in the officer's direction, the improvident speaker would sooner or later find himself on the receiving end of a midnight visit from all three of the—visitants. In the face of that monumentally understated threat, the would-be masters of the world proved themselves only too eager to cooperate with the police.

Stillman presented the thoroughly disgruntled experimenters to the duty officer, together with their signed confessions attesting to their respective intentions to murder one another, a collar which was sure to gain him a commendation at the least, and possibly even a promotion. It was worth the aches and pains to see the look on the lieutenant's face when each prisoner meekly handed over his confession. It further developed that all three men were additionally wanted on various minor charges, from theft of scientific equipment and art supplies to failing to return an overdue book from the University's Special Collections library.

The members of the unnatural trio who had propitiated this notable sequence of events waited behind the station to congratulate Stillman when he clocked off duty. He winced as he stretched, studying each of them in turn.

"So—what're you guys gonna do now?" he asked curiously. "If you'd like to hang around the city, I know for a fact you could probably each get a tryout with the Bears."

"Bears?" the Monster rumbled. "I like to eat bear."

"No, no. It's a professional sports team. You know? Pro football? No," he reflected quietly, "maybe you don't know."

"If it be His will, we shall each of us make our way to a place of solitude and contentment. For such as we be, there is a special path for doing so. But we must wait for the coming of day to find the true passageways."

Stillman nodded. "Seems a shame after what you've done tonight to have to hang out here, by yourselves, in this crappy weather."

Mary Stillman came out of the kitchen to greet her returning husband. She was drying a large serving dish with a beige towel spotted with orange flowers.

"Mary," Stillman called out, "I'm home! And I've brought some friends over for a little late supper. Do we have any of that Christmas turkey left?"

"Urrrrr—Christmas!" the Monster growled like a runaway eighteen-wheeler locking up its brakes at seventy per, and his sentiment if not his words were echoed by his companions.

While the Golem skillfully caught the dish before it struck the floor, the well-mannered Afreet performed the same service for a falling Mary Stillman. When she recovered consciousness and her husband hastily explained matters to her, she nodded slowly and went to see what she could find in the kitchen, whereupon they all shared a very nice late-night snack indeed, wholly in keeping with the spirit of the Seasons.

Copyright © 1993 by Alan Dean Foster

Larry Niven is a former Worldcon Guest of Honor, a frequent bestseller, a five-time Hugo winner, and the creator of the Known Space *series. This marks his third appearance in* Galaxy's Edge *(and his second with an original Draco Tavern story). He recently teamed up with Brad R. Torgersen and Matthew Harrington to produce* Red Tide, *a Stellar Guild book published by Arc Manor/Phoenix Pick.*

CLOSING SALE

by Larry Niven

It started in February with a tight knot of brilliant stars in a patch of southern sky, almost between the two Magellanic Clouds, ten of them blooming over a span of less than three weeks. Astronomers said they were all Type 1A supernovae.

The world speculated. In the past this might have seemed urgent, but not now, not since the first Chirpshithra spacecraft arrived half a century ago. We'd get an explanation eventually, when the next ship came.

Remember when we used to do our own research?

In July a sizeable near-sphere made orbit around the Moon: *Wildflower Flavors*, with a small crew and a score of passengers of varied species. A lander settled near the Draco Tavern and the place filled up with visitors. Then another ship arrived, *Guns Set Aside*. Two ships orbiting the Moon have been a rare thing these past fifty years.

Then seven more over the course of a week, a sudden pileup of interstellar vessels around the Moon.

The Draco Tavern wasn't nearly big enough to hold the traffic. Landers settled all over the ice around us, and then pressure tents sprang up in various sizes and shapes, and caverns and castles carved from the ice itself. The Tavern was still jammed. Our translation systems don't usually show any sign of self-awareness, but now they were complaining about the overcrowding. I kept notes regarding these dozens of new species, but I knew that I was falling behind.

Mashisthet, one of the Chirpsithra officers aboard *Wildflower Flavors*, tried to explain what we were seeing. "Of course they do look like a certain common variety of supernova, but to the right eyes it's clear. Rick, they're not really supernovae, they're beacons. We're sorry for the confusion. You thought what? Dark energy? What in any cosmos is dark energy? Are you addicted to comic books?"

I asked, "But why do they all clump up?"

"Of course they couldn't all have lit up at once. They're not in one region, they're strung halfway across the galaxy. We're looking at a nearly straight line of lights, foreshortened because it's running toward Sol system. We believe some radicals at Sagittarius Transit Control are interfering with the interstellar traffic system, in furtherance of a union strike."

"How dangerous could *that* get?"

Mashisthet touched her fingers to a sparker. "Sss… Merely awkward, we hope. The Centrists won't seek a high death rate. They only seek disruption. I think you'll be seeing more ships."

I needed a bigger staff while the ships were in, but hiring was easy: I always have volunteers. The Draco Tavern is a wonderful place to do business, not least because of the privacy shields. I could watch interactions among groups standing shoulder to thorax to eyegrid yet completely ignoring each other, and I could speculate what it was all about. I heard snatches as I moved about with sparkers and drinks and chemical mash. Something was being bought, something sold. I caught the phrase, "To a good home," from one of the Chirpsithra, and I asked her.

"I've sold a translator," Tarashishpiff said. And one of the translators broke in to add, "I go to California Institute of Technology. We'll have so much to learn from each other."

"You never sold translation devices before," I said.

Tarashishpiff said, "They're smarter than human and they're doing their own negotiating. Rick, we didn't want to share our technology, but with so many ships, we need to buy many resources."

Visitors came: Dr. Cheri Kaylor and Carlos Magliocco, from the United Nations, with a few staff. I'd thought we'd just talk, but they set up a pressure tent on the ice. "We're here to observe," Cheri said. "Our bosses are afraid what happened with those fish might happen again." She meant the virtual takeover of the equatorial Pacific by Sea People.

I asked, "How would you stop it?" The UN has grown more powerful over the decades, particularly since the interstellar ships came, but they're no match for any aliens.

Carlos Magliocco said, "We have no idea. Fill us in, will you? What's going on?"

I said, "We've got lots more toilets. It's a double arc now. Installing those went fast. I didn't get involved. A couple more airlocks too, but that wasn't much of a problem. There must be limits to how big or how contorted sapient beings can get and still travel."

"There's marketing. Suddenly a lot of marketing," Carlos said. "Our pressure tent, it came out of a department store, but it's Chirpsithra technology. That's nothing. There are little cold fusion plants being sold—"

Cherie jumped in. "Very hard to control. Easy power in everybody's hands. Terrorists too. Every nation on Earth is going to have to deal with that."

"But there's not a lot of power flow," said Carlos. "You can't run the cold fusion plants hot. Good for a household, but not a good weapon, praise the Lord. Then there are medical—"

"Right. Rick, the Gligstith(click)optok are selling immortality—"

"Longevity," I corrected her.

"Yeah, okay, you can still die, but yeah. It's like a logjam came loose somewhere. What's happening?"

I said, "Too many ships. They all want resources, and some of those resources have to be bought. They're rigorous about that. All these aliens are willing to pay in knowledge. Eager. The Tavern is a great place for brokering deals."

The UN folk hung around, living in their mansion of a tent, using the Tavern's communications and buying drinks and some meals. Trade continued. I brokered some of the deals. One day Cheri asked me, "Sand?"

"Yeah. They're getting silica from the Moon, but they're paying for it because we've got a claim. Aluminum too. But they're buying seawater here on Earth."

"Why not go to Europa?" Cherie asked.

"Oh, they're talking to the fingerfish, but Europa's charging too high for water, and they own rights in the other moons too. The fingerfish have been space-going for a long time. And we've got rising seas, so why not sell some water?"

"They're buying produce in the markets, in Australia and Europe and the States," Magliocco said. "There's some secrecy. They're trying to auction off Glig medical methods, but those techniques leak out. They're selling easy turn-on-and-off pregnancy, and extended childhood, and regeneration. They're buying spices with the money."

Some of what was being sold was irresistible. I bought some healing and reshaping products for me and Jehaneh. I bought into some Glig mental exercises. That was weird: they worked, and for humans. I asked about telekinesis and teleportation and got laughed at, but I could do amazing things with mathematics and I could remember where everything was in the vast variety of the bar—a wonderful aid to not poisoning customers. I could fix a broken toilet, sometimes.

Rumor said that the Folk—who look like wolves with their heads on upside down, and act like that too—had started hunting expeditions in South America, with drug running gangs as targets. I tried to find out more about that, and couldn't. I waited with some uneasiness for Carlos or Cherie to bring it up, but they never did. Maybe nobody was complaining to the UN.

A Quarasht sold a computer system to make instant movies, with any background and any deceased actors you like. As with books and publishers, suddenly the problem isn't making a movie, it's getting publicity for it, and doing it better than the next ten thousand film makers.

News from the outer world filtered back to the Draco Tavern, but sporadically. Walter Dass, one of my staff, was keeping better track than I was. "It feels like we can do anything," he told me. "There's a Mith-hakak team selling weather control. The drought's over in California, and they're gearing up to flood the Sahara. There's a new species that came aboard *Special Haven*, construction artists like evolved beavers? They're selling buildings that grow themselves out of ice or ocean water. They still need

The BEST OF GALAXY'S EDGE 2013-2014

Larry Niven
C. L. Moore
Nick DiChario
Robert T. Jeschonek
Tina Gower
Mercedes Lackey
Ralph Roberts
Ken Liu
Marina J. Lostetter
Andrea G. Stewart
Eric Cline
Tom Gerencer
Nancy Kress
Sabina Theo
Gio Clairval
Steve Cameron
Brad R. Torgersen
Eric Leif Davin
Kary English
Lou J. Berger
Brian Trent
K. C. Norton
Leena Likitalo
James Aquilone

Edited by
Mike Resnick

THE ORIGINAL HUGO- AND
NEBULA-WINNING NOVELLA

THE MOUNTAINS OF MOURNING

LOIS McMASTER BUJOLD

A MILES VORKOSIGAN ADVENTURE

WINNER
HUGO
AWARD

WINNER
NEBULA
AWARD

a crew to keep them growing right. Boss, it's as if we're turning godlike. By the way, I'm getting rich off all of this."

✧

So was I, but I barely had time to notice. Twelve ships now. Too many staff; no time to train them. I was constantly needed to point them toward or away from iffy chemicals. Airlocks running hot, day and night. Noise overflow from the overloaded translators. I barely noticed when it started to ease off.

Yes, the ships were leaving.

It didn't happen all at once. One day a few pressure tents were gone. The Tavern crowds thinned until I had moments to myself, to think, and the noise dwindled some too. The glowing dots around the Moon were fewer.

"*Wildflower Flavors* is going too, but some of the crews will stay," Mashisthet told me. She was sitting with me and four UN staff and a silent Qarasht. "One or two ships, for awhile. The buildings, weather control, the Sea People all need tending, for awhile. Glig sometimes make mistakes, and that will need watching. But this is all the traffic you're likely to get for twenty or thirty years."

"No more ships?" I wondered.

"No, Rick."

"Good grief! What does that do to the Tavern?"

The Chirp didn't answer. I kept thinking…and decided. "I'll keep the Tavern going. You've given us a lot to absorb in just the past year. It'll take us decades. I should add a library."

"We can build our own ships now," Carlos Magliocco said. "You finally sold us the techniques we need. The radiation shield was what we needed most."

Sheri Kaylor said, "With that…maybe now we can take back Mars."

I didn't laugh. "Hold up, Dr. Kaylor. Let's not get above ourselves. The legal decision went against us. Besides, the Chirpsithra ships have been trading with Europa too, haven't you, Mashisthet?"

"Yes. Our decision was final. Europa will keep Mars. But you own a plot of land on Mars, Rick. You could open an embassy."

✧

The departing ships have left humanity weirdly changed. We're ready to expand into the solar system.

Europa and Mars and some moons of Jupiter and Saturn are claimed by the fingerfish. We might try to claim the rest. If we were looking for habitable worlds, we'd have to go interstellar. I think that is beyond us, for now.

We certainly would want to steer clear of red dwarf stars. Those planets belong to the Chirpsithra.

Copyright © 2015 by Larry Niven

Jody Lynn Nye is the author of forty novels and more than one hundred stories, and has at various times collaborated with Anne McCaffrey and Robert Asprin. Her husband, Bill Fawcett, is a prolific author, editor, and packager, and is also active in the gaming field.

BOOK REVIEWS

by Bill Fawcett and Jody Lynn Nye

Coming Home
by Jack McDevitt
Ace Science Fiction/Headline—2014
ISBN: 978-1472207579

A search for lost relics of the pre-collapse civilization, *Coming Home* is the seventh in a series, though it stands well alone. There is something wonderful about a well written series of novels. When you discover them, you have the excitement of knowing there are many hours of enjoyable reading ahead. Familiar characters become both better known and evolve, and the world becomes deeper and more appealing. Perhaps the only dark side is when you get deeply involved in something brilliant and then discover the next book, and the fate of characters you have learned to care about, is yet to be written. (Yes, George R. R. Martin, get to work…)

The Alex Benedict novels are certainly a great read. To review these books I had to ask myself why they work so well. Certainly, Jack McDevitt's skill at wordsmithing is part of it. To give him the ultimate compliment on the mystery itself, I did not see its solution coming at all… and should have. Jack McDevitt also accomplishes something even harder to find. All the Alex Benedict books, including *Coming Home*, are set a whopping seven thousand years in the future, though the society and people and how they love and think are in many ways not uncomfortably different from us today. The people are people and the characters feel real. This distant future is also familiar because, like Western civilization today, this interstellar civilization is less than a millennium from the end of a very extended Dark Age.

The impressive thing is how McDevitt handles this future. The differences appear, but do not slap you in the face. Two parallel plots, one the attempt to find a trove of pre-collapse artifacts and the other a rescue attempt for a space liner popping in and out of time, are the focus of the main character's concerns. The lost artifacts at the basis of the mystery are valued in a space traveling society seven millennia up time: early NASA objects. The hero works for a man who specializes in the sale and recovery of relics, just as some dealers today do with ancient Egyptian items. But in the far future such things as Neil Armstrong's coffee cup from his Apollo mission have become valued and tinged with the aura of capital "H" History. The secondary plot, trying to find a way to save those on the temporally suspended space liner, dwells less on the science than on the social and political hazards of performing any well publicized rescue mission. If you can only save a few hundred of three thousand in the first attempt, who gets saved? How much risk is acceptable to save them all now, versus a chance to maybe do so more safely in five or fifty years?

This author has brought you into a very futuristic, but probable and easily entered world of the far future with no trumpet blasts, no jarring shocks, or Archeological Road Show inside jokes. It is a unique future, but one that adds to and does not get in the way of the mystery. I was struggling to find a way to explain just how skillful an author Jack McDevitt is when SFWA did it for me. He is being given the Heinlein Award at this year's Nebula Ceremony.

Who should read this series? Those who enjoy a good mystery with a twist. Those who like to read about well-developed characters and anyone who likes to look at a future that is both different and yet still filled with people you could meet at a SF convention. A good read, a strong mystery, and fascinating look set in a future that is both different and familiar.

☼

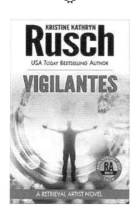

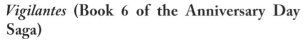

Vigilantes (Book 6 of the Anniversary Day Saga)
by Kristine Katherine Rusch
WMG Publishing—2015
ASIN: B00SCDPDTK

A question you have to ask yourself when reading a book in the middle of a series is, does it make you want to go back and read the others? In the case of Kristine Katherine Rusch's *Vigilantes*, the answer is yes. As the author of long-running series myself, I know that it's not an easy thing to produce a book that tells a stand-alone story, lest this be the only one of the line a reader can find. It also must have enough of the overarching plot without giving away everything that happened before, but yet provide enough background to understand what's going on.

In this sixth volume of this saga, the action begins twelve days after the Anniversary Day massacre and only days following the Peyti Crisis. In the midst of the Moon trying to recover from the two events, in which thousands of people died, a brutal murder takes place that no one seems to want to investigate. Miles Flint, retrieval artist, has to cope with his grieving daughter, Talia, who also has to deal with her own secret that was made all the worse by the current events. Rusch tells a good story from several characters' points of view. I'm looking forward to reading the rest of the series and seeing how the multiple storylines come together. If you would enjoy following in the footsteps of determined investigators through a well-drawn universe, you'll enjoy this book.

☼

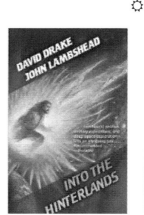 

Into the Hinterland and **Into the Maelstrom**
by David Drake and John Lambshead
Baen Books—2012 and 2015
ISBN: 978-1451638424, Hinterland
ISBN: 978-1476780283, Maelstrom

History provides a wonderful basis for science fiction novels. Alternate history novels such as Harry Turtledove's *Guns of the South* or Eric Flint's *1632* series have literally created their own genre. Another variant in using history is to move a familiar element from the past to an alien environment. This was the premise of David Drake's *Ranks of Bronze* and Harry Turtledove's *Videssos* novels where in each a Roman Legion is moved to a strange world and yet triumphs. This also happens to an American Civil War regiment from Maine in William R. Forstchen's *Lost Regiment* novels. Two more recent science fiction series from David Drake change this equation again. These series use the events of history, but place them in a technologically-advanced future. David Drake's Lieutenant Leary (*Lightning* and *Reaches*) novels actually are based on incidents that occurred during the Punic Wars between Rome and Carthage. Even more fun is that his heroes are on the side of the loser, Carthage, and so their cause is doomed.

This new series, which begins with *Into the Hinterlands*, is a retelling of the American Revolution as seen through the eyes of a George Washington-inspired character. It is has as a basis one of the most appealing and unique methods of interstellar travel I have seen in more than half a century of reading SF, but I won't spoil it for you here. The first novel is a far future and high tech reflection of the French and Indian wars. It even contains a version of the incident that may have been young George Washington's worst mistake, and one that was an actual cause of that historical war. It also parallels much about the first American president that is not normally found in any history books, involving Washington's long romantic interest in the fiancée and then wife of a friend (Sally Fairfax in history and Saria in the novels). Washington was a lesser aristo at best who married money, and only inherited any real wealth when his older brother died unexpectedly. Looking at the parallels is part of the fun of this series, but hardly all of it. As you would expect from any Dave Drake or John Lambshead book, the military action is vivid, real, and gritty. The characters are well drawn in their own right, even ignoring history; knowing the way the actual events unfolded does not lessen the suspense or excitement. The second volume, *Into the Maelstrom*, has also just become available. These books will provide you with a rousing read. If you enjoy military SF, history, or just good war stories, you should enjoy them.

Time's Mistress
by Steven Savile
Wordfire Press—2014

ISBN-13: 978-1614752400

Time's Mistress is a collection of deeply compelling and highly emotional stories and vignettes. In these pages, you will find tales about loss and lost love. Savile will tear at your heart by showing you the dark palace where gods who have no more followers are banished forever, unable to die. He creates deep, sorrowful moods through imagery that is often very powerful, and characters that are very human. The stories will never cheer the despondent, but they will evoke emotions and reactions from you that may surprise you with their intensity. If you want to wake up thinking about the story you read the day before, then Steven Savile's *Time's Mistress* is worth your attention.

The Stars My Destination
by Alfred Bester
iPicturebooks edition—2011
ISBN-13: 978-1876963460

In each column we are going to take the liberty of suggesting a classic of science fiction or fantasy. Some books from half a century ago or longer were highly praised and innovative back them, but simply have not held up. Others are as fresh and exciting as when they first appeared. Certainly one of the most outstanding of the latter is the Hugo-nominee *The Stars My Destination* by Alfred Bester. There are not that many books by Alfred Bester, but most are considered gems and retain their gleam, and this is among his best.

The Stars My Destination first appeared as a four part serial in *Galaxy Magazine* in 1956. In the UK it was released as a novel titled, *Tiger! Tiger!* The story is one of a common spaceman, Gully Foyle, who has great potential and no ambition. This changes when his ship is ambushed and he, as sole survivor, is stranded as bait on the wreck deep in space. He saves himself and sets out to gain his revenge on those who stranded him, those who chose not to rescue him, and also on the aristocratic oligarchy that rules the solar system, and in so doing, he just sort of incidentally and unintentionally changes the future of all mankind.

Beyond amazing writing and pulse-rising action, this novel also includes a unique means of travel, an insightful look at the highest and lowest levels of a society that could evolve from that of today, interstellar espionage, and a deep and driven central character. This book stands the test of time. The society, its excesses and wonders, and Bester's bigger-than-life characters feel as real today as they did more than fifty years ago. For those who want to be well read in the field, and enjoy hard, character-driven science fiction, this is a must read, not just because it is an acknowledged classic, but because you are likely to find that it is still one best SF novels ever written.

Gregory Benford is a Nebula winner and a former Worldcon Guest of Honor. He is the author of more than thirty novels, six books of non-fiction, and has edited ten anthologies. This previously appeared in Aliens: The Anthropology of Science Fiction, *Southern Illinois University Press.*

EFFING THE INEFFABLE

by Gregory Benford

Their light of pocket-torch, of signal flare,
Licks at the edge of unsuspected places,
While others scan, under an arc-lamp's glare,
Nursery, kitchen sink, or their own faces.
-Kingsley Amis

There is probably no more fundamental theme in science fiction than the alien. The genre reeks of the desire to embrace the strange, the exotic and unfathomable nature of the future. Often the science in SF represents knowledge—exploring and controlling and semi-safe. Aliens balance this desire for certainty with the irreducible unknown.

A lot of the tension in SF arises between such hard certainties and the enduring, atmospheric mysteries. And while science is quite odd and different to many, it is usually simply used as a reassuring conveyor belt which hauls the alien on stage.

Of course, by alien I don't merely mean the familiar ground of alienation which modern literature has made its virtual theme song. Once the province of intellectuals, alienation is now supermarket stuff. Even MTV knows how commonly we're distanced and estranged from the modern state, or from our relatives, or from the welter of cultural crosscurrents of our times.

Alienation has a spectrum. It can verge into the fantastic simply by being overdrawn, as in Kafka's "The Metamorphosis," which describes a man who wakes up one morning as an enormous insect. Only one step beyond is Rachel Ingalls's recent Mrs. Caliban, in which a frog man appears. He simply steps into a kitchen, with minimal differences from ordinary humans. He is merely a puppet representing the "good male," and in fact can be read as a figment of the protagonist's imagination. The novel isn't about aliens, of course; it's a parable of female angst.

We don't describe our neighbors as alien just because they drive a Chevy and we have a Renault. What SF does intentionally, abandoning lesser uses to the mainstream, is to take us to the extremes of alienness. That, I think, is what makes it interesting.

I deplore the *Star Trek* view, in which aliens turn out to be benign if you simply talk to them kindly; this is Hubert Humphrey in space. That fits into a larger program of some SF, in which "friendly alien" isn't seen for the inherent contradiction it is. Friendliness is a human category. Describing aliens that way robs them of their true nature, domesticates the strange.

Yet much early SF was permeated with the assumption that aliens had to be like us. In *Aelita, or The Decline of Mars* by Alexei Tolstoi (1922), the intrepid Soviet explorers decide even before landing that Martians must necessarily be manlike, for "everywhere life appears, and over life everywhere manlike forms are supreme: it would be impossible to create an animal more perfect than man—the image and similitude of the Master of the Universe."

We've come a long way since such boring certitudes—through the marauding Martins of H.G. Wells, the inventive and Disney-cute Mars of Stanley Weinbaum's 1934 short story "A Martian Odyssey," and into hard SF's meticulously constructed worlds for fantastic creatures. Aliens have been used as stand-in symbols for bad humans, or as trusty native guides, as foils for expansionist empires, and so on.

Yet for me, the most interesting problem set by the alien is in rendering the alienness of it. How do you set the ineffable in a frame of scientific concreteness? This is a central problem for SF. Very seldom has it been attempted in full, using the whole artistic and scientific arsenal.

ARTFUL ALIENS

Of course, we all know that one cannot depict the totally alien. This is less a deep insight than a definition. Stanislaw Lem's *Solaris* asserts that true contact and understanding is impossible. It was a vivid remainder twenty years ago. As genre criticism, it seems nowadays ponderously obvious.

Since then, its targets—anthropomorphism, the claustrophobic quality of intellectual castles, and cultural relativism—have become rather cold meat. Indeed, everybody now assumes without discussion that, in writing about the very strange, we must always gesture toward something known, in order to make analogies or provide signs. So we're careful, because unless we keep reminding the reader that this creature is to be taken literally, it readily becomes (surprise, surprise) a metaphor.

In the mainstream, walk-on aliens come with metaphors and labels worn on the sleeve. How could they not? In "realistic" fiction, aliens can't be real. SF insists that they are—and that important issues turn upon admitting alien ways of knowing.

Even in SF, though, I must inveigh against the notion that we make statements about the alien in the form of a work of art.

Not so. While this reductionist view is useful for inquiring into epistemology, or diagnosing contemporary culture, or other worthy purposes, it has little to do with what happens when we confront the alien in fiction.

Naturally, there are always people who want to put art to use for some purpose—political, social, or philosophical. But it is so easy to forget, once we're done using art, that it is not only about something, but that it is something.

The alien in SF is an experience, not a statement or an answer to a question. An artistic—that is, fulfilling, multifaceted, resonant—rendering of the alien is a thing in the world itself, not merely a text or a commentary on the world.

All the deductions we can make from a story about the truly alien give us conceptual knowledge. So does science. But the story should—must—also give us an excitation, captivating and enthralling us. When SF works, it gives us an experience of the style of knowing something (or sometimes, as I'll discuss, not knowing).

This means that a prime virtue in depicting the truly alien alien is expressiveness, rather than "content"—a buzzword which provokes the style/substance illusion in criticism. We don't read *The*

War of the Worlds for its views on Martian biology or psychology, but for the sensations of encounter.

This may well be the most original thing which SF does with the concept of irreducible strangeness. It's worthwhile inquiring into the underlying ideas and approaches scholars and writers take in pursuit of it.

SCIENCE AND "SENSAWONDA"

Most SF which takes the idea of the alien seriously (though not necessarily solemnly) deploys a simple strategy:

First, use scientifically sound speculative ideas to construct either the background or the actual physical alien. Garnish the strange planet with whatever ecology looks workable, always favoring the more gaudy and spectacular effects.

Next, deploy a logical sequence of deductions about how an alien would evolve in this place. Stick to concepts like Darwinian evolution, or some later modifications ("punctuated equilibria" in evolution, for example). Then make the alien behave in keeping with this world. Present his/her/its actions, getting the maximum effect of the detailed world view. Only slowly make known how the alien got that way. This guarded unfolding spices the story with mystery.

This usually works well to make a situation strange and intriguing to the reader. Isaac Asimov's *The Gods Themselves* uses a speculative physics and well-rendered oceanic imagery to evoke strangeness. Larry Niven and Jerry Pournelle's *The Mote in God's Eye has* three-legged Moties with well-thought-through implications. On the other hand, Hal Clement's classic *Mission of Gravity* uses a gargantuan planet of crushing gravity; yet the aliens come over more like Midwesterners. (Maybe this was necessary at the time. The planet was so *outré*, Clement may have used ordinary aliens to keep things manageable.)

An obvious pitfall of this whole class of approach is that the reader—who may be quite technically adept and can catch the author in a lapse of world building—may find all this apparatus merely clever and engaging, a fresh kind of problem story. He'll get no sense of strangeness.

What writers are after here is what the fans call "sense of wonder"—an indefinable rush when be-

holding something odd and new and perhaps a bit awesome. "Dat ole sensawonda" is the essential SF experience. No alien should leave home without it.

Beyond this approach there are refinements. Chad Oliver's *The Shores of Another Sea* treats a chilling alien form which is never more than glimpsed, but whole strangeness slowly comes across, through the way it uses animals in Africa. Some writers have tried to render alien perceptions, grounding their effects in the sciences. Damon Knight's short story "Stranger Station" treats the anguish of a human trying to enter into an alien's way of thinking. The human emerges with provisional explanations of how a vastly powerful alien society sees us. (There is a strong hint, though, that he has merely projected his own childhood traumas on the huge creature, so this is really another failed attempt at real contact.)

What I find most interesting about this area is the tricky way it can make so many of our cherished ideas disappear up our own assumptions.

ALIEN CHAT

Scientists often say that communication with aliens could proceed because, after all, we both inhabit the same physical universe. We should agree on the basic laws—gravitation, electromagnetism, stellar evolution, and so on. This is the gospel of the universal language. I'm not so sure. After all, we must frame our ideas in theory, or else they're just collections of data. Language can't simply refer to an agreed-upon real world, because we don't know if the alien agrees about reality.

There's an old anthropologists' joke about this. In the outback, one anthropologist is trying to learn a native's language by just pointing at objects until the native tells what the object is in the language. He wanders around pointing and gradually getting more excited. He tells a colleague that these people have built into their language the concept that nature is all one essence, because whatever he points to, the native says the same word.

It is a great discovery. Only much later do they discover that the word the native means "finger."

So we can't just rely on raw data. We must somehow convey concepts—which means theory. And in science, theory inevitably leads to mathematics.

Indeed, the standard scenario for communicating by radio with distant civilizations relies on sending interesting dit-dah-dit patterns, which the receiving creatures dutifully decompose into pictures. Those sketches show us, our planetary system, some physical constants (like the ratio of the proton mass to the electron mass), and so most confidently on and on.

Let's play with some notions that go against this grain. Suppose the aliens don't even recognize the importance of dit-dah-dit? Why not? Their arithmetic could be nonnumerical, that is, purely comparative rather than quantitative. They would think solely in terms of whether A was bigger than B, without bothering to break A and B into countable fragments.

How could this arise? Suppose their surroundings have few solid objects or stable structures—say, they are jelly creatures awash in a soupy sea. Indeed, if they were large creatures requiring a lot of ocean to support their grazing on lesser beasts, they might seldom meet even each other. Seeing smaller fish as mere uncountable swarms—but knowing intuitively which knot of delicious stuff is bigger than the others—they might never evolve the notion of large numbers at all. (This idea isn't even crazy for humans. The artificial intelligence researcher Marvin Minsky told me of a patient he had once seen who could count only up to three. She could not envision six as anything other than two threes.)

For these beings, geometry would be largely topological, reflecting their concern with overall sensed structure rather than with size, shape, or measurement, a la Euclid. Such sea beasts would lack combustion and crystallography, but would begin their science with a deep intuition of fluid mechanics. Bernoulli's Law, which describes simple fluid flows, would be as obvious as gravitation is to us.

Of course these creatures might never build a radio to listen for us. But even land-based folk might not share our assumptions about what's obvious.

Remember, our concepts are unsuited to scales far removed from those of our everyday experience. Ask what Aristotle would've thought of issues in quantum electrodynamics and you soon realize that he would have held no views, because the subject lies beyond his conceptual grasp. His natural world

didn't have quanta or atoms or light waves in it. In a very limited sense, Aristotle was alien.

Perhaps only in the cool corridors of mathematics could there be genuinely translatable ideas. Marvin Minsky takes this view. He believes that any evolved creature—maybe even intelligent whorls of magnetic field, or plasma beings doing their crimson mad dances in the hearts of stars—would have to dream up certain ideas, or else make no progress in surviving, or mathematics, or anything else. He labels these ideas Objects, Causes, and Goals.

Are these fundamental notions any alien must confront and use? We've cast a pale shadow of doubt over Objects, and I wonder about Causes. Causality isn't a crystal-clear notion even in our own science. There are puzzles about quantum cats and, as I elaborated in my novel *Timescape*, fundamental worries about the sequence of time, too.

Why should Objects, Causes, and Goals emerge in some other-worldly biosphere? Minsky holds that the ideas of arithmetic and of causal reasoning will emerge eventually because every biosphere is limited. Basically, it's economics—eventually, some inevitable scarcity will crop up. The smart bunny will turn into a fast-track achiever since he'll get more out of his efforts. Such selection will affect all his later biases. Minsky has framed technical arguments showing that these notions must turn up in any efficient (and, presumably, intelligent) computer.

I have my doubts, but others have gone a long way toward making math alone carry the burden of communication. Hans Freudenthal's LINCOS is a computer language designed to isolate the deepest ideas in logic itself and to build a language around it. It uses binary symbols typed out in lines. LINCOS stands ready the moment we run into something green, slimy, and repulsive, and yet with that restless urge to write.

Math is central to the whole issue of communication because it allows us to describe "things" accurately and even beautifully without even knowing what they are. Richard Feynman once said, to the horror of some, that "the glory of mathematics is that we do not have to say what we are talking about" (emphasis his).

This is quite a threat to the humanists, who often wish that scientists would become more fluent in communicating. Feynman means that the "stuff" that communicates fields, for example, will work whether we call it wave or particle or thingamabob. We don't have to have cozy pictures, as long as we write down the right equations.

I'm reasonably comfortable with this idea. As David Politzer of Caltech once remarked, "English is just what we use to fill in between the equations." Maybe scientists will themselves make useful models for aliens.

Delving into the artistic pursuit of alienness always brings up the problem of talking. As I've sketched here, there are sound reasons to believe that some aliens are genuinely unreachable. We must share a lot to even recognize aliens as worth talking to—note how long it's taken us to get around to thinking about whales and dolphins.

But suppose we finesse the communication card for a moment. How does a writer assume that some chat can occur and then create the sensation of strangeness?

THE TRAPDOOR MOMENT

One of my favorite SF stories is Terry Carr's "The Dance of the Changer and the Three," in which a human visiting a world remarks that he "was ambassador to a planetful of things that would tell me with a straight face that two and two are orange."

This reminds me of surrealism in its deliberate rejection of logic. Notice, though, that even while it is commenting on the fundamental strangeness of the aliens, this sentence tries to impose a human perspective—why should the natives have a "strange face" at all? Or any face?

The story deals with creatures on the rather ordinary world of Loarra, and their folk legends are shown in loving detail. This takes most of the text and the unwary reader thinks he is reading a pleasant bit of pseudoanthropology. Then the aliens suddenly kill most of the expedition. Why? "Their reason for wiping out the mining expedition was untranslatable. No, they weren't mad. No, they didn't want us to go away. Yes, we were welcome to the stuff we were taking out of the depths of the Loarran ocean. And, most importantly, no, they couldn't

tell me whether they were likely ever to repeat their attack."

The story concludes two paragraphs later, with the humans unable to decide what to do next. Notice that the use of "mad" can be read here as either colloquial for angry, or else genuinely crazy. And through the aliens' rejection of prediction they deny the very notion of science as we would hold it. This seems to rule out the universal language dogma.

I like the story because it strings the readers along and then drops the trapdoor just as we're lulled into a pleasant sensation of Loarran pseudopolynesian simplicity. The ideas revealed this way are startling, but the core of the story is that sideways lurch into the strange.

For contrast, consider one of the most famous stories about alien encounter, Fredric Brown's "Arena" (1944). A man is trapped inside a desert-floored dome and told he must fight it out with an implacable alien foe for mastery of the galaxy. In their struggle, the alien "roller" reaches the man telepathically (avoiding the whole language problem).

He felt sheer horror at the utter alienness, the differentness of those thoughts. Things that he felt but could not understand and could never express, because no terrestrial language had the words, no terrestrial mind had images to fit them. The mind of a spider, he thought, or the mind of a praying mantis or a Martian sand-serpent, raised to intelligence and put in telepathic rapport with human minds, would be a homely and familiar thing, compared to this.

But if the roller were utterly alien, it would be incomprehensible. As the critic John Huntington has pointed out, it is understandable alienness that so horrifies the human. In fact, it is horrible because it stimulates difficult, inexpressible feelings in the man! He understands the alien by reading his own feelings. He can't deal with them, so he attacks their origin.

"Arena" is usually read as a paean to hard-boiled, Cambellian rationality. I think you can read it as covertly pushing unconscious emotionality. This program is completely different—intellectually and emotionally—from Carr's.

MODERNIST ALIENS

Oscar Wilde remarked that in matters of supreme moment, style is always more important than substance. So, too, here. We cannot know the true deep substance of the totally alien, but we can use conscious and conspicuous style to suggest it. Some of the best SF takes this approach. It is quite different from the careful scientific explanations in the style of Hal Clement.

In Robert Silverberg's short story "Sundance," the text surges back and forth between points of view, changes tenses, and ricochets between objective description and intense personal vision—all to achieve a sense of dislocation, of reality distortion, of fevered intermittent contact that one cannot quite resolve into a clear picture. "It is like falling through many trapdoors, looking for the one room whose floor is not hinged."

The story culminates in rapidly reflecting and refracting visions of the same "reality," seeing slaughtered aliens for one moment as objects and then experiencing them from the inside. The narrative voices lurch and dive and veer, always pulling the trapdoor from under any definitive view. The story concludes "And you fall through." There is no solid ground.

This is one of the best examples of how SF has used styles and approaches first developed in the dawning decades of the twentieth century, in what critics term modernism. Breaking with the whole nineteenth-century vision, modernism evolved methods to undermine consensual reality and achieve a more personal, dislocated view. In the Joycean stream of consciousness, in the Faulknerian wrenchings of "The Sound and the Fury," literary devices dynamite cozy assumptions.

When science fiction uses such methods, they have different content. This is, I think, one of the most important contributions the genre has made to literature as a whole. Run-on sentences don't merely mean internal hysteria, flooding of the sensorium, runaway ennui, and so on. Instead, the method suggests genuinely different ways of perceiving the world, emerging not from psychology and sociology, but from evolution, genetics, even physics.

Unnoticed, SF has taken "mainstream" methods of breaking down traditional narrative and turned them to achieve uniquely SF ends. (I'd almost term it—delving into jargon myself—using modernism to achieve a kind of SF postrealism.) Nor has this ground been fully explored. I believe it is only now being pioneered. One of the most interesting uses is that, in SF, these can translate as a rendering of the scientifically unknowable—or, at least, unfathomable by humans. The blizzard-of-strangeness motif is a persistent notion, even among hard-science types.

Time and again in SF, encounters with the alien swamp mere humans. In Fred Hoyle's *The Black Cloud*, Chris Kingsley, the eccentric and brilliant scientist protagonist, is driven into a kind of overloaded insanity when he attempts full contact with a huge, intruding superintelligent cloud. To accommodate the immense flood of new ideas and perceptions, Kingsley "decided to accept the rule that the new should always supersede the old whenever there was trouble between them." This is an SF article of faith. But in the end, contradictions are unmanageable.

The new information settling into the same neural brain sites makes life itself impossible. Kinglsey (an echo of Kingsley Amis?) dies. Hoyle is no stylist, but I find it significant that he is drawn to the same notion of contact. Others later expanded on this insight.

Thus, one underlying message in SF is that the truly alien doesn't just disturb and educate, it breaks down reality, often fatally, for us. Here SF departs quite profoundly from the humanist tradition in the arts. Science fiction nowhere more firmly rejects—indeed, explodes—humanism than in treating the alien. Humanist dogma holds that man is the measure of all things, as Shakespeare put it. SF makes a larger rejection of this than did modernism or surrealism, because it even discards the scientists universal language and the mathematicians' faith in Platonic "natural" ideas. SF even says that the universe may be unknowable, and its "moral" structure might forever lie beyond humanity's ken.

This makes Camus and Sartre and nihilism seem like pretty small potatoes. If you're shopping for literary alienation, SF offers the industrial-strength, economy-size stuff. Yet it also contains the symbols of certainty, through science.

I suspect that the longstanding antagonism between the literary world and the SF community isn't merely the old story of the stylish effetes versus the nerd engineers. Instinctively, without much overt discussion, the two groups dispute the fundamental ideals behind humanism. SF writers take different views of the universe and can't be reconciled by a few favorable notices in the "New York Times Review of Books."

EROTICA AND STRANGENESS

Writers as diverse as Philip Jose Farmer ("The Lovers"), James Tiptree, Jr. ("And I Awoke and Found Me Here on a Cold Hill's Side"), and Gardner Dozois (Strangers) have dwelled upon the erotic component in the alien. It turns up in such drive-in movie classics as "I Married a Monster from Outer Space."

In discussing as personal a subject as sex, I might as well drop the convenient cover of dispassionate critic and write about my own work. At least this approach minimizes the number of potential lawsuits.

When I began thinking about the alien in detail, one of the first stories I wrote was "In Alien Flesh." I constructed it more or less unconsciously, piecing the story together from parts written at separate times over a period of months. For a long time, I didn't know where the tale was going.

In it, a man named Reginri has been hired to crawl up into a huge, beached whalelike alien on the shore of an alien sea. He is an ordinary worker, not a scientist. He simply finds sites to plunge sensors directly into the inner reaches of the being, called the Drongheda. Direct contact floods him with images, feelings—that sensual overload. It provokes ineffable thoughts. And he gets trapped inside the beast.

I wrote most of the story, but had no ending. So I retreated, building a frame around the central tale, which makes the main narrative a flashback. In the frame, Reginri is looking back on his nearly fatal encounter with the Drongheda. I put into this part an approaching fog which humans must avoid, a damaging mist of another planet. Only after I wrote the last lines of the story did I suddenly see what the

end of the flashback portion had to be. "There was something ominous about it and something inviting as well. He watched as it engulfed trees nearby. He studied it intently, judging the distance. The looming presence was quite close now. But he was sure it would be all right."

That done—though not understood, at least by me—I quickly retreated to the point where Reginri is smothered in the alien mountain of flesh and in desperation taps directly into the Drongheda's nerves. I started writing again, filling in action without thinking or planning very much.

Shaken by the flood of strange mathematics and sensation he has gotten from the Drongheda. Reginri finds his way out. Standing in the wash of waves as the Drongheda moves off on its inexplicable way, Reginri learns that one of his fellow workers has been crushed by the alien. Looking back, he sees that the hole he had used to crawl up into the Drongheda, pushing and worming his way in, was not "something like a welt"—the description I'd written before and let stand—but in fact was quite obviously a sexual orifice.

Until I wrote those lines, I had no clue what the story was really about. What a field day for Freudian analysis! A critic's playground! Effing the ineffable!

I decided to let the frame stand. Having written the thing by intuition, I didn't dare tinker with it in the cool light of a critical eye. There's always a point in writing when you have to let go, for fear that you'll tinker away all the life in a piece. So, whatever the tale means, or says about my own disquieting interior, there it is.

Although I have now applied the reductionist hammer—which I scorned at the beginning of this essay—to one of my own works, I must say that I thin postreadings do tell part of the story. Still, once you've dissected a salamander, you know more about it, sure—but it's dead.

As for my own way of assembling the story, I prefer this manner of pondering, shuffling back and forth, and by bits and pieces trying to artistically render the alien—intuitively, not seeking final answers, and with a certain lack of embarrassment, as well.

I'll return to my first assertion, too, and maintain that performing the usual critical slice-and-dice on "In Alien Flesh" misses the thrust of it. Rendering the alien, making the reader experience it, is the crucial contribution of SF. Such tales can argue over communication, spring trapdoors, inundate the reader with stylistic riverruns—all to achieve the end of a fresh experience. That's what the alien is really about.

Views expressed by guest or resident columnists are entirely their own.

FROM THE HEART'S BASEMENT

by Barry N. Malzberg

Barry N. Malzberg won the very first Campbell Memorial Award, and is a multiple Hugo and Nebula nominee. He is the author or co-author of more than 90 books.

The Briars and the Brambles

Nobody got to know Alice Sheldon. (Not even Sheldon, or she would never have showed at our party.) Julie Phillips' 2006 biography was a good try, about as good as a literary biography can get, and it is not Phillips' fault that she missed the point. Alice was so seductive. Alice knew how to please. Even in her most despairing work the pact with the reader is clear: *You and I can sort this out together. We stand apart from the fools, we know the real truths.*

But here is another real truth: Sheldon was a fraud from the hair on her chinny-chin-chin to her dancing twinkletoes, a bigger fraud than her and my own deeply-admired Alfred Bester and those making excuses for her ("this was her truest self") are like the people making excuses for John Campbell. ("He was just trying to shake them up.")

She was a narcissist, and at the end a murderer. She killed her husband. Planned it for years. Blame it on her mother if you will, or circumstance or fate or karma, but those are facts. Bester, whose external attitudes were quite similar, was at his core just silly, a silly kid playing with the family firecrackers. Sheldon? She wanted to destroy the world, and the world begins at home. Oh the rage! Ah, the rage!

This is not a popular position. Tiptree was embraced by feminism from the spring day in 1976 that she made her identity public. "She is one of us! She masqueraded as a man for a dozen years, and no one suspected! Silverberg fell for it! Joanna Russ fell for it! U.K. LeGuin fell for it! The whole community fell for it! What a neat practical joke on those chauvinists. Her fiction made her more of a man than the men."

In her memory years later came the Tiptree Award, financed by bake sales and the feminist press. "A distinguished work of fiction which illuminates and expands the concept of gender."

A question: What is the concept of gender? Isn't it something which you are? (Subject increasingly to medical, not conceptual, intervention.)

Sheldon might have made merry over the Tiptree Award. It is a mug's game to predict the opinions of the dead, but she certainly left enough on the record. In the late 60s she was writing to her academic mentor (who guided her to a degree in clinical psychology which she never practiced) of this charming and eccentric group of crazies with whom she had become involved in epistolary fashion. But don't tell anyone. Those crazies were her secret indulgence. We were to her what the hookers were to Frank Harris. Her Secret Life.

Bester was another with a secret life. I wrote about him in the previous column. Our greatest genius, our principal failure. Gilded Manhattan's gilded emissary to the underworld. The Jacob Riis of *Holiday*. How the other half lives. His stories were demonstrations of the dimensions of the trap, the hamster wheel of science fiction. Like the Men Who Murdered Muhammed, Bester's great career and great collapse were demonstration that the harder, more desperately you ran, the more you were slammed into the walls of containment. Heinlein (the subject a column earlier) was another runner: push at the limits however industriously, frantically, brilliantly and what you found in exhaustion's mirror was your own screaming face. Run through

the briars and run through the brambles. Run through the bushes where the rabbits wouldn't go. Run so fast the hounds couldn't catch him, down the Mississippi to the Gulf of Mexico. (Astounding, November 1949. The *ubermensch*.) And then there is the issue of Sturgeon, who was alive and well until he wasn't. Let us not, within this context, approach the issue of Dianetics. Not present at the creation but early enough and canisters of bad charge.

Was it science fiction itself which propitiated odysseys like this? Was it the solipsism, the meglo-mania at the center of the genre itself, which made narratives like this possible? "The capitalist will sell you the rope with which you will hang him," Marx is reputed to have said or written—and the science fiction writer will furnish, lavishly, the materiel for her own destruction, for the eager reader who is always looking for a way out, a special, flaming odyssey which will mark her sensitivity and originality. James Blish wrote of this phenomenon more than six decades ago, the audience ever slack-jawed and in search of greater thrills, greater sensation. Blish identified the slack-jawed as the enemies of the form, the fulcrum for all that was meretricious, but I have long been struggling toward another view. Blish's slack-jawed were not the enemies or the hinging factor against the True Quill, Blish's folks *were* science fiction, the heart of the artichoke. It was from its modern origin—Verne, Wells, Mary Shelley Moskowitz's *Science Fiction by Gaslight* people—profoundly opposed to the common reality. And in that opposition, in that contempt for limits, it took its practitioners in the same direction that the post-technological culture had taken the West... toward oblivion.

Virginia Woolf thought that human nature itself had changed profoundly at the time of the First World War. My culprit, if not hers, was the technology with which the best and worst of Gernsback and Campbell manipulated. Sheldon's central insight was that *everything* associated with science fiction was intimately linked to death. Bester was not so clear, he had pizzazz, he came out of comic books and serial radio, he interposed *dazzle!* and *enchantment!* but he saw it as did Sheldon, and if he did not end as spectacularly as Alice in the Underground he ended as definitively.

Like Kuttner's shuffling, clanging, weeping robot in "Home There's No Returning," science fiction lurched through the corridors of its creation and dialectic looking for an exit, glinting its mechanical style, weeping its metal tears. A fascinating variant or descendant of Frankenstein. The monster undone by the fact of his construction.

Did Sheldon see any of this? Was her final decision the greatest ka-boom that she could generate from the playpen for which she had such initial contempt and ultimate fear? Or was it no decision at all but simply the end of yet another Van Vogt narrative of the cosmic seesaw? Lift up your heads, oh ye gates, and spy in the ebullient darkness the Vault of the Beast.

Oh well. Just a few thoughts on the cusp of the Equinox. Anyway, here come the Nebulas. Ruling the Sevagram!

Copyright © 2015 by Barry N. Malzberg

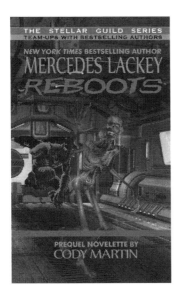

Zombies and Werewolves in space
What could possibly go wrong?

Joy Ward is the author of one novel. She has several stories in press, at magazines and in anthologies, and has also done interviews, both written and video, for other publications.

David Brin is a former Worldcon Guest of Honor, the winner of three Hugos and a Nebula, creator of the Uplift Universe, and a frequent bestseller.

THE *GALAXY'S EDGE* INTERVIEW

Joy Ward interviews David Brin

Dr. David Brin, the brilliant and puckish author of some of science fiction's most innovative work such as The Postman, Sundiver, The Uplift War, and many others kindly opened his home to my interview team.

Joy Ward: How did you get into writing?

DB: I've always known that I would be a writer. I come from a family of writers going back generations. It was fun and I always knew I would be good at it.

But as a teenager I did something that all science fiction writers do. I read a lot of history and something struck me. History is gruesome. It's awful. It's filled with errors and above all, delusion. Delusion is the great human talent. We authors cater to it by providing incantations that can cause miracles of subjective reality to erupt in the readers' heads. This art is great. It's wonderful. But when artists tell you that art is rare that's when they lie.

Art fizzes out of the pores of probably fifty percent of all human beings. All the great scientists I've known practiced an artistic avocation at almost a professional level.

There has been almost no civilization that I know of without art. It is the most natural human undertaking after sex, love, and eating. If you kill all the artists in a society, and it's been tried, the next year you'll get more art. Art is not rare. Great art may be, but the essentially delusional nature of human beings makes art one of the most profoundly easy things to do. All the propaganda spread by artists notwithstanding, because it is on their best interest to talk about how rare and brilliant they are.

When I realized this, I also saw that my life in 1950s, 60s America was pretty good and for the first time we had a civilization that at least paid lip service to rights, decency, and knowledge. Something different was happening.

For the first time a civilization was employing millions of people not to reinforce what they passionately believed to be true but to honestly experiment and find out what is true. That had never happened before.

So I decided I was going to join those people. I would be a scientist and do my art part time.

Probably the most evil limitation on human nature is the zero sum game; the assumption that for every victory there must be a loss, for every winner there must be a defeated. If you are good at something it means you can be good at nothing else. This propaganda that we are inherently limited beings.

The most powerful concept that a modern person can grasp is that of the positive sum game—that is the notion is that one person may win more than another but the other doesn't have to be a loser. Competitiveness in marketplaces or science can result in everyone getting richer. You can be a good parent, spouse, citizen, co-worker and still find a way to be an artist.

Science fiction was very badly named. Just the name "science fiction" helps to foist a pallor of hostility across the genre in a thousand university campuses in America. In only twenty or thirty has the science fiction instructor been given tenure, even though science fiction is the literature of which Americans should be most proud: perhaps the name has something to do with it. Only ten percent or so of science fiction authors are scientifically trained as I am. But that doesn't stop many of them from doing terrific scientific science fiction.

There are English majors out there who write the hard stuff as easily as I do with bold extrapolations and adventures that will be mediated by science and technology. Some of the best examples would be Kim Stanley Robinson, Nancy Kress, Greg Bear, none of whom could parse a simple derivative if their lives depended on it. They learned the simple trick in our field which is that scientists, the best of them, will give very cheap consultations to science fiction authors for the price of pizza and beer or naming a character after them. One or two of the best experts held out for their character to have sex on stage or to die gruesomely, depending on their personalities. I was happy to oblige, especially the latter. The point is that if ten percent or so of SF authors are scientifically trained, almost one hundred percent read history voraciously.

Quite frankly, the field was badly named. It should have been speculative history because that's most of what we do. We speculate what history would have been like if this or that had happened or the rules had been different. What might that past truly have been like, but above all how might we extrapolate this gorgeously stupid, poignantly horrific litany of errors that is called the human experience?

Indeed, that may be one explanation for the Fermi Paradox of why we haven't been contacted by aliens. Our struggles may be so interesting to them. We're the miniseries that they want to see renewed and never end.

JW: You were talking earlier about how humans are really deluded in this idea of zero sum game. How has that come through your writing?

DB: First off this is a concept that is absolutely essential, and if I urge your readers to pick up any nonfiction book from the past twenty years it would be Robert Reich's *Non Zero* because once you understand the concept of the positive sum game all your politics change. You start to understand ninety-nine percent of human history across six thousand years was kept tragic by zero sum or sometimes negative sum cultures in which cabals or gangs of large men would pick up large instruments, call themselves kings, lords, and priests and took away the wheat and women from other men. I say this in a sexist manner quite deliberately because women were in no position to object across those six thousand years. It quickly became the natural human social order, variations on feudalism, societies shaped like a pyramid with a few at the top lording over others. Those lords, their top priority over competing with each other was to suppress the ambitions of those below.

Fantasy novels portray this kind of social structure. It is the one common thread in most modern fantasy novels except urban fantasy and steam punk, which fields I respect. It is the assumption of society's changelessness that I consider to be the grotesque but highly natural story telling riff that distinguishes science fiction from fantasy.

This was best expressed by the great author and my dear friend the late Ann McCaffrey. Regularly in interviews she would be referred to as a "fantasy author." Always she would rear up in anger and deny this. She would say, "I'm a science fiction author." People would smirk because she had dragons, people riding dragons with swords. She had sword fights. She had castles and keeps and long passages about medieval crafts like macramé, sewing and weaving. The ambiance was very similar to a fantasy novel so why would she say that?

It's truly simple. In her dragonriders cosmology the people of the planet Pern have a feudal social order. They have lords, tenant farmers, they have their great knights on their charging steeds of the sky, but at some point in the second novel they discover a truth that they were colonists on this planet who had been beaten down by a catastrophe. The feudal order with all of its lovely crafts and its ornate culture and all the cool aspects, were all fallback positions. Once their ancestors had flown through the sky but they had had the germ theory of disease and their children didn't die in their arms. Once they had flush toilets, printing presses, and networked tablets. The thing that distinguishes Ann McCaffrey's characters from those who wallow in mindless sameness in Tolkien and so many fantasies is this; Ann McCaffrey's characters want those things back. They are determined to get them back, and if their lords and the dragonriders help them get these things back

then there might be nominal lords in the future. If they stand in their way they will be grease spots. This is what made Ann McCaffrey without a scintilla of doubt a science fiction author.

The true distinction is that science fiction admits to the possibility of fundamental change and deals with it. Fantasy harkens to an older tradition going back to the *Iliad*, the *Odyssey*, the *Vedas* of India. The notion that the demigod is more important than the citizens and the social order, there may be dramatic variations on who gets to be king, but there will always be kings.

JW: Your work goes in the face of that. I'm thinking about your work dealing with nonhumans.

DB: I'm not the first to speak of uplifting animals to human levels of intelligence. But those authors did what perhaps I would have done in their situation. They told the simplest possible version of that story, one that writes itself and that is it's a Frankenstein situation. We created these new beings in order to be slaves, we're cruel to them, and we get our comeuppance for having the arrogance and hubris for picking up God's powers.

Well, this has been done and I'm not convinced that picking up God's powers is automatically punishable. There are passages in the Bible that suggest it's what we were made to do. So in my Uplift universe I decided to try something different. What if we give the Promethean gift of sapience to other creatures with the very best of intentions, openly, submitting the project to endless criticism, avoiding as many errors as we could and correcting those we come across? Wouldn't that still be a fascinating story? Wouldn't there still be dramatic and tragic errors? Would not the intermediate generations suffer from a poignancy of both progress and pain? That could make for good art. In fact, I think the potential mixed feelings of such creatures would be made more interesting in a milieu of kindness than deliberate grotesque caricature of cruelty.

JW: Is there a lesson that we need to learn from the way the creatures—the chimps, the dolphins—come across in your writing?

DB: We need to become unafraid of complexity. I believe that one of the attractions of fantasy stories is the notion of the simple, old-fashioned social order. You knew who you were; you knew what your role was. We know what our role is compared to the other animals on Earth. If they start talking to us, if the robots start asking for rights, if aliens come here, perhaps domineering or curious or as refugees, life becomes ever more complex. We have dealt with complexity so vastly more intricate and so much more successfully than any of our ancestors ever would have predicted. Our only chance of survival is to do the same. That is the real contribution of science fiction.

JW: How have you seen science fiction change?

DB: I am no stranger to writing dark fiction. Certainly my graphic novel, *The Life Eaters*, set in a future where the Nazis and the Norse gods won World War II is plenty dystopic. But there again I like to veer in a different direction.

The Postman was not about an individual or a small gang achieving triumph, instead a complex and fretful demi-hero reluctantly coming to realize that he had the power to lie and that his lies could inspire survivors to remember one simple thing—that once upon a time they had been citizens.

Dystopias are useful and interesting to the extent that they point out errors or possibilities. The greatest dystopias include George Orwell's *1984*, Harry Harrison's *Soylent Green*, *Silent Spring*, *On the Beach*, *Dr. Strangelove*. What did all of these have in common? They were self-preventing prophecies. Each of them pointed out a potential failure mode so vividly that millions became determined to prevent it from ever coming true. This trait cannot be ascribed to the tsunami of simple-minded, grotesquely clichéd dystopias and post-apocalyptic tales that we're seeing today.

If you want to get your heroes into pulse-pounding action by starting with a premise of a holocaust, fine. That's lazy, but go for it. On the other hand, if your failure mode has nothing interesting or realistic or chillingly likely about it, then your only reason for taking us to this place is authorly laziness.

I had an essay in *Locus Magazine* that got a lot of attention. People can see it on my website. It's called "The Idiot Plot." It describes the underlying reason why Hollywood and so many authors are pounding us flat with dystopias after apocalypse.

It's not that they really believe that they live in such a world. Were any of the directors or authors to find themselves in trouble they would dial 911 and they would be pissed off if skilled professionals did not leap to their aid. Yet none of their characters ever do that. Or if they dial 911 the phone lines are down or if they get through the operator is incompetent. If the police come, they come late. If they come on time they are incompetent. If they're incompetent that's the surest sign that they are in cahoots with the bad guy. With one exception. There is a sliding scale of competence that civilization is allowed, depending on how bad-ass the villains are. When you have someone unlike the Joker in Batman, the cops are allowed to be haplessly competent; just enough to get in Batman's way. When the villains are as humongously bad-ass, as the Independence Day aliens, the government and military of the United States of America is allowed to be simultaneously good and competent.

I don't begrudge authors and directors for making this choice deliberately, that the simplest way to keep their heroes in pulse-pounding jeopardy for ninety minutes or three hundred pages, is to assume no institution works and that you can never count on your neighbors because they are hopeless sheep. But for them to make this clichéd choice out of habit and sheer laziness that's contemptible because every dystopia that's like this, that says, "I'm not offering you a failure mode that you could do something about, you viewers or readers. I am immersing you in gloom with the fundamental lesson that thou shall never trust any institution, no matter how many citizens fight to make it useful and better and above all, never put any confidence in your neighbors.

The exceptions are actually very heart-warming. In every Spiderman movie, and they are not great art, the hero saves New Yorkers ninety percent of the film. But there is always a scene wherein the New

Yorkers save Spiderman. Now that's sweet. It's an homage to a civilization that has actually been pretty good to all of us, and this notion is that civilization might be a character in your work, it's flaws, it's failures, but also the good aspects the hero might call upon.

This is the fundamental distinction between *Star Wars* and *Star Trek*. In *Star Wars* the ship is a World War I fighter plane. The heroic pilot, silk scarf and all, is the demigod, going back to comic books, going back to World War I, going back to Achilles. And there's room on the fighter plane for perhaps his brave gunner or droid. The ship is a knight's charger; there is no room for civilization.

In George Lucas' epic saga, you never see civilization doing anything. The Republic never does anything. It never even takes any actions that may be called mistakes. It does nothing. The other institution, the Jedi Council, is dumber than a bag of hammers.

This is an ancient story-telling motif. It writes itself, which you can tell from the writing quality of the three prequels.

In *Star Trek* the ship is a naval vessel. The captain is at most way above average and needs the expertise and skill of not only main cast members but also every episode somebody from below decks must rise up and contribute to the team effort. The ship deals with complexities. One of the major cargoes and passengers of the Enterprise and Voyager is civilization, the Federation. Does it make mistakes? Absolutely. These are topics of shows; mistakes to correct, mistakes to reveal and expose, but also thought experiments about how our grandchildren might be better than us.

All of these are possible when civilization is a topic and you don't fall for the old demigods trap. When the Enterprise encounters a demigod what is the reaction? Folded arms and a skeptical expression looking at this pretentious being and saying, "Okay, what's your story?" Individualism is a core message in our culture, and those who use the demigod motif actually convince themselves that they are writing stories in praise of individualism because they have a hero, the hero overcomes all odds and villainy

and caricature villains with red glowing eyes. In fact, they are wrong. They are deceiving themselves. They are not promoting individualism because individual human beings can be cantankerous, egotistical, and self-centered, but they only achieve really valid goals, ironically, in the context of the civilization. It is indeed ironic that those tales that have a functioning civilization in the background are the ones that speak to individualism most valuably, most realistically, and offer insights that go beyond resentment, revenge, and rage.

JW: Where is your work going?

DB: My novel *Kiln People* was a cry for help. I have a substantial public speaking career and I consult about many future oriented issues. This plus three kids, teaching, all in all I've been neglectful of my core writing career. Hence, I dreamed of having a machine where I could make cheap copies of myself every day. In *Kiln People* everyone gets such a machine. The notion in so many science fiction novels is here's a new piece of scientific progress, let's assume it's hoarded in secret and hence you get all Michael Crichton plots.

I like to see what happens if everybody gets it. So in this world any morning you could put your face on your home copies and out steps a cheap, clay golem image of yourself. Good for one day. It will melt after twenty-four hours. It knows everything you know; has your personality, and it's one chance of continued existence is to do what needs to be done and come home and download the memories of the day. As a result, you were five people yesterday. You had five days yesterday. Today you might make six copies because there's a lot to be done. It's a world in which you have a list of things to accomplish you can do them all. Can you see now why it is a wish fantasy? You make two cheap green copies to do all the errands, fix all the things around the house, and do all the cleaning. You make an expensive ebony copy to go to the library and study. You make a battle version to go to the arena and get killed, but have its head put on ice so that you can remember.

In *Existence*, we have the genre of novel that I conveyed also in "Earth." These are my two, big, sprawling near future extrapolations from *Chronos*. The motif is based upon John Brunner's *Stand on Zanzibar*, filled with extracts from media and events happening around the characters, portraying a complex society that we might plausibly live to see. By the way, folks can go to DavidBrin.com and see a three minute trailer for *Existence* with gorgeous art and portrayals of the characters by the great web artist Patrick Farley. I guarantee you the most fun you'll have in three minutes with your clothes on. My wife made trailers for two older novels, *Glory Season* and *Heart of the Comet*.

I was among the Killer Bees, Greg Bear and myself who were asked by the Asimov Estate to write the second Foundation Trilogy. These are stand alone novels that also tie together. Isaac's widow was very kind calling it the best non-Isaac.

But putting that braggadocio aside, I find a lot of the new folks truly wonderful. They are very bright, knowledgeable, and better writers than I am. Still, I like to think that I'm one of the last truly great science fiction authors for one simple reason. Dentistry. *(With tongue firmly in cheek)* These new whippersnappers are geniuses, brilliant writers, but they have got almost no fillings in their mouths so they don't pick up radio waves from Aldegeberon Six in the Twilight Dimension. Hence, I have an unlimited supply of ideas.

SERIALIZATION
Melodies of the Heart *(novella)*

Part 3

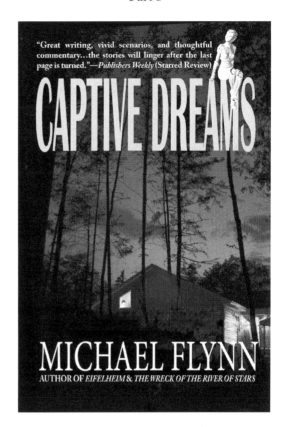

"Great writing, vivid scenarios, and thoughtful commentary...the stories will linger after the last page is turned."—*Publishers Weekly* (Starred Review)

CAPTIVE DREAMS

MICHAEL FLYNN
AUTHOR OF *EIFELHEIM* & *THE WRECK OF THE RIVER OF STARS*

"Melodies of the Heart" is the lead novella in the collection, CAPTIVE DREAMS.
by Michael Flynn
Phoenix Pick, 2012
Trade Paperback: 266 pages.
ISBN: 978-1-61242-059-2

MELODIES OF THE HEART
[serialization – Part 3 of 3]

Michael Flynn

Once at the Home, I sought out Mae in her garden retreat, hoping that she was in a better mood than yesterday. I had a thousand questions to ask. A dozen puzzles and one hope. But when she saw me coming, her face retreated into a set of tight lines: Eyes, narrowed; mouth and lips, thin and disapproving.

"Go away," said Mae Holloway.

"I only wanted to ask a few—"

"I said, go away! Why are you always pestering me?"

"Don't mind her," said a voice by my elbow. "She's been that way since yesterday." I turned and saw Jimmy Kovacs, the retired printer. "Headache. Maybe you should give her something."

"You don't need a doctor to take aspirin."

He shook his head. "Aspirin didn't work. She needs something stronger. Might be a migraine. I had an allergy once. To hot dog meat. Every time I had a frank, my head felt like fireworks going off inside. So, my doc, he tells me—"

"I'll see what I can do," I said. Old folks chatter about little else than their ailments. They compare them the way young boys compare…Well, you know what I mean. "Mine is bigger than yours." They have contests, oldsters do, to see who has the biggest illness. The winner gets to die.

I sat on the stone bench beside Mae. "Jimmy tells me you have a headache," I said.

"Jimmy should mind his own affairs."

"Where does it hurt?"

"In my haid, jackass. That's what makes it a headache."

"No, I mean is it all over or in one spot? Is it a dull ache or sharp points. Is it continual, or does it come in bursts? Do you see or hear anything along with the headache?"

She gave me a look. "How do you make a headache into such a contraption?"

I shrugged. "There are many things that can cause a headache. When did it start?" If I could relieve her pain, she might be willing to answer the questions I had about her family history.

She squinted at the ground, her face tight as a drum. I heard her suck in her breath. Bees danced among the flowers to our right; the fragrances hung in the air. "Yesterday afternoon," she said. "Yesterday afternoon, after you left. It was like the sun come up inside my head. I was lying down for a nap when everything turned blind white for a few seconds and I heard a chorus a-singing hymns. I thought I'd surely died and gone to heaven." She took a deep breath and massaged her left temple with her fingers. "Somedays I'ud as lief I were dead. All these here aches and pains…And I cain't do the things I used to. I used to dance. I used to love to dance, but I can't do that no more. And everybody who ever mattered to me is a longtime gone."

Her parents. Little Zach. Green Holloway. Gone a very long time, if I was right. Joe Paxton. Ben Wickham. There must have been plenty of others, besides. Folks in Cincinnati, in California, in Wyoming. She left a trail of alienation behind her every place she had ever been. It was a cold trail, in more ways than one.

"When the white light faded out, I saw it weren't an angel choir, after all. It were Christy's Minstrels that time when they come to Knoxville, and Mister and me and…" She frowned and shook her head. "Mister and me, we tarryhooted over to hear 'em. Doc, it was the clearest spell I ever had. I was a-settin' in the audience right down in front. I clean forgot I was a-bedded down here in Sunny Dale."

Sometimes migraines triggered visions. Some of the saints had suffered migraines and seen the Kingdom of God. "Yes?" I prompted.

"Well, Mister was a-settin' on my left holding my hand; and someone's man-child, maybe fifteen years, was press't up agin me on my right—oh, we was packed in almighty tight, I tell you—but, whilst I could see and hear as clear as I can see and hear you, I couldn't feel any of them touching me. When I thunk on it, I could feel that I was lying a-bed with the sheets over me."

I nodded. "You weren't getting any tactile memories, then. I think your—"

She didn't hear me. "The troupe was setting on benches, with each row higher than the one in front—Tiers, that be what they call 'em. They all stood to sing the medley, 'cept 'Mr. Interlocutor,' who sat in a chair front and center. Heh. That was the out-doin'est chair I ever did see. Like a king's throne, it was. They sang *Jim Along Josie* and *Ring, Ring the Banjo*. I h'ain't heared them tunes since who flung the chuck. The interlocutor was sided by the soloists on his right and the glee singers—what they later called barbershop singers—on the left." She gestured, moving both hands out from the center. "Then the banjo player and the dancer. Then there was four end-men, two t' either side. Those days, only the end-men were in the Ethiopian business."

"The Ethiopian business?"

"You know. Done up in black-face."

Images of Cantor singing "Mammy." Exaggerated lips; big, white, buggy eyes. An obscene caricature. "Black face!"

My disapproval must have shown in my voice, for Mae grew defensive. "Well, that was the only way us reg'lar folks ever got to hear nigra music back then," she said, rubbing her temple. "The swells could hear 'em any time; but the onlyest nigras I ever saw 'fore I left the hills was Will Biddle and his kin, and they didn't do a whole lot of singing and dancing."

"Nigras?" That was worse than black-face. I tried to remind myself that Mae had grown up in a very different world.

Mae seemed to refocus. Her eyes lost the dreamy look. "What did I say? Nigra? Tarnation, that isn't right, anymore, is it? They say 'coloreds' now."

"African-American. Or black."

She shook her head, then winced and rubbed her temple again. "They weren't mocking the col— the black folks. The minstrels weren't. Not then. It was fine music. Toe-tapping. And the banjo… Why, white folks took that up from the coloreds. But we'uns couldn't go to dark-town shows, and they couldn't come to us—not in them days. So, sometimes white folks dressed up to play black music. Daddy Rice, he was supposed to be the best, though I never did see him strut *Jim Crow*; but James Bland that wrote a lot of the tunes was a black man his own self. I heared he went off to France later 'cause of the way the white folks was always greenin' him."

"I see. Has your headache subsided since then?" *Minstrel shows*, I thought.

"It's all so mixed up. These memories I keep getting. It's like a kalidey-scope I had as a young 'un. All those pretty beads and mirrors…"

"Your headache, Mrs. Holloway. I asked if it was still the same." Try to keep old folks on the track. Go ahead, try it.

She grimaced. "Why, it comes and goes, like ocean waves. I seen the ocean oncet. Out in Californey. Now, that was a trek, let me tell you. Folks was poor on account of the depression, so I took shank's mare a long part of the way, just like Sweet Betsy." She sighed. "That was always a favorite of mine. Every time I heared it, it was like I could see it all in my mind. The singing around the campfire; the cold nights on the prairie. The Injuns a-whooping and a-charging…" She began to sing.

The Injuns come down in a great yelling horde. And Betsy got skeered they would scalp her adored. So behind the front wagon wheel Betsy did crawl. And she fought off the Injuns with powder and ball.

Mae tried to smile, but it was a weak and pained one. "I went back to Californey years later. I taken the *Denver Zephyr*, oh, my, in the 1920s I think it was. Packed into one of them old coach cars, cheek by jowl, the air so thick with cigar smoke. And when you opened the window, why you got coal ash in your face from the locomotive."

"Look, why don't you come to the clinic with me and I'll see if I have anything for that headache of yours."

She nodded and rose from her bench, leaning on her stick. She took one step and looked puzzled. Then she staggered a little. "Dizzy," she muttered. Then she toppled forward over her stick and fell to the ground. I leaped to my feet and grabbed her by the shoulders, breaking her fall.

"Hey!" I said. "Careful! You'll break something."

Her eyes rolled back up into her head and her limbs began to jerk uncontrollably. I looked over my shoulder and saw Jimmy Kovacs hurrying up the garden path. "Quick," I said. "Call an ambulance! Call Dr. Khan! Tell her to meet us at the hospital."

Jimmy hesitated. He looked at Mae, then at me. "What's wrong?" he said.

Sail to Success

a unique writers' workshop on board a luxury cruise ship

Intensive manuscript critique by
Toni Weisskopf (head of Baen Books)
and
Nancy Kress (bestselling, Hugo/Nebula-winning author)

PLUS

Writing and business (publishing) seminars by
Mike Resnick
Jack Skillingstead
Eric Flint
and
Eleanor Wood (head of Spectrum Literary Agency)

Class size restricted to only 22 students
December 7-11, 2015

All-inclusive pricing starting at $999 (as of April 2015; subject
to change). Prices include cruise, food, entertainment
and all materials needed for the workshop.

www.SailSuccess.com

SAIL TO SUCCESS 2012

The Sail to Success 2012 writer's workshop, sponsored by Arc Manor/Phoenix Pick press and organized by Shahid Mahmud, was held onboard the *Norwegian Sky* cruise liner, sailing from Miami on December 3 and returning December 7 after a tour of the Bahamas, including Grand Bahama Island, Nassau, and Great Stirrup Cay. Onboard instructors were authors Kevin J. Anderson, Paul Cook, Nancy Kress, Rebecca Moesta, Mike Resnick, and Jack Skillingstead, publisher and editor Toni Weisskopf, and literary agent Eleanor Wood. *Locus* was invited to attend, and design editor Francesca Myman was on board to represent the magazine.

Over the four days, 17 panel-style classes and two critique sessions were scheduled from 9:00 a.m. to 11:00 p.m., with a five- to six-hour break each day for cruise activities. Most students attended a majority of the classes, though there was no requirement to do so. Students had excellent social access to instructors, with three scheduled group meals and the opportunity to make individual appointments to discuss the industry or just share a drink.

Overall, the focus was on the seminars, with classes slanted towards providing an insider perspective on the business of science fiction and fantasy publishing, but also including the history of science fiction, a solid introduction to writing basics, and some advanced technique. Highlights included Kevin Anderson and Rebecca Moesta's well-known "Professional Approach to Writing" seminars, Eleanor Wood's insider look at the intricacies of contract negotiation, and manuscript critique sessions with Nancy Kress and Toni Weisskopf. Critique sessions were structured as a kind of "speed-dating" version of traditional workshopping, with the instructors offering comments on manuscripts submitted prior to the cruise and a brief opportunity for fellow students to comment. Additional optional follow-up critique sessions were available with Kress.

Arc Manor/Phoenix Pick provided plenty of swag, including T-shirts and bags printed with the Sail to Success logo and instructor names, and a 550-page perfect-bound book with glossy cover containing all the students' manuscript submissions bound into a single volume.

The *Norwegian Sky* itself was a handsome 848-foot-long ship with a friendly crew of 934 and a Hawaiian-luau atmosphere: hibiscus flowers painted on the hull. bright aqua carpets with tropical fish swimming down the hallways, etc. Onboard amenities included three *plein-air* pools on the top decks, five Jacuzzis, three "free" restaurants, three luxe "paid" restaurants, five bars, a fitness center and volleyball court, a spa offering massages and facials for purchase, a video arcade, and the requisite shops and casino. Despite these glitzy offerings, the overall atmosphere for workshop participants was quiet, with a preference for sharing time with instructors and classmates, enjoying the clean salt sea air on the many open decks, and even writing! (Kevin J. Anderson was spotted writing away with his signature giant headphones affixed, in the forward lounge. According to Anderson, he continued writing even when a dance class started up around him.) The cruise line offered classes in everything from dancing to cupcake decoration to circus skills like juggling, plate spinning, and devil sticks, which might have challenged even Anderson's concentration.

There was a bewildering (and exciting) array of shore excursions available, including visits to the recently opened billion-dollar Atlantis Aquaventure resort development, scuba diving, various flavors of snorkeling – including the usual variety and a variant with powered scooters, sailing, fishing, kayaking, parasailing, and dolphin and sea lion encounters. Various tours were available by glass-bottom boat, underwater motorbike, semi-submarine. Harley-Davidson (I'm not joking), Segway, bike, off-road jeep, horseback, and catamaran. Workshop participants tended towards milder away expeditions, including historical tours and self-made adventures, though many also opted for at least one good snorkel or swim. Participants and instructors all had positive things to say about the experience in the evaluations, and many instructors have chosen to return next year at Mahmud's invitation. Confirmed faculty members include Kevin J. Anderson, Eric Flint, Nancy Kress, Rebecca Moesta, Mike Resnick, Jack Skillingstead, Toni Weisskopf, and Eleanor Wood.

The 2013 workshop will be held aboard *Norwegian Sky* from December 2-6, sailing again from Miami to the Bahamas. Further information will be available at <www.sailsuccess.com> and <www.phoenixpick.com>.

– Francesca Myman ∎

Transportation to Nassau Island, where Thoraiya Dyer, Jeff Giese, and Francesca Myman explore the local hotspots

Eva Eldridge asks Mike Resnick to sign a book

Attendees (l to r): Therese Pieczynski, Lou Berger, Ron S. Friedman, Shahid Mahmud (sponsor), Ilana Harris, Eva Eldridge, Kelly Varner, Alvaro Zinos-Amaro, Gamaliel Martinez, Frank Morin; front: Jessica Carlson, Sandra Odell, Thoraiya Dyer

Instructors (l to r): Paul Cook, Kevin J. Anderson, Rebecca Moesta, Mike Resnick, Toni Weisskopf, Eleanor Wood, Nancy Kress, Jack Skillingstead

"Hurry! I think she's having another stroke."

Jimmy rushed off and I turned back to Mae. Checkout time, I thought. But why now? Why now?

I have always loved hospitals. They are factories of health, mass producers of treatments. The broken and defective bodies come in, skilled craftsmen go to work—specialists from many departments, gathered together in one location—and healthy and restored bodies emerge. Usually. No process is one hundred percent efficient. Some breakdowns cannot be repaired. But it is more efficient to have the patients come to the doctor than to have the doctor waste time traveling from house to house. Only when health is mass produced can it be afforded by the masses.

Yet, I can see how some people would dislike them. The line is a thin one between the efficient and the impersonal.

Khan and I found Mae installed in the critical care unit. The ward was shaped like a cul-de-sac, with the rooms arranged in a circle around the nurses' station. White sheets, antiseptic smell. Tubes inserted wherever they might prove useful. Professionally compassionate nurses. Bill Wing was waiting for us there. With clipboard in hand and stethoscope dangling from his neck, he looked like an archetype for The Doctor. We shook hands and I introduced him to Khan. Wing led us out into the corridor, away from the patient. Mae was in a coma, but it was bad form to discuss her case in front of her, as if she were not there.

"It was not a stroke," he told us, "but a tumor. An astrocytoma encroaching on the left temporal lobe. It is malignant and deeply invasive." Wing spoke with an odd Chinese-British accent. He was from Guandong by way of Hong Kong.

I heard Khan suck in her breath. "Can it be removed?" she asked.

Wing shook his head. "On a young and healthy patient, maybe; though I would hesitate to perform the operation even then. On a woman this old and weak…" He shook his head again. "I have performed a decompression to relieve some of the pressure, but the tumor itself is not removable."

Khan sighed. "So sad. But she has had a long life."

"How much longer does she have?" I asked.

Wing pursed his lips and looked inscrutable. "That is hard to say. Aside from the tumor, she is in good health…for a woman her age, of course. It could be tomorrow; it could be six months. She has a time bomb in her head, and no one knows how long the fuse is. We only know that the fuse…"

"Has been lit," finished Khan. Wing looked unhappy, but nodded.

"As the tumor progresses," he continued, "her seizures will become more frequent. I suspect there will be pain as the swelling increases." He paused and lowered his head slightly, an Oriental gesture.

"There must be something you can do," I said. Khan looked at me.

"Sometimes," she said, "there is nothing that can be done."

I shook my head. "I can't accept that." Holloway could not die. Not yet. Not now. I thought of all those secrets now sealed in her head. They might be fantasies, wild conclusions that I had read into partial data; but I had to know. I had to know.

"There is an end to everything." Noor Khan gazed toward the double doors that led to the medical CCU. "Though it is always hard to see the lights go out.

I drew my coat on. "I'm going to go to the University Library for a while."

Khan gave me a peculiar look. "The Library?" She shrugged. "I will stay by her side. You know how she feels about hospitals. She will be frightened when she recovers consciousness. Best if someone she knows is with her."

I nodded. "She may not regain consciousness for some time," I reminded her. "What about your patients?"

"Dr. Mendelson will handle my appointments tomorrow. I called him before I came over."

All right, let her play the martyr! I tugged my cap onto my head. Khan didn't expect thanks, did she? I could just picture the old crone's ravings. The hysteria. She would blame Khan, not thank her, for bringing her here.

As I reached the door, I heard Khan gasp. "She's singing!"

I turned. "What?"

Khan was hovering over the bed. She flapped an arm. "Come. Listen to this."

As if I had not listened to enough of her ditties. I walked to the bedside and leaned over. The words came soft and slurred, with pauses in between as she sucked in breath: "There was an old woman…at the foot of the hill…If she ain't moved away…she's living there still…Hey-diddle…day-diddle…de-dum…" Her voice died away into silence. Khan looked at me.

"What was that all about?"

I shook my head. "Another random memory," I said. "The tumor is busy, even if she is not."

It was not until mid-afternoon, buried deep in the stacks at the University Library, that I remembered my promise to call Brenda. But when I phoned from the lobby, Consuela told me that she had gone out and that I was not to wait up for her.

But the summer faded, and a chilly blast
O'er that happy cottage swept at last;
When the autumn song birds woke the dewy morn,
Our little "Prairie Flow'r" was gone.

In the year before Deirdre was born, Brenda and I took a vacation trip to Boston and Brenda laid out an hour-by-hour itinerary, listing each and every site we planned to visit. Along the way, she kept detailed logs of gas, mileage, arrival and departure times at each attraction, expenses, even tips to bellboys. It did not stop her from enjoying Boston. She did not insist that we march in lockstep to the schedule. "It's a guide, not a straitjacket," she had said. Yet, she spent an hour before bed each night updating and revising the next day's itinerary. Like an itch demanding a scratch, like a sweet tooth longing for chocolate, satisfying the urge to organize gave her some deep, almost sensual pleasure.

Now, of course, everything was planned and scheduled, even small trips. Sometimes the plan meant more than the journey.

Brenda frowned as I pulled into the secluded lot and parked in front of an old, yellow, wood-frame building. A thick row of fir trees screened the office building from the busy street and reduced the sound of rushing traffic to a whisper.

"Paul, why are we stopping? What is this place?"

"A lab," I told her. "That phone call just before we left the house…Some work I gave them is ready."

"Can't you pick it up tomorrow when you're on duty?" she said. "We'll be late."

"We won't be late. The Sawyers never start on time, and there'll be three other couples to keep them busy."

"I hope that boy of theirs isn't there. He gives me the creeps, the way he stares at people…"

"Maybe they changed his medication," I said. "Do you want to come in, or will you wait out here?"

"Is there a waiting area?"

"I don't know. I've never been here before."

Brenda gave a small sound, halfway between a cough and a sigh. Then she made a great show of unbuckling her seat belt.

"You don't have to come in if you don't want to," I said.

"Can you just get this over with?"

Inside the front door was a small lobby floored with dark brown tiles. The directory on the wall listed three tenants in white, plastic, push-pin letters: a management consulting firm, a marriage counselor, and the genetics lab.

When Brenda learned that S/P Microbiology was situated on the third floor, she rolled her eyes and decided to wait in the lobby. "Don't be long," she said, her voice halfway between an order, a warning, and a plaintive plea to keep the schedule.

The receptionist at S/P was a young redhead wearing a headset and throat mike. He showed me to a chair in a small waiting room, gave me a not-too-old magazine to read, and spoke a few words into his mouthpiece. When the telephone rang, he touched his earpiece once and answered the phone while on his way back to his station. Clever, I thought, to have a receptionist not tied to a desk.

I was alone only for a moment before Charles Randolph Singer himself came out. He was a short, slightly rumpled-looking man a great deal younger than his reputation had led me to expect. His white lab coat hung open, revealing a pocket jammed full of pens and other instruments. "Charlie Singer," he said. "You're Doctor Wilkes?"

"Yes."

He shook my hand. "You sure did hand us one larruping good problem." Then he cocked his head sideways and looked at me. "Where'd you get the samples?"

"I'd…rather not say yet."

"Hunh. Doctor-patient crap, right? Well, you're paying my rent with this job, so I won't push it. Come on in back. I'll let Jessie explain things."

I followed Singer into a larger room lined with lab benches and machines. A dessicator and a centrifuge, a mass spec, a lot of other equipment I didn't recognize. A large aquarium filled with brackish water, fish, and trash occupied one corner. The plastic beverage can rings and soda bottles were dissolving into a floating, liquid scum, which the fish calmly ignored.

"Jessie!" Singer said. "Wilkes is here."

A round-faced woman peered around the side of the mass spectrometer. "Oh," she said. "You." She was wearing a headset similar to the receptionist's.

"Jessica Burton-Peeler," said Singer introducing us, "is the second-best geneticist on the face of the planet."

Peeler smiled sweetly. "That was last year, Charlie." She spoke with a slight British accent.

Singer laughed and pulled a stick of gum from the pocket of his lab coat. He unwrapped it and rolled it into a ball between his fingers. "Tell Doctor Wilkes here what we found." He popped the wad of gum into his mouth.

"Would you like some tea or coffee, Doctor? I can have Eamonn bring you a cup."

"No, thanks. My wife is waiting downstairs. We were on our way to a dinner party, but I couldn't wait until tomorrow to find out."

Singer gave me a speculative look. "Find out what?"

"What you found out."

After a moment, Singer grunted and shrugged. "All right. We cultured all three cell samples," he said. "The 'B' sample was normal in all respects. The cells went through fifty-three divisions."

"Which is about average," Peeler added. "As for the other two…One of them divided only a dozen times—"

"The 'A' sample," I interjected.

"Yes," she said after a momentary pause. "The 'A' sample. But the 'C' sample…That one divided one hundred and twenty-three times."

I swallowed. "And that is…abnormal?"

"Abnormal?" Singer laughed. "Doc, that measurement is so far above the Gaussian curve that you can't even see abnormal from there."

"The 'A' sample wasn't normal, either," said Peeler quietly.

I looked at her and she looked at me calmly and without expression. "Well," I said and coughed. "Well."

"So, what's next?" Singer demanded. "You didn't send us those tissue samples just to find out they were different. You already knew that—or you suspected it—when you sent them in. We've confirmed it. Now what?"

"I'd like you to compare them and find out how their DNA differs."

Singer nodded after a thoughtful pause. "Sure. If the reason is genetic. We can look for factors common to several 'normal' samples but different for your 'A' and 'C' samples. Run polymerase chain reactions. Tedious, but elementary."

"And then…" I clenched and unclenched my fists. "I've heard you work on molecular modifiers."

"Nanomachines," said Singer. "I have a hunch it'll be a big field someday, and I'm planning to get in on the ground floor." He jerked a thumb over his shoulder at the aquarium. "Right now I'm working on a bacterium that eats plastic waste."

"Dear Lord," said Burton-Peeler in sudden wonder. "You want us to modify the DNA, don't you?"

Singer looked from me to his wife. "Modify the DNA?"

"Yes," I started to say.

Burton-Peeler pursed her lips. "Modify the 'A' sample, of course. Whatever factor we find in the 'C' sample that sustains the cell division…You want us to splice that into the short-lived sample."

I nodded, unable to speak. "I thought it might be possible to bring it up to normal."

Singer rubbed his jaw. "I don't know. Splicing bacterial DNA is one thing. Human DNA is another. A universe more of complexity. Of course, there is that business with the multiple sclerosis aerosol. They used a modified rhinovirus to carry the mucus-producing genes into the lungs. If the factor is gene specific, we could do something similar. Infect the cells with a retrovirus and…"

"Then you can do it?"

"Now hold on. I said no such thing. I said *maybe* it was possible, *if* the chips fall right. But there'll be some basic research needed. It will cost. A lot."

"I'll…find the money. Somehow."

Singer shook his head slowly. "I don't think you can find that much. You're talking about maybe three to five years research here."

"Three to—" I felt the pit of my stomach drop away. "I don't have three to five years." Dee-dee would be dead by then. And Mae, too, taking the secret in her genes with her.

"We'll do it at cost," said Burton-Peeler. Singer turned and looked at his wife.

"What?"

"We'll do it at cost, Charlie. I'll tell you why later." She looked back to me. "Understand, we still cannot promise fast results. When you set off into the unknown, you cannot predict your arrival time."

Go for broke. Damn the torpedoes. "Just try is all I ask."

✡

Burton-Peeler saw me out. On the landing to the stairwell she stopped. "You're the father of the young girl with progeria," she said. "I saw it in the paper a few years ago. The 'A' sample was hers, wasn't it?"

I nodded. "Yes, and the second sample was my own. For comparison." I turned to go.

Peeler stopped me with an arm on my sleeve. She looked into my eyes. "Whose was the third sample?" she asked.

I smiled briefly and sadly. "My faith, that the universe balances."

✡

In the lobby, Brenda was just handing a tea cup and saucer back to Singer's red-haired receptionist when she saw me coming. With a few brisk motions she collected her things and was already breezing out the door as I caught up with her.

"I'll drive," she said. "We're way behind schedule now, thanks to you."

I said nothing and she continued in what was supposed to be an idly curious tone. "Who was that woman with you? The one on the landing."

"Woman? Oh, that was Jessica Burton-Peeler. Singer's wife."

Brenda arched an eyebrow and made a little moue with her lips. "She's a little on the plump side," she said. "Do you find plump women attractive?"

I didn't have the time to deal with Brenda's insecurities. "Start the car," I told her. "We'll be late for dinner."

> They say we are aged and gray, Maggie
> As spray by the white breakers flung;
> But to me you're as fair as you were, Maggie,
> When you and I were young.

Mae Holloway lay between white sheets, coupled to tubes and wires. She lay with her eyes closed, and her arms limp by her sides atop the sheets. Her mouth hung half-open. She seemed gray and shrunken; drawn, like a wire through a die. Her meager white hair was nearly translucent.

She looked like a woman half her age.

Noor Khan was sitting near the wall reading a magazine. She looked up as I entered the room. "They told you?"

"That Mae has recovered consciousness? Yes. I'm surprised to see you still here."

Khan looked at the bed. "I have made arrangements. She has no family to keep watch."

"No," I agreed. "They are long gone." Longer than Khan could suppose. "Is she sleeping?"

She hesitated a moment, then spoke in a whisper. "Not really. I think that as long as she keeps her eyes closed she can pretend she is not in hospital. Those memories of hers…The consciousness-doubling, you called it. I think they play continually, now. The pressure from the tumor on the temporal lobe."

I nodded. Suppress all external stimuli and Mae could—in a biological kind of virtual reality—live again in the past. If we spoke too loudly, it would bring her back to a time and place she did not want. "Why don't you take a break," I said. "I'll sit with her for a while."

Khan cocked her head to the side and looked at me. "You will."

"Yes. Is that so surprising?"

She started to say something and then changed her mind. "I will be in the cafeteria." And then she fluttered out.

When she was gone, I pulled the chair up to the bedside and sat in it. "Mae? It's Doctor Wilkes." I touched her gently on the arm, and she seemed to flinch from the contact. "Mae?"

"I hear yuh," she said. Her voice was low and weak and lacked her usual snap. I had to lean close to hear her. "It'ud pleasure me if you'd company for a mite. It's been mighty lonely up hyar."

"Has it? But Doctor Khan—"

"I kilt the b'ar," she whispered, "but it stove up Pa something awful. He cain't hardly git around no more, so I got to be doin' for him." She paused as if listening. "I'm not so little as that, mister; I jest got me a puny bone-box. I ain't no yokum. I been over the creek. And I got me a Tennessee toothpick, too, in case you have thoughts about a little girl with a crippled-up Pa. What's yore handle, mister?"

"Mrs. Holloway," I said gently. "Don't you know me?"

Mae giggled. "Right pleased to meet you, Mister Holloway. Greenberry's a funny name, so I'll just call you Mister. If you'll set a spell, I'll whup you up a bait to eat. H'ain't much, only squirrel; but I aim to go hunting tomorry and find a deer that'll meat us for a spell."

I pulled back and sat up straight in my chair. She was reliving her first meeting with Green Holloway. Was she too far gone into the quicksand of nostalgia to respond to me? "Mae," I said more loudly, shaking her shoulder. "It's Doctor Wilkes. Can you hear me?"

Mae gasped and her eyes flew open. "Whut…? Where…?" The eyes lighted on me and went narrow. "You."

"Me," I agreed. "How are you feeling, Mrs. Holloway?"

"I'm a-gonna die. How do you want me to feel?"

Relieved? Wasn't there a poem about weary rivers winding safe to the sea? But, no matter how long and weary the journey, can anyone face the sea at the end of it? "Mrs. Holloway, do you remember the time you were on the White House lawn and the president came out?"

Her face immediately became wary and she looked away from me. "What of it?"

"That president. It was Lincoln, wasn't it?"

She shook her head, a leaf shivering in the breeze.

I took a deep breath. "The Sanitary Commission was the Union Army's civilian medical corps. If you were wearing that uniform, you were remembering the 1860s. That business on the lawn. It happened. I looked it up. The dancing. *Listen to the Mockinbird*. Lincoln coming outside to join the celebration. The whole thing. You know it, but you won't admit it because it sounds impossible."

"Sounds impossible?" She turned her head and looked at me at last. "How could I remember Lincoln? I'm not *that* old!"

"Yes, you are, Mae. You are that old. It's just that those early memories have gone all blurry. It's become hard for you to tell the decades apart. Your oldest memories had faded entirely, until your stroke revived them."

"You're talking crazy."

"I think it must be a defense mechanism," I went on as if she had not spoken. "The blurring and forgetting. It keeps the mental desktop cleared of clutter by shoving the old stuff aside."

"Doc…"

"But, every now and then, one of those old, faded memories would pop up, wouldn't it? Some impossible recollection. And you would think…"

"That I was going crazy." In a whisper, half to herself, she said, "I was always afraid of that, as long back as I can remember."

No wonder. Sporadic recollections of events generations past…Could a sane mind remember meeting Lincoln? "Mae. I found your name in the 1850 Census."

She shook her head again. Disbelief. But behind it…Hope? Relief that those impossible memories might be real? "Doc, how can it be possible?"

I spread my hands. "I don't know. Something in your genes. I have some people working on it, but…I think you have been aging slow. I don't know how that is possible. Maybe it has never happened before. Maybe you're the only one. Or maybe there were others and no one ever noticed. Maybe they were killed in accidents; or they really did go mad; or they thought they were recalling past lives. It doesn't matter. Mae, I've spent the last week in libraries and archives. You were born around 1800."

"No!"

"Yes. Your father was a member of Captain James Scott's settlement company. The Murrays, the Hammontrees, the Holloways, the Blacks and others. The overmountain men, they were called. They bought land near Six Mile Creek from the Overhill Cherokees."

I paused. Mae said nothing but she continued to look at me, slowly shaking her head. "Believe me," I said. "Your father's name was Josh, wasn't it?"

"Josiah. Folks called him Josh. I…I had forgotten my folks for such a long time; and now that I can remember, it pains me awful."

"Yes. I overheard. A bear mauled him."

"Doc, he was such a fine figure of a man. Right portly—I mean, handsome. He cut a swath wherever he walked. To see him laid up like that…Well, it sorrowed me something fierce. And him always saying I shouldn't wool over him."

"He died sometime between 1830 and 1840, after you married Green Holloway."

She looked into the distance. "Mister, he was a long hunter. He come on our homestead one day and saw how things stood and stayed to help out. Said it wasn't fittin' for a young gal to live alone like that with no man to side her. 'Specially a button like I was. There was outlaws and renegades all up and down the Trace who wouldn't think twice about bothering a young girl. When Pa finally said 't was fittin', we jumped the broom 'til the preacher-man come through." She stopped. "Doc?"

"Yes?"

"Doc, you must have it right. Because…Because, how long has it been since folks lived in log cabins, and long hunters dressed up in buckskins?"

"A long time," I said. "A very long time."

"Seems like just a little while ago to me, but I know it can't be. The Natchez Trace? I just never gave it much thought."

Have you ever seen a neglected field overgrown with weeds? That was Mae's memory. Acres of thistle and briar. All perspective lost, all sense of elapsed time. "Your memories were telescoped," I said. "Remember when you sang *Sweet Betsy from Pike* for me, and you said how real it all seemed to you? Well, after the Civil War, sometime during the Great Depression of the 1870s, you went out west, probably on one of the last wagon trains, after they finished the railroad. After that, I lost track."

She stayed quiet for a long time and I began to think she had dozed off. Then she spoke again.

"Sometimes I remember the Tennessee hills," she said in a faraway voice, "all blue and purple and cozy with family." She sighed. "I loved them mountains," she said. "We had us a hardscrabble, side-hill farm. The hills was tilted so steep we could plow both sides of an acre. And the cows had their legs longer on the one side than the other so's they could stand straight-up." She chuckled at the hillbilly humor. "Oh, it was a hard life. You kids today don't know. But in the springtime, when the piney roses and star-flowers and golden bells was in bloom, and the laurel was all purpled up; why, doc, you couldn't ask God for a purtier sight." She sighed. "And other times…Other times, I remember a ranch in high-up, snow-capped mountains with long-horned cattle and vistas where God goes when He wants to feel small. There was a speakeasy in Chicago, where the jazz was hot; and a bawdy house in Frisco, where I was." She let her breath out slowly and closed her eyes again. "I remember wearing bustles and bloomers, and linen and lace, and homespun and broadcloth. I've been so many people, I don't know who I am."

She opened her eyes and looked at me. "But I was always alone, except in them early years. With Mister. And with Daddy and my brother Zach." A tear dripped down the side of her face. I pulled a tissue from the box and blotted it up for her. "There weren't nobody left for me. Nobody."

I hesitated for a moment. Then I said, "Mae, you never had a brother."

"Now what are you talking about? I remember him clear as day."

"I've checked the records. Your mother died and your father never remarried."

Mae started to speak, then frowned. "Pa did tell me oncet that he'd never hitch ag'in, because he loved the dust of Ma's feet and the sweat of her body more than he loved any other woman. But Zach—"

"Was your own child."

She sucked in her breath between clenched teeth. "No, he weren't! He was near my own age."

"You remember Zach from 1861 when he followed your husband into the army. He was twenty-two then, and you…Well, you seemed to be thirty-seven to those around you. So, in your memory he seems like a brother. By the time you rejoined him on his ranch in Wyoming, he was even a bit older than your apparent age. Remembered how you thought he resembled Mister? Well, that was because he was Mister's son. I think…I think that was when you started forgetting how the years passed for you. Mae, no one ever ran out on you. You just outlived them. They grew old and they died and you didn't. And after a while you just wouldn't dare get close to anyone."

Tears squeezed from behind her eyes. "Stop it! Every time you say something, you make me remember."

"In all this time, Mae, you've never mentioned your child. You did have one; the clinical evidence is there. If Zach wasn't your boy, who was? Who was the boy sitting next to you at the minstrel show in Knoxville?"

She looked suddenly confused, and there was more to her confusion than the distance of time. "I don't know." Her eyes glazed and she looked to her right. I knew she was re-seeing the event. "Zach?" she said. "Is that you, boy? Zach? Oh, it is. It is." She refocused on me. "He cain't hear me," she said plaintively. "He hugged me, but I couldn't feel his arms."

"I know. It's only a memory."

"I want to feel his arms around me. They grow up so fast, you know. The young 'uns. One day, they're a baby, cute as a button; the next, all growed up and gone for a soldier. All growed up. I could see it happening. All of 'em, getting older and older. I thought there was something wrong with me. That I'd been a bad girl, because I kilt my Ma; and the Good Man was punishing me by holding me back from the pearly gates. If'n I never grew old, I'd never die. And if I never died, I'd never see any of my kin-folk again. Doc, you can't know what it's like, knowing your child will grow old and wither like October corn and die right before your eyes."

For a moment, I could not breathe. "Oh, I know," I whispered. "I know."

"Zach…I lived to see him turn to dust in the ground. He died in my own arms, a feeble, old man, and he asked me to sing *Home, Sweet Home*, like I used to when he was a young 'un. Oh, little Zach!"

And she began to cry in earnest. She couldn't move her arms to wipe the tears away, so I pulled another tissue from the box on the tray and dabbed at her cheeks.

She reached out a scrawny hand and clutched my arm. "Thank you, doc. Thank you. You helped me find my child again. You helped me find my boy."

And then I did an odd thing. I stood and bent low over the bed and I kissed Mae Holloway on her withered cheek.

I'm going there to see my mother.
She said she'd meet me when I come.
I'm only going over Jordan,
I'm only going over home.

My days at the Home passed by in an anonymous sameness, dispensing medicines, treating aches and pains. Only a handful of people came to see me; and those with only trivial complaints. Otherwise, I sat unmolested in my office, the visitor's chair empty. I found it difficult even to concentrate on my journals. Finally, almost in desperation, I began making rounds, dropping in on Rosie and Jimmy and the others, chatting with them, enduring their pointless, rambling stories; sometimes suggesting dietary or exercise regimens that might improve their well-being. Anything to feel useful. I changed a prescription on Old Man Morton, now the Home's Oldest Resident, and was gratified to see him grow more alert. Sometimes you have to try different medications to find a treatment that works best for a particular individual.

Yet, somehow those days seemed empty. The astonishing thing to me was how little missed Mae Holloway was by the other residents. Oh, some of them asked after her politely. Jimmy did. But otherwise it was as if the woman had evaporated, leaving not even a void behind. Partly, I suspect, it was because they were unwilling to face up to this reminder of their own mortality. But partly, too, it must have been a sense of relief that her aloof and abrasive presence was gone. If she never had any friends Mae had told me, she wouldn't miss them when they were gone. But neither did they miss her.

I usually stopped at the hospital on my way home sometimes to obtain a further tissue sample for Singer's experiments, sometimes just to sit with her

Often, she was sedated to relieve the pain of the tumor. More usually, she was dreaming; adrift on the river of years, connected to our world and time by only the slenderest of threads.

When she was conscious, she would spin her reminiscences for me and sing. Rosalie, the Prairie Flower. Cape Ann. Woodsman, Spare that Tree. Ching a Ring Chaw. The Hunters of Kentucky. Wait for the Wagon. We agreed, Mae and I, that a wagon was just as suitable as a Chevrolet for courting pretty girls, and Phyllis and her wagon was the ancestor of Daisy and her bicycle, Lucille and her Oldsmobile, and Josephine and her flying machine. And someday, I suppose, Susie and her space shuttle.

It was odd to see Mae so at peace with her memories. She no longer feared them; no longer suppressed them. She no longer fled from them. Rather, she embraced them and passed them on to me. When she sang, *Roisin the Beau*, she remarked casually how James Polk had used its melody for a campaign song. She recollected without flinching that she had voted for Zachary Taylor. "Old Rough and Ready," she said. "There was a man for you. 'Minds me some'at of that T.R. Too bad they pizened him, but he was out to break the slave power." It gave her no pause to recall how at New Orleans, "*There stood John Bull in martial pomp / And there stood Old Kentucky.*" It must have been an awful relief to acknowledge those memories, to relax in their embrace.

There were fond memories of her "bean," Green the Long Hunter. Of days spent farming or hunting or spinning woolen or cooking 'shine. Of nights spent 'setting' by the fire, smoking their pipes, reading to each other from the Bible. Quiet hours from a time before an insatiable demand for novelty—for something always to be *happening*—had consumed us. Green had even taken her down to Knoxville to see the touring company of *The Gladiator*, a stage play about Spartacus. Tales of slave revolts did not play well elsewhere in the South, but the mountaineers had no love for the wealthy flatland aristocrats.

She recalled meeting Walt Whitman, a fellow nurse in the Sanitary Commission. "A rugged fellow and all full of himself," she recalled, "but as kind and gentle with the men as any of the women-folk."

She still confused her son sometimes with a brother, with her father, with Green. He was younger, he was older, he was of her own age. But there were childhood memories, too, of the sort most parents have. How he had "spunked up with his gal," "spooned with his chicken," or "lollygagged with his peach," depending on the slang of the decade. How they had "crossed the wide prairie" together after the War and set up a ranch in Wyoming Territory. How he met and wed Sweet Annie, a real "piece of calico."

Not all the memories were pleasant—Sweet Annie had died screaming—but Mae relished them just the same. It was her life she was reclaiming, and a life consists of different parts, good and bad. The parts make up a whole. I continued to record her tales and tunes, as much because I did not know what else to do as because of any book plans, and I noticed that, while her doubling episodes often hopscotched through her life—triggered by associations and chance remarks—the music that played in her mind continued its slow and inexorable backward progression, spanning the 1840s and creeping gradually into the mid-thirties.

Slowly, a weird conviction settled on me. When the dates of her remembered tunes finally reached 1800, she would die.

✿

Time was running short. Most brain tumor patients did not survive a year from the time of first diagnosis; and Mae was so fragile to begin with that I doubted a whole year would be hers. Reports from Singer alternated between encouragement and frustration. Apparent progress would evaporate with a routine, follow-up test. Happenstance observation would open up a whole new line of inquiry. Singer submitted requests for additional cell samples almost daily. Blood, skin, liver. It seemed almost as if Mae might be used up entirely before Singer could pry loose the secret of her genes and splice that secret into my Deirdre.

I began to feel as if I were in a race with time. A weird sort of race in which time was speeding off in both directions. A young girl dying too old. An old woman dying too young.

One day, Wing was waiting for me when I entered the hospital. Seeing the flat look of concern on his face, my heart faltered. *Not yet*, I thought; *not yet!* My heart screeched, but I kept my own face composed. He took me aside into a small consultation room. Plaster walls with macro designs painted in happy, soothing colors. Comfortable chairs; green plants. An appallingly cheerful venue in which to receive bad news.

But it was not bad news. It was good news, of an odd and unexpected sort.

"Herpes?" I said when he had told me. "Herpes is a cure for brain tumors?" I couldn't help it. I giggled.

Wing frowned. "Not precisely. Culver-Blaese is a new treatment and outside my field of specialty, but let me explain it as Maurice explained it to me." Maurice LeFevre was the resident in genetic engineering, one of the first such residencies in the United States. "Several years ago," said Wing, "Culver and Blaese successfully extracted the gene for the growth enzyme, thymidine kinase, from the herpes virus, and installed it into brain tumor cells using a harmless retrovirus."

"I would think," I said dryly, "that an enzyme that facilitates reproduction is the last thing a brain tumor needs spliced into its code."

Wing blinked rapidly several times. "Oh, I'm sorry. You see it's the ganciclovir. I didn't make that clear?"

"Ganciclovir is—?"

"The chemical used to fight herpes. It reacts with thymidine kinase, and the reaction products interfere with cell reproduction. So if tumor cells start producing thymidine, injecting ganciclovir a few days later will gum up the tumor's reproduction and kill it. There have been promising results on mice and in an initial trial with twenty human patients."

"What is 'promising'?"

"Complete remission in seventy-five percent of the cases, and appreciable shrinkage in all of them."

I sucked in my breath. I could hardly credit what Wing was telling me. Here was a treatment, a *deus ex machina*. Give Singer another year of live tissue experiments and he would surely find the breakthrough we sought. "What's the catch?" I asked. There had to be a catch. There was always a catch.

There were two.

"First," said Wing, "the treatment is experimental, so the insurance will not cover it. Second…Well, Mrs. Holloway has refused."

"Eh? Refused? Why is that?"

Wing shook his head. "I don't know. She wouldn't tell me. I thought if I caught you before you went to see her…"

"That I could talk her into it?"

"Yes. The two of you are very close. I can see that."

Close? Mae and I? If Wing could see that, those thick eyeglasses of his were more powerful than the Hubble telescope. Mae had not been close to anyone since her son died. *Since her child died in her arms, an old, old man.* Inwardly, I shuddered. No wonder she had never gotten close to anyone since. No wonder she had lost an entire era of her life.

"I'll give it a try," I said.

When I entered her room, Mae was lying quietly in her bed, humming softly. Awake, I knew, but not quite present. Her face was curled into a smile, the creases all twisted around in unwonted directions. There was an air about her, something halfway between sleep and joy, a *calm* that had inverted all those years of sourness, stood everything on its head, and changed all her minus signs to plus.

Setting on her cabin porch, I imagined, gazing down the hillside at the laurel hells, and at a distant, pristine stream meandering through the holler below. At peace. At last.

I pulled the visitor's chair close by the bedside and laid a hand lightly on her arm. She didn't stir. "Mae, it's me. I've come to set a spell with you."

"Howdy there, doc," she whispered. "Oh, it's such a lovely sunset. All heshed. I been telling Li'l Zach about the time his grandpap and Ol' Hickory went off t' fi't the Creeks. I was already fourteen when Pa went off, so I minded the cabin while he was away."

I leaned closer to her. "Mae, has Dr. Wing spoken to you about the new treatment?"

She took in a long, slow breath; and let it out as slowly. "Yes."

"He told me you refused."

"I surely did that."

"Why?"

"Why?" She opened her eyes and looked at me; looked sadly around the room. "I been hanging on too long. It's time to go home."

"But—"

"And what would it git me, anyways. Another year? Six months? Doc, even if I am nigh on to two hunnert year, like you say, and my bone-box only thinks it's a hunnert, *that's still older'n most folks git.* Even if that Doctor LeFevre can do what he says and rid me of this hyar tumor, there'll be a stroke afore long or my ticker'll give out, or something. Doc, *there ain't no point to it.* When I was young, when I was watching everyone I knew grow old and die, I wanted to go with them. I wanted to be with them. Why should I want to tarry now? If the Lord'll have me, I'm ready." She closed her eyes again and turned a little to the side.

"But, Mae…"

"And who'll miss me, beside," she muttered.

"I will."

She rolled out flat again and looked at me. "You?"

"Yes. A little, I guess."

She snorted. "You mean you'll miss whatever you want that you're wooling me over. Always jabbing me with needles, like I was a pincushion. There's something gnawing away at you, Doc. I kin see it in your eyes when you think no one is looking. Kind of sad and angry and awful far away. I don't know what it is, but I know I got something to do with it."

I drew back under her speech. Her words were like slaps.

"And suppose'n they do it and they do git that thang outen my brain. Doc, what'll happen to my music? What'll happen to my memories?"

"I—"

"You done told me they come from that tumor a-pressing against the brain. What happens if it's not pressin' any longer?"

"The memories might stay, now that they've been started, even with the original stimulus removed. It might have been a 'little stroke' that started it, just like we thought originally."

"But you can't guarantee it, can you?" She fixed me with a stare until I looked away.

"No. No guarantees."

"Then I don't want it." I turned back in time to see her face tighten momentarily into a wince.

"It will relieve the pain," I assured her.

"Nothing will relieve the pain. Nothing. Because it ain't that sort of pain. There's my Pa, my Ma, Green, Little Zach and his Sweet Annie. Ben and Joe and all the others I would never let cozy up to me. They're all waiting for me over in Gloryland. I don't know why the Good Man has kept me here so long.

H'isn't punishment for killing Ma. I know that now. There must be a reason for it; but I'm a-weary of the waiting. If'n I have this operation like you want, what difference will it make? A few months? Doc, I won't live those months in silence."

My Chloe has dimples and smiles, I must own;
But, though she could smile, yet in truth she could frown.
But tell me, ye lovers of liquor divine,
Did you e'er see a frown in a bumper of wine?

There is something about the ice cold shock of a perfect martini. The pine tree scent of the gin. The smooth liquid sliding down the throat. Then, a half second later, wham! It hits you. And in that half second, there is an hour of insight; though, sometimes, that hour comes very late at night. You can see with the same icy clarity of the drink. You can see the trail of choices behind you. Paths that led up rocky pitches; paths beside still waters. You can see where the paths forked, where, had you turned that way instead of this, you'd not be here today. You can even, sometimes, see where, when the paths forked, people took different trails.

"Paul!"

And you can wonder whether you can ever find that fork again.

I turned to see Brenda drop her briefcase on the sofa. "Paul! I *never* see you drinking."

Subtext: Do you drink a lot in secret when I can't see you? Sub-subtext: Are you an alcoholic? Holding a conversation with Brenda was a challenge. Her words were multi-layered; and you never knew on which layer to answer.

I placed my martini glass, still half-full, carefully down upon the sideboard, beside the others. It spilled a little as I did, defying the laws of gravity. I faced her squarely. "I'm running out of time," I said.

She looked at me for a moment. Then she said, "That's right. I'd wondered if you knew."

"I'm running out of time," I repeated. "She'll die before I know."

"*She*…" Brenda pulled her elbows in tight against her sides. "I don't want to hear this."

"That old woman. To live so long, only to die just now."

"The old woman from the home? *She* has you upset? For God's sake, Paul." And she turned away from me.

"You don't understand. She could save Dee-dee."

Brenda's head jerked a little to the left. Then she retrieved her briefcase and shook herself all over, as if preparing to leave. "How can a dying old woman save a dying old girl?"

"She's yin to Dee-dee's yang. The universe is neutral. There's a plus sign for every minus. But she wants to go over Jordan and I…can't stop her. And I don't understand why I can't."

"You're not making any sense, Paul. How many of those have you had?"

"She's two centuries old, Brenda. Two centuries old. She was a swinger and a sheba and a daisy and a pippin. She hears songs, in her head; but sometimes they're wrong, except they're right. The words are different. Older. *Old Zip Coon*, instead of *Turkey in the Straw. Lovely Fan'*, instead of *Buffalo Gals. Bright Mohawk Valley*, instead of *Red River Valley*. She read *Moral Physiology*, when it first came out. Mae did. Do you know the book? *Moral Physiology*, by Robert Dale Owen? No, of course not. It was all about birth control and it sold twenty-five thousand copies even though newspapers and magazines refused to carry the ads *and it was published in 18-god-damned-30*. She voted for Zachary Taylor, and her Pa fought in the Creek War, and her husband died at Resaca, and she saw Abraham-fucking-Lincoln—"

"Paul, can you hear yourself? You're talking crazy."

"Did you know *The Gladiator* debuted in New York in 1831? 'Ho! slaves, arise! Freedom…Freedom and revenge!'" I struck a pose, one fist raised.

"I can't stand to watch you like this, Paul. You're sopping drunk."

"And you're out late every night." Which was totally irrelevant to our discussion, but the tongue has a life of its own.

Through teeth clenched tight, she answered: "I have a job to keep."

I took a step away from the sideboard, and there must have been something wrong with the floorboards. Perhaps the support beams had begun to sag, because the floor suddenly tilted. I grabbed for the back of the armchair. The lamp beside it wobbled and I grabbed it with my other hand to keep it still.

Awkwardly twisted, half bent over, I looked at Brenda and spoke distinctly. "Mae Holloway is two centuries old. There is something in her genes. We think. Singer and Peeler and I. We think that with enough time. With enough time. Singer and Peeler can crack the secret. They can tailor a…Tailor a…" I hunted for the right word, found it scuttling about on the floor and snatched it. "Nanomachine." Triumph. "Tailor a nanomachine that can repair Dee-dee's cells. But Mae is dying. She has a brain tumor, and it's killing her. There's a treatment. An experimental treatment. It looks very good. But Mae won't take it. She doesn't want it. She wants to sleep."

I don't know what I expected. I expected hope, or disbelief. I expected a demand for proof, or for more details. I expected her to say, "do anything to save my daughter!" I expected anything but indifference.

Brenda brushed imaginary dust from her briefcase and turned away. "Do what you always do, Paul. Just ignore what she wants."

I was in the clinic at the Home the next day when I received the call from the hospital. My head felt as if nails had been driven into it. I was queasy from the hangover. When the phone rang and I picked it up, a tinny voice on the other end spoke crisply and urgently and asked that I come over right away. I don't remember what I said, or even that I said anything; and I don't suppose my caller expected a coherent answer. My numb fingers fumbled the phone several times before it sat right in its cradle. *Heart attack*, I thought. And as quickly as that, the time runs out.

But they hadn't said she was dead. They hadn't said she was dead.

I hope that there was no traffic on the road when I raced to the hospital, for I remember nothing of the journey. Three times along the way I picked up the car phone to call the hospital for more information; and three times I replaced it. It was better not to know. Half an hour, with the lights right and the speed law ignored. That was thirty minutes in which hope was thinkable.

Smythe, the cardio-vascular man, met me in the corridor outside her room. He grabbed me by both my arms and steadied me. I could not understand why he was grinning. What possible reason could there be?

"She'll live, mon," he said. "It was a near thing, but she'll live."

I stared at Smythe without comprehension. He shook me by the arm, hard. My head felt like shattered glass.

"She'll live," he said again. His teeth were impossibly white.

I brushed him off and stepped into the room. *She'll live?* Then there was still time. Everything else was detail. My body felt suddenly weak, as if a stopcock had been pulled and all my sand had drained away. I staggered as far as the bedside, where I sank into a steel and vinyl chair. Smythe waited by the door, in the corridor, giving me the time alone.

Dee-dee lay asleep upon the bed, breathing slowly and softly through a tube set up her nose. An intravenous tube entered her left arm. Remote sensor implants on her skull and chest broadcast her heartbeat and breathing and brain waves to stations throughout the hospital. Smythe was never more than a terminal away from knowing her condition. I reached out and took her right hand in mine and gently stroked the back of it. "Hello, Dee-dee, I came as fast as I could. Why didn't…" I swallowed hard. "Why didn't you wait for me to tuck you in."

Dee-dee was still unconscious from the anesthetic. She couldn't hear me; but a quiet sob, quickly stifled, drew my attention to the accordion-pleated expandable wall, drawn halfway out on the opposite side of the bed. When I walked around it, I saw Consuela sitting in a chair on the other side. Her features were tightly leashed, but the tracks of tears had darkened both her cheeks. Her hands were pale where they gripped the arms of the chair.

"Connie!"

"Oh, Paul, we almost lost her. We almost lost her."

It slammed against my chest with the force of a hammer, a harder stroke for having missed. *Someday we will.* I took Connie's hand and brushed the backside of it as I had brushed Dee-dee's. "It's all right now," I said.

"She is such a sweet child. She never complains."

Prognosis: The life span is shortened by relentless arterial atheromatosis. Death usually occurs at puberty.

"She's all right now."

"For a little while. But it will become worse, and worse; until…" She leaned her head against me and I cradled her; I rubbed her neck and shoulders, smoothed her hair. With my left hand, I caressed her cheek. *It is not the end; but it is the beginning of the end.*

"We knew it would happen." The emotions are a very odd thing. When all was dark, when I believed myself helpless, I could endure that knowledge. It was my comfort. But now that there was a ray of light, I found it overwhelming me, crushing me so that I could hardly breathe. A sliver of sunshine makes a darkened room seem blacker still. I could live with Fate, but not with Hope. I found that there was a new factor in the equation now. I found that I could fail.

"Where is Brenda?" I asked.

Connie pulled herself from my arms, turned and pulled aside the curtain that separated her from Deirdre. "She didn't come."

"What?"

"She didn't come."

Something went out of me then, like a light switch turned off. I didn't say anything for the longest time. I drifted away from Connie over toward the window. A thick stand of trees filled the block across the street from the hospital. Leaves fresh and green with spring. Forsythia bursting yellow. A flock of birds banked in unison over the treetops and shied off from the high tension lines behind. I thought of the time when Brenda and I first met on campus, both of us young and full of the future. I remembered how we had talked about making a difference in the world.

I found Brenda at home. I found her in the family room, late at night after I had finally left the hospital. She was still clad in her business suit, as if she had just come from the office. She was standing rigidly by the bookcase, with her eyes dry and red and puffy, with Dee-dee's book, *The Boxcar Children*, in her hands. I had the impression that she had stood that way for hours.

"I tried to come, Paul," she said before I could get any words out. "I tried to come, but I couldn't. I was paralyzed; I couldn't move."

"It doesn't matter," I said. "Connie was there. She'll stay until I get changed and return." I rubbed a hand across my face. "God, I'm tired."

"She's taken my place, hasn't she? She feeds Deirdre, she nurses her, she tutors her. Tell me, Paul, has she taken over *all* my duties?"

"I don't know what you mean."

"I didn't think there was room in your life for anyone beside your daughter. You've shut everyone else out."

"I never pushed you away. You ran."

"It needs more than that. It needs more than not pushing. You could have caught me, if you'd reached. There was an awful row at the office today. Crowe and FitzPatrick argued. They're dissolving the partnership. I was taking too long to say yes to the partnership offer; so Sèan became curious and…He found out Walther had wanted a 'yes' on a lot more, so we filed for harrass…Oh, hell. It doesn't matter anymore; none of it."

She was talking about events on another planet. I stepped to her side and took hold of the book. It was frozen to her fingers. I tugged, and pried it from her grasp. Slowly, her hands clenched into balls, but she did not lower her arms. I turned to place the book on the shelf and Brenda said in a small voice, "It doesn't go there, Paul."

"Damn it, Brenda!"

"I'm afraid," she said. "Oh, God, I'm afraid. Someday I will open up the tableware drawer and find her baby spoon; or I'll look under the sofa and find a ball that had rolled there forgotten. Or I'll find one of her dresses bundled up in the wash. And I won't be able to take it. Do you understand? Do you know what it's like? Do you have any feelings at all? How can you look at that shelf and remember that *her* book had once lain there? Look at that kitchen table and remember her high chair and how we played airplane with her food? Look into a room full of toys, with no child anymore to play with them? Everywhere I look I see an aching void."

With a sudden rush of tenderness, I pulled her to me, but she remained stiff and unyielding in my arms. Yet, we all mourn in our own ways. "She did not die, Brenda. She'll be okay."

"This time. But, Paul, I can't look forward to a lifetime looking back. At the little girl who grew up and grew old and went away before I ever got to know her. Paul, it isn't right. It isn't right, Paul. It isn't right for a child to die before the parent."

"So, you'll close her out of your mind? Is that the answer? Create the void now? You'll push all those memories into one room and then close the door? You can't do that. If we forget her, it will be as if she had never lived."

She softened at last and her arms went around me. "What can I do? I've lost her, and I've lost you, and I've lost…everything."

We stood there locked together. I could feel her small, tightly controlled sobs trembling against me. Sometimes the reins have been held so close for so long that you can never drop them, never even know if they have been dropped. The damp of her tears seeped through my shirt. Past her, I could see the shelf with *The Boxcar Children* lying flat upon it and I tried to imagine how, in future years, I could ever look on that shelf again without grief.

> *Tell me the tales that to me were so dear*
> *Long, long ago; long, long ago.*
> *Sing me the songs I delighted to hear*
> *Long, long ago, long ago.*

Dee-dee was wired. There was a tube up her nose and another in her arm. A bag of glucose hung on a pole rack by her bed, steadily dripping into an accumulator and thence through the tube. A catheter took her wastes away. A pad on her finger and a cuff around her arm were plugged into a CRT monitor. I smiled when I saw she was awake.

"Hi, daddy…" Her voice was weak and hoarse, a byproduct of the anaesthesia.

"Hi, Dee-dee. How do you feel?"

"Yucky…"

"Me, too. You're a TV star." I pointed to the monitor, where red and yellow and white lines hopped and skipped across the screen. Heart rate, blood pressure. Every time she breathed, the white line crested and dropped. She didn't say anything and I listened for a moment to the sucking sound that the nose tube made. A kid trying for the last bit of soda in the can. The liquid it carried off was brown, which meant that there was still a little blood. "Connie is here." I nodded to the other side of the bed.

Dee-dee turned her eyes, but not her head. "Hello, Connie. I can't see you."

Consuela moved a little into her field of vision. "Good morning, Little One. You have a splendid view from your window."

"Nurse Jeannie told me that…Wish I could see…"

"Then, I will tell you what it looks like. You can see the north end of town—all those lovely, old houses—and far off past them, on the edge of the world, the blue-ridge mountain wall and, in the very center of it, the Gap; and through the Gap, you can see the mountains beyond."

"It sounds beautiful…"

"Oh, it is. I wish I could be here instead of you, just so I could have the view."

I looked up at Connie when she said that and, for a moment, we locked gazes with one another. I could see the truth of her words in her eyes.

And then I saw surprise. Surprise and something else beside. I looked over my shoulder—and Brenda was standing there in the doorway, smartly dressed, on wobbly legs, with her purse clutched tightly in her hands before her.

"The nurses," she said. "The nurses said she could only have two visitors at a time." Visiting was allowed every three hours, but only for an hour and only two visitors at a time. I was a doctor and Connie was a nurse and the staff cut us a little slack, but the rules were there for a reason. Consuela stood.

"I will leave."

Brenda looked at her and caught her lower lip between her teeth. She laid her purse with military precision on a small table beside the bed. "I would like to spend some time with Deirdre, Paul. If you don't mind."

I nodded. As I stood up I gave Dee-dee a smile and a little squeeze on her arm. "Mommy's here," I told her.

Connie and I left them alone together (a curious expression, that—"alone together") and waited in the outer nursing area. I didn't eavesdrop, though I did overhear Brenda whisper at one point, "No, darling, it was never anything that *you* did wrong." Maybe it wasn't much, not when weighted against those years of inattention. It wasn't much; but it wasn't nothing. I knew—maybe for the first time—how much it cost Brenda to take on these memories, to take on the risks of remembering; because she was right. If in later years you remembered nothing, you would feel no pain.

And yet, I had seen two centuries of pain come washing back, bringing with it joy.

Children recover remarkably well. Drop them, and they bounce. Maybe not so high as before, but they do rebound. Dee-dee bore a solemn air about her for a day or two, sensing, without being told, that she had almost "gone away." But to a child, a day is a lifetime, and a week is forever; and she was soon in the recovery ward, playing with the other children. Rheumatic children with heart murmurs; shaven-headed children staring leukemia in the face; broken children with scars and cigarette burns…They played with an impossible cheerfulness, living, as most children did, in the moment. But then, the Now was all most of them would ever have.

There came a day when Dee-dee was not in her room when I arrived. Connie sat framed in a bright square of sunlight, reading a book. She looked up when I walked in. "Deirdre has gone to visit a new friend," she said.

"Oh." A strange clash of emotions: Happy she was up and about again, even if confined to a wheelchair; disappointed that she was not there to greet me.

"She will return soon, I think."

"Well," I said, "we had wanted her to become more active."

Consuela closed her book and laid it on the small table beside her. "I suppose you will no longer need my services," she said. She did not look at me when she said it, but out the window at the new-born summer.

"Not need you? Don't be foolish."

"She has her mother back, now."

Every morning before work; every evening after. Pressing lost years into a few hours. "She still needs you."

"The hospital staff cares for her now."

I shook my head. "It's not that she *needs* you, but that she needs *you*. You are not only her nurse."

"If I take on new clients," she went on as if I had not spoken, "I can do things properly. I can visit at the appointed times, perform my duties, and leave; and not allow them such a place in my heart when they are gone."

"If people don't leave a hole in your life when they are gone, Consuela, they were never in your life at all."

She turned away from the window and looked at me. "Or two holes."

I dropped my gaze, looked instead at the rumpled bed.

"In many ways," I heard her say, "you are a cold man, Doctor. Uncaring and thoughtless. But it was the fruit of bitterness and despair. I thought you deserved better than you had. And you love her as deeply as I. If death could be forestalled by clinging tight, Deirdre would never leave us."

I had no answer for her, but I allowed my eyes to seek out hers.

"I thought," she said, "sometimes, at night, when I played my flute, that because we shared that love… That we could share another."

"It must be lonely for you here, in a strange country, with a strange language and customs. No family and fewer friends. I must be a wretched man for never having asked."

She shook her head. "You had your own worry. A large one that consumed you."

"Consuela Montejo, if you leave, you would leave as great a hole in my life as in Dee-dee's."

"And in Mrs. Wilkes'." She smiled a little bit. "It is a very odd thing, but I believe that if I stayed I might even grow to like her."

"She was frightened. She thought she could cauterize the wound before she received it. It was only when she nearly lost Dee-dee that she suddenly realized that she had never had her."

Consuela stood and walked to the bed. She touched the sheet and smoothed it out, pulling the wrinkles flat. She shook her head. "It will hurt if I go; it will hurt if I stay. But Mrs. Wilkes deserves this one chance."

I reached out and took her hand and she reached out and took mine. Had Brenda walked in then, I do not know what she would have made of our embrace. I do not know what I made of it. I think I would

have pulled Brenda in with us, the three of us arm in arm in arm.

The really strange thing was how inevitable it all was in hindsight.

When I left Consuela, I went to visit Mae. It had been nearly two weeks since I had last seen her and it occurred to me that the old bat might be lonely, too. And what the hell, she could put up with me and I could put up with her.

I found my Dee-dee in Mae Holloway's room. The two of them had their heads bent close together, giggling over something. Deirdre was strapped to her electric wheelchair and Mae lay flat upon her bed; but I was struck by how alike they looked. Two gnarled and bent figures with pale, spotted skin stretched tight over their bones, lit from within by a pure, childlike joy. Two old women; two young girls. Deirdre looked up and saw me.

"Daddy! Granny Mae has been teaching me the most wonderful songs."

Mae Holloway lifted her head a little. "Yours?" she said in a hoarse whisper. "This woman-child is yours?"

"Yes," I said, bending to kiss Dee-dee's cheek. "All mine." No. Not *all* mine. There were others who shared her.

"Listen to the song Granny Mae taught me! It goes like this."

I looked over Dee-dee's head at the old woman "She didn't tell you?"

"Noor brought her in, but didn't say aye, yea, or no. Just that she thought we should meet."

Dee-dee began singing in her high, piping voice.

The days go slowly by, Lorena.
The snow is on the grass again.
The years go slowly by Lorena…

"Her days are going by too fast, ain't they?" Mae said. I nodded and saw how her eyes lingered on my little girl. "Growing old in the blink of an eye," she said softly. "Oh, I know how that feels."

"Granny Mae tells such interesting stories," Dee-dee insisted. "Did you know she saw Abraham Lincoln one time?" I rubbed her thinning hair. Too young to know how impossible that was. Too young to doubt.

Mae's hand sought out Dee-dee's and clenched hold of it. "Doc, I'll have me that operation."

"What?"

"I'll have me that operation. The one that's supposed to make this tumor of mine go away. I'll have it, even if my music and my memories go with it."

"You will. Why?"

"Because I know why you been poking me and taking my blood. And I know why the Good Lord has kept me here for all this long time."

Noor Khan was waiting in the hallway when I stepped out of the room.

"Ah, doctor," I said. "How are things at Sunny Dale?"

"Quiet," she said. "Though the residents are all asking when you will be back."

I shrugged. "Old people dislike upsets to their routine. They grew used to having me around."

Khan said, "I never knew about your little girl. I heard it from Smythe. Why did you never tell me?"

I shrugged again. "I never thought it was anyone's business."

Khan accepted the statement. "After you told Wing and me of Mae's remarkable longevity…I knew you were taking blood samples to that genetic engineering firm—"

"Singer and Peeler."

"Yes. I thought you had…other reasons."

"What, that I would find the secret of the Tree of Life?" I shook my head. "I never thought to ask for so much. Mae has lived most her life as an old woman. I would not count that a blessing. But to live a normal life? To set right what had come out wrong? Yes, and I won't apologize. Neither would you, if it were your daughter."

"Is Singer close? To a solution?"

"I don't know. Neither do they. We won't know how close we are until we stumble right into it. But we've bought a little time now, thanks to you. Is that why you did it? Because you knew that meeting my daughter would convince Mae to accept the Culver-Blaese gene therapy?"

Khan shook her head. "No. I never even thought of that."

"Then, why?"

"Sometimes," said Khan, looking back into the room where the young girl and the old girl taught each other songs. "Sometimes, there are other medicines, for other kinds of hurts."

I seek no more the fine and gay,
For each does but remind me
How swift the hours did pass away
With the girl I left behind me.

They are all gone now. All gone. Mae, Dee-dee, all of them. Consuela was first. Brenda's partnership arrangement with FitzPatrick—telecommuting, they called it—left no place for her at the house. She came to visit Dee-dee, and she and Brenda often met for coffee—what they talked about I do not know—but she stopped coming after Dee-dee passed on and I have not seen her in years.

Brenda, too. She lives in LA, now. I visit her when I'm on the Coast and we go out together, and catch dinner or a show. But she can't look at me without thinking of *her*; and neither can I, and sometimes, that becomes too much.

There was no bitterness in the divorce. There was no bitterness left in either of us. But Dee-dee's illness had been a fault line splitting the earth. A chasm had run through our lives, and we jumped out of its way, but Brenda to one side and I, to the other. When Dee-dee was gone, there was no bridge across it and we found that we shared nothing between us but a void.

The operation bought Mae six months. Six months of silence in her mind before the stroke took her. She complained a little, now and then, about her quickly evaporating memories; but sometimes I read to her from my notes, or played the tape recorder, and that made her feel a little better. When she heard about seeing Lincoln on the White House lawn, she just shook her head and said, "Isn't that a wonder?" The last time I saw Mae Holloway, she was fumbling after some elusive memory of her Mister that kept slipping like water through the fingers of her mind, when she suddenly brightened, looked at me, and smiled. "They're all a-waiting," she whispered, and then all the lights went out.

And Dee-dee.

Dee-dee.

Still, after all these years, I cannot talk about my little girl.

They call it the Deirdre-Holloway treatment. I insisted on that. It came too late for her, but maybe there are a few thousand fewer children who die now each year because of it. Sometimes I think it was worth it. Sometimes I wonder selfishly why it could not have come earlier. I wonder if there wasn't something I could have done differently that would have brought us home sooner.

Singer found the key; or Peeler did, or they found it together. Three years later, thank God. Had the breakthrough followed too soon on Deirdre's death, I could not have borne it. The income from the book funded it and it took every penny, but I feel no poorer for it.

It's a mutation, Peeler told me, located on the supposedly inactive Barr body. It codes for an enzyme that retards catabolism. There's a sudden acceleration of fetal development in the last months of pregnancy that almost always kills the mother, and often the child, as well. Sweet Annie's dear, dead child would have been programmed for the same future had she lived. After birth, aging slows quickly until it nearly stops at puberty. It only resumes after menopause. In males, the gene's expression is suppressed by testosterone. Generations of gene-spliced lab mice lived and died to establish that.

Is the line extinct now? Or does the gene linger out there, carried safely by males waiting unwittingly to kill their mates with daughters?

I don't know. I never found another like Mae, despite my years of practice in geriatrics.

When I retired from the Home, the residents gave me a party, though none of them were of that original group. Jimmy, Rosie, Leo, Old Man Morton…By then I had seen them all through their final passage. When the residents began approaching my own age, I knew it was time to take down my shingle.

I find myself thinking more and more about the past these days. About Mae and the Home; and Khan—I heard from my neighbor's boy that she is still in practice, in pediatrics now. Sometimes, I think of my own parents and the old river town where I grew up. The old cliffside stairs. Hiking down along the creek. Hasbrouk's grocery down on the corner.

The memories are dim and faded, brittle with time.

And I don't remember the music, at all. My memories are silent, like an old Chaplin film. I've had my house wired, and tapes play continually, but it isn't the same. The melodies do not come from within; they do not come from the heart.

They tell me I have a tumor in my left temporal lobe, and it's growing. It may be operable. It may not be. Wing wants to try Culver-Blaese, but I won't let him. I keep hoping.

I want to remember. I want to remember Mae. Yes, and Consuela and Brenda, too. And Dee-dee most of all. I want to remember them all. I want to hear them singing.

THE BEST OF THE NEW AND THE OLD

✶New and Old Stories by Masters of Science Fiction and Fantasy✶

✶New Stories by Emerging New Talents✶

✶PLUS Columns, Book Reviews and Interviews✶

✶Serializations of Great Novels & Stories✶

DON'T MISS OUT ON ANY ISSUE

SUBSCRIBE

www.GalaxysEdge.com/sub.htm

Or send a check for $37.74 for a one-year (six-issue) subscription (save 10% off the cover price) with this form to :

Subscriptions: Galaxy's Edge

Arc Manor Publishers

P.O. Box 10339

Rockville, MD 20849

Currently, subscription to the paper edition is only available within the United States.

Your Name_____

Full Address_____

_____

_____

Ph. No._____ Email_____

Manufactured by Amazon.ca
Bolton, ON

19895896R00061